Unforgettable Novels

of the West

by Jack Ballas . . .

TOMAHAWK CANYON: Cole Mason came to New Mexico Territory looking for a good graze—and found a bloody range war instead . . .

DURANGO GUNFIGHT: Quint Cantrell wants to bury his past. But the Hardester clan wants to bury *him* . . .

MAVERICK GUNS: Clay Mason's brother has been marked for death by a sly killer—but when you take on one of the Mason clan, you take on *all* of the Mason clan . . .

MONTANA BREED: Young Rafe Gunn wanted to look into his family's past. But first he had to look death square in the face . . .

APACHE BLANCO: Trace Gundy has a chance to make a small fortune and a fresh start. But in helping a rich man's son escape from prison, he could get himself locked up—or worse . . .

GUN BOSS: Raised by an Apache tribe, Trace Gundy never forgot his lessons in survival. Now, to avenge the loss of his beloved wife, he will call upon the fighting spirit he learned as a boy . . .

POWDER RIVER: Case Gentry was no longer a Texas Ranger. But he had to call those old instincts back the night the two-bit gunhand rode up to his cabin . . .

ANGEL FIRE

JACK BALLAS

JOVE BOOKS, NEW YORK

ANGEL FIRE

A Jove Book / published by arrangement with
the author

PRINTING HISTORY
Jove edition / February 1996

The Putnam Berkley World Wide Web site address is
http://www.berkley.com

ISBN: 0-515-11805-2

A JOVE BOOK®
Jove Books are published by The Berkley Publishing Group,
200 Madison Avenue, New York, New York 10016.
JOVE and the "J" design are trademarks
belonging to Jove Publications, Inc.

PRINTED IN THE UNITED STATES OF AMERICA

10 9 8 7 6 5 4 3 2 1

*To my granddaughter, Paula,
who has always been there for me,
and to my granddaughters,
Vanessa and Joanna,
whom I love very much.*

CHAPTER 1

MELANIE CORBIN SAT in front of the window of her Newton, Kansas, hotel room, angry, scared, but determined to find someone she could trust—someone to teach her to handle guns, to kill.

The weather, hot and muggy that early summer day, stifled her, and frustration made it worse. She couldn't take a nap, she'd tried that, but lying on the bed made her perspire even more.

She stared at the street below, thinking, wondering if the three men chasing her were there before her eyes. Of the three men, she knew only one.

She couldn't run forever. She'd missed tying in with a wagon train in Independence by two days. Now, she and her two companions, both darkies who'd been with her family since their birth, had to go it alone.

Her stomach churned, tied itself in knots. She faced the prospect of having to kill three men. That they were out to kill her, she doubted not. In addition to wanting her land and money, at least one of them wanted *her*. But, the thing she was most certain of: *they all wanted her dead.* She carried knowledge that could get them hung.

Her gaze traveled from one end of the main street to the other, and back again. Each time her look came back to the high-shouldered, lean man slouched against the saloon's wall across the street, she hesitated in her search. Was he one of the three who hunted her? He stood tall, she thought he might be over six feet, and he wore a side gun, the holster tied low on his thigh, his posture indolent. He wasn't the one she knew, the one who'd threatened her, but that one had spoken of two brothers. Was the man across the street one of them?

Two men, both slim, one redheaded, the other with white

1

hair, crossed the street toward the tall man, their right hands not swinging but held close to the guns at their sides, their attitude threatening. Melanie held her breath, her own troubles forgotten for the moment. Fascinated, her eyes locked on the scene below. For some reason fear washed over her for the lone man facing the two.

Abruptly, the man leaning against the saloon wall straightened and stepped away from the wall. The two men stopped about ten yards from the high-shouldered man, hands now brushing the holsters at their sides. The redheaded one spoke; Melanie heard him plainly even though his voice was soft.

"Buckner, we done traveled a distance to find you. You brung our partner in across his saddle. Killed 'im when it warn't none o' yore business to do so. Now it's yore turn."

"Mister," said the man called Buckner; his voice deep, yet soft, came to Melanie, "I don't know who your partner was, but he broke the law or I'd a left 'im alone."

The white-haired man cut in, "Don't make no difference who he wuz. You cut 'im down for bounty money. You filled yore pockets with dirty money, now fill yore hand with that side gun."

"No. I'll not draw first, but after I kill you, I'll be wanting to collect the bounty on your scalps. There's certain to be money on your heads, an' after I think on it a moment it'll come to me who you are. If you're set on killin' me, get at it—or drop your gun belts."

The two took a couple of steps to the side to open a space between them. The lone man facing them said, his voice now deadly, "Separate one more step and I'll blow you to hell." They turned as though to walk away, and when their holster sides turned away from him, each flashed a hand for his gun.

Looking as though he had all day, the tall man drew, thumbed off two shots, walked to where they lay, and stared down at them.

The redheaded one still had enough life to try and trigger a shot. His neck muscles stood out with the effort to bring his gun to bear on the tall man. His arm shook with the effort, then relaxed. The gun dropped into the street's dust.

He sucked in a deep breath, and tried to push words from his mouth, but the only thing that passed his lips was a trickle of blood. It flowed from the corners of his lips to paint a red streak down his cheek. He shuddered, kicked once, and stared at the vast blue sky above through sightless eyes. The white-haired one lay a few feet to the side, already dead.

The high-shouldered man calmly opened the loading gate, removed spent shells, and punched good shells into the chamber.

Melanie gasped. A quiver of revulsion shook her. Two men lay in the dusty street below, and the man responsible for their death seemed not to care a whit.

A slight breeze wafted the acrid smell of gunpowder mixed with smells from the stockyards through her window. She shook her head, not wanting to believe what she looked at. Two men dead, and the townspeople treated it like some sort of sporting event. Perhaps thirty men crowded close to gawk at the bodies.

The scene left her mouth dry and a tightness in her chest—but *that* man still standing was the kind she looked for. She wanted to talk with him, let her intuition tell her whether to trust him. She'd heard somewhere bounty hunters were cold, hard men, who cared nothing about life, and from the words of one of the dead men, the tall one *was* a bounty hunter. She'd have to see for herself.

The scene she'd witnessed and the smells brought home how far she'd come from her sheltered life in Virginia.

Kurt Buckner eased his Colt .44 into its holster and took a couple of deep breaths. His nerves relaxed a little, and his stomach stopped turning over. He became aware of people gathered around. Voices, sounding like hundreds, crashed on his hearing. A glance showed only thirty or so in the crowd gathered around him. One of the crowd wore a badge.

"You got lucky, gunfighter, I seen 'em bring it to you. Wish I hadn't. I'd like an excuse to lock you up."

A smile touched the corners of Buckner's lips. "Win some, lose some, Marshal. Better luck next time." He nodded, stepped away, and turned back. "And, Marshal, you owe me some money. One of those men is Whitey Terrence, the other is Red Costner. There's a thousand dollars on each o' them. Send a wire for it. I'll get it from you in the mornin'." He headed toward the saloon.

Outwardly cold and uncaring, the man felt bile flow to the back of his tongue. He'd not wanted to kill those men. They had taken up the fight of their saddle partner, one he'd brought to the law because he made good money for that service.

He thought of the others he'd brought in. There had been eleven, three of them dead. He hoped he'd not have to kill more, but if he did . . . He shrugged. So be it. His fingers touched the bulge of his money belt. He had over eight thousand dollars; now that count would go to ten thousand dollars that no other job could bring him. This money would be a nice start in some other line of work.

He stood at the bar, ordered a whisky, knocked it back, felt its pleasant warmth burn its way to his stomach, and ordered another. He sipped his second drink, all the while feeling dagger-like stares spearing his back. To hell with them.

Finished with his drink, Buckner glanced at his watch. Five-thirty, time for supper.

The town's citizens' hard, unfriendly stares accompanied his walk to the hotel. Buckner set his face in a stiff, emotionless mask. He cared nothing for what they thought of him. They didn't have the backbone to take care of their own problems. They yelled for others to do their fighting, and then turned on them when a killing took place. They were contemptible.

He'd not had time to order supper when a girl he guessed to be between twenty and twenty-five years of age walked to his table and looked down at him. He stood.

"Mr. Buckner?"

He nodded. "Yes, ma'am. Won't you have a seat?"

She hesitated, nodded, and when he held her chair, sat. He smiled, finding it easy to smile when looking at her. She was breathtakingly beautiful: chestnut hair, blue eyes, patrician features, and a body . . . well, enough thinking along those lines. "Is there something I can do for you, ma'am?"

Again she hesitated, then nodded. "I think—Oh, I don't know. We need to talk, then I'll make up my mind."

Amused, he stared at her a moment. "If it involves me, I figure I'll have something to say about it too? What's your name?"

"Melanie Corbin, and of course you'll have a say in it."

He introduced himself even though she already knew his name from some source. The waitress walked to their table. He looked questioningly at Melanie. "Have dinner with me? We'll talk while we eat."

She picked up the menu.

They ate like two hungry people would—in silence. Then when the waitress put their coffee in front of them, Melanie locked gazes with him. "Mr. Buckner, I saw you shoot those men this afternoon, and yes, I know you had to do it or be killed. That leads me to think you're the man I need for a job."

"Miss Corbin, I don't need a job. What makes you think I might hire out to you?"

"Sir, I didn't imply you either wanted or needed a job. I thought, though, you might listen to my offer."

He allowed himself a slight smile and nodded. "Let's hear it."

She toyed with her napkin a moment, staring at it while she pulled its edges through her fingers. She looked up. "There are three of us; two darkies, old, almost a part of my family, and me. We left Virginia in the dark of night to get away from three brothers, one of whom, or perhaps all three, want my land and—and what little money I have left.

"Sir, I haven't seen them, but I know they're back there, and out here where no one knows me, or will miss me, I'm certain they'll not stop short of murder." She took a sip of her coffee. "I want to hire you, or some reliable man, to teach me about weapons, help me fight those men if need be, and—and shoot me if it looks like they're going to win the fight. I refuse to fall into their hands." She stared into her cup, obviously pondering whether to say more.

When she looked up, she nodded. "There's more than

what I've told you. I know something about them that would mean a hangman's knot for them from any court. That's why they will kill me. I'll not burden you with it unless you agree to take the job."

Buckner stared at her in disbelief. "Ma'am, it's not those behind you to give you worry. Do you realize you're askin' me to take you across Kiowa, Arapaho, an' part of Comanche lands? Why didn't you hook up with a wagon train in Independence?"

Her chin lifted and set in stubborn lines. "I'm not stupid, sir. I missed joining a wagon train by two days, and knowing those men were closing in on me, I left."

"Ma'am, I have to ask you this: how do you know they're followin' you? You could have gone anywhere in the West. Out of Independence you could have taken the Oregon Trail or the Santa Fe Trail. Fact is, wagon trains leave there for both places pretty often."

"Mr. Buckner, I'm not well versed in how to avoid being tracked. From my plantation, across to the Mississippi I left a trail a blind man could follow. Heavy wagon tracks from home to the first settlement, and in each town thereafter I asked questions how to get to the next town." She sighed. "And in Independence there were probably twenty merchants who could have told those asking after me where I headed, because I asked questions and was advised by almost all of them to not try to follow the Santa Fe Trail alone, but I was desperate."

Buckner took his pipe from his pocket and looked questioningly at her. She nodded. "Go ahead, I like the aroma."

While he tamped tobacco into the bowl and put fire to it, he felt the girl studying him, apparently wondering how much more to tell. When he sat back and looked into her eyes, she sighed and said, "I hated to abandon our plantation, it was a beautiful place, but these three carpetbaggers, brothers, want it, and they influenced the Yankee tax assessor to raise my taxes such that they would be impossible to pay—and the one I know by sight wanted *me* more than land, or money. Then I witnessed the act that put the fat in the fire—and they know I know.

"We had to leave. After dark that very night, Mama Tilde and Uncle Ned helped me pack a wagon and we lit out. They can have the plantation. It won't do me any good if I'm dead."

Buckner tilted his cup, studied its bottom through coffee grounds, pulled his handgun to a more comfortable position, and let silence hang between them. He didn't need a job. He had enough money to do pretty much whatever came to mind. This girl needed help, but by taking on the job he might get her killed, probably a more horrible death than the three chasing would commit. Also why had she picked him? There were others qualified to do what she asked.

He looked at her. "Ma'am, you don't know me. I could be as bad as those you're running from, and you don't know the danger you're asking me to take you into." He shook his head. "I won't do it, Miss Corbin."

Her shoulders slumped, and her face lost its expression of hope. "Very well, sir. I had to try. I know it was asking a lot—but I had to try."

Abruptly, not knowing why he did it, he covered her small hand lying on the table with his. "Miss, let me take back those words, let me think on it overnight. If it's all right with you, we'll meet here for breakfast. I'll give you my answer then." The way her face lit up, Buckner knew what his answer would be—damned fool that he was.

She stood. "In the morning then, about six-thirty?"

"That'll be fine, ma'am." He nodded. "In the morning."

When Buckner left the table, he went back to the saloon, wanting to play poker. On entering, he studied the people in the room and saw no one he thought might bring him trouble. One table at the back had an empty seat. He went to it and stood, studying the game and the players a moment. Although he didn't know the man who sat across the table, he'd heard of him. Bill Hickok, long blond hair, flowing mustache, red sash, and twin guns. Hickok looked up, nodded, and turned his attention back to the game. Buckner reckoned there were few in the West who hadn't heard of Hickok.

Another of the players he'd never seen or heard of, but his type could be found in most saloons from Independence to Santa Fe: small, bigmouthed, drinking too much, losing, and argumentative. The other four looked to be well-to-do cattlemen.

"Mind if I sit in?"

The man with a pack of cards in his hands looked up. "Fifty-dollar takeout, table stakes, five-card stud, three raises—no other game."

Buckner pulled several double eagles from his pocket, twisted the chair out, and sat. "Name's Buckner."

Each man around the table mentioned his own name. When it came to Hickok, he nodded. "Heard 'bout you, Buckner." A slight, cold smile crinkled the corners of his eyes. "Most of it good."

Buckner nodded his greeting. "Reckon there isn't a man west o' the Mississippi hasn't heard of you, Marshal. Thought you were carrying the badge for Abilene."

"That's right," Hickok said, "goin' back in the mornin'."

Buckner's eyes flicked to the short drunk; his name was Sneed. The man stared back, a sneer twisting his face. "This ain't no tea party. Get on with it." The little man's eyes turned toward the dealer. "Deal the damned cards."

An hour into the game, Buckner dragged another pot, one he figured would bring him about even. He glanced at the man who lost. The short, dirty drunk stared at the pile of Buckner's money, knocked back the drink in front of him, and snarled, "You jest about as slick with them cards as you are with them guns, ain't you."

Buckner, his hands busy stacking his winnings, locked gazes with him. "Meaning?"

"Meanin', seems like ever' time I figure I got a lock at you, you somehow get to drag the pot."

Buckner stuck the little man with a hard look. "Gonna tell you somethin', Sneed, only a damned fool plays poker when he's drunk. And that gun you're wearin' better stay in the holster. Don't push your luck."

He finished stacking his money, then pinned the mouthy one with another look. "Mister, you're not big enough to figure you could whip me. The only thing about you that makes us equal is that big iron you're carryin', an' even drunk I hope you got better sense than to try to use it. So, I figure you as a little bastard with a big mouth. Now, shut the hell up before I get too much of your jawin' and whip your ass, despite your size."

One of the players spoke, "You better do like the man said, Crowley. Mr. Buckner ain't one to make idle threats." It was Hickok who'd spoken.

The sore loser stood, gathered his change, and walked from the saloon. Hickok looked at Buckner. "Want to swap sides so you can watch the door? He'll be back."

Buckner shook his head. "Win, lose, or draw, I'm gonna play three more hands and get some sack time, an' that chair you're sittin' in seems lucky. Wouldn't ask you to give it up. Thanks anyway." He smiled. "If he comes back, let me know in time to turn around."

Hickok nodded.

Buckner lost two pots and won the third. He dragged the pot and stacked the money when Hickok said, "Behind you, friend. You got trouble."

Buckner threw himself to the side, aware at the same time every player at the table did the same. His hand flashed to his gun. Three shots tore the jumble of voices. With the last shot, a burning streak creased his shoulder.

The drunk stood inside the batwing doors. He fanned another shot toward the poker table. Buckner thumbed off two shots. Two black holes tore through the loser's shirt; one in his left shoulder, another between his elbow and side. The slugs turned him around. He caught himself, and tried to step forward. He stuck his hand out to trigger another shot, but his hand was empty. He'd dropped his gun when the first bullet belted him.

Buckner looked at his own torn and bloody shirtsleeve, then looked at Hickok. "Thanks, Hickok, figure he'd a got me."

Hickok only nodded. A glance showed Buckner one of

the other players with blood on his shirt. He looked into the man's eyes. "Bad?"

The wounded player shook his head. "Had rope burns worse."

The tall, high-shouldered man walked through the acrid stench of gunpowder to the one he'd just shot. "If you still had a gun in your hand, I'd kill you." He reached down, picked up the runt's gun, and stuck it in his own belt.

The mouthy man stared at Buckner a moment. "Tell you somethin', bounty hunter. You better watch yore back every trail you ride 'cause I'm gonna make you pay for this."

The town marshal walked up. "So you did it again, huh, bounty hunter? This time I *am* gonna cart you off to the hoosegow."

"In my town, Marshal, we try to hear both sides of a story before arresting a man."

The marshal's head snapped around to pin Hickok with a gaze. "Who the hell're you to tell me how to run my town, Hickok? This's my town, and I'm tired of slick guns killin' our citizens."

It looked to Buckner like a sheet of ice dropped over Hickok's eyes. "This man, in fact all of us playin' poker at that table," he flicked a thumb toward the table, "were attacked by that one bleedin' yonder. He fired three shots before any o' us had a chance to get a gun out. Buckner could have killed 'im, but he put his shots where he wanted 'em."

The Newton lawman turned his eyes back to Buckner. "Sounds like you lucked out again, gunfighter. You even swat a fly in my town again and I'll lock you up."

Buckner's neck muscles tightened, and anger boiled into his throat. "Mister, my hotel room's paid for an' I'm gonna use it. Then you're gonna pay me two thousand dollars for savin' you the trouble o' hangin' those men this afternoon, *then*, Mr. Marshal, I'm leavin' town." Buckner slipped his .44 gently back into its holster. "Now, you called me a gun fighter the second time. Don't do it again, or I'll make you prove it."

"You threatening me?"

Buckner let a thin smile bend his lips. "No, Marshal, they call it a promise where I come from. And, Marshal, be sure you have my money in the mornin'."

Hickok stepped between the two and steered Buckner toward the door. "You kill 'im, right or wrong, it'd put you on the wrong side o' the law. You don't want that." They walked across the dusty street and stopped in front of the hotel. "Where you headin' in the morning?"

"Dodge, I reckon—probably end up in New Mexico Territory or Colorado. Why?"

Hickok lit a cigar, inhaled a large drag, blew it out, and said, "Thought if we were headin' the same direction we could ride together. Heading back to Abilene, though, so that's out."

"Much obliged, Hickok, but I been offered a job. I might take it; if not, well hell, I might go to Abilene."

They talked a few more minutes and parted. Hickok to find a game in another saloon, Buckner headed for bed.

Long after he put his head on the pillow he thought of the girl who asked for his help. He wanted to do what she asked, but feared to get involved. He wanted to see the other side of the hills. The girl's problems would throw a huge kink in his freedom. But his conscience nagged him. Of course her beauty had something to do with his wanting to help her. He admitted to himself it did. But he couldn't afford to get involved.

He'd dreamed of finding a valley, somewhere high in the mountains. He could see it now behind his closed lids. His valley would be good for raising horses. He'd build his cabin before snow, sit out the winter, then get on with life.

He tossed and turned a couple of hours, gnawing at the girl's problem. Before sleep took him, he knew he would do what she asked.

CHAPTER 2

BUCKNER FINISHED HIS first cup of coffee when Melanie came through the doorway. He looked at his watch, six-thirty sharp. She was a woman of her word. He seated her, and before she could ask, he smiled. "Reckon we'll be trail partners for a while."

The way her face lighted up, he wished he could have the moment again. He sobered. "Ma'am, I'm gonna do this against my better judgement. You and your two friends will have to be willing to do as I say, as soon as I say it, without thinking, or we may all be killed. I'm not trying to scare you, ma'am, I'm just sayin' it like it is." She nodded.

"Now, I want to take a look at your rig, see what shape it's in, and check your provisions, guns, ammunition, everything. We'll go from here to Hutchinson, about three, three and a half days' travel. There we'll stock what supplies you're short on, including handguns and rifles for each of you." He pinned her with a gaze that brooked no argument. "All right?"

She nodded. "You're in charge, Mr. Buckner, but why Hutchinson, why not here?"

He cocked an eyebrow, smiled, and signaled the waitress. "We'll not stock up here, ma'am, because the town marshal and I don't rightly see eye-to-eye. He'll use any excuse to jail me. We'll go where I've not had trouble."

"I watched him yesterday. He didn't bother you then."

"Only because what I did was within the law—self-defense. Where is your wagon? I want to check it over before we pull out."

"It and my friends are at the edge of town. I'll get my bags and we can walk there together." She hesitated. "But we haven't talked about what you're going to charge me."

He hadn't given that any thought. He figured she couldn't

pay what he'd been making. He couldn't offer to do it for nothing for fear of hurting her feelings, yet she needed help. He smiled. "Why don't I charge you what a top hand would make, say, sixty a month?"

She nodded. "That'll be fine, sir. Now, I think I'd better get my things together."

"Take your time. The marshal has somethin' of mine. I'll pick it up first."

When she went upstairs, Buckner went to the livery stable, saddled his horse, went to the marshal's office, collected his money along with an order to get out of town, and then he rode across the street to the hotel.

Melanie waited for him at the hotel's desk. He took her bag, and they headed for the wagon. Buckner walked alongside her, leading his horse and carrying her valise.

On the way, he kept a sharp lookout for friends of the men he had killed the day before—and for anyone looking as though they threatened the girl. The only way he'd know those in either bunch would be if they attacked—then it might be too late.

As soon as he spotted the wagon, he liked what he saw. He'd been afraid it would be a light rig. Instead he looked on a heavy Studebaker, and a team of eight oxen grazing off to the side. Standing by the wagon were the two old darkies Melanie spoke of: the man, large, brawny, with just a sprinkling of gray at his temples; the woman, small, bird-like.

"Mama Tilde, Uncle Ned, I've brought a friend to help us."

Buckner stepped forward and shook hands. "Kurt Buckner. I'm pleased to meet you folks. We'll be spending long days and nights together, so call me Kurt." He looked over his shoulder at Melanie. "You too, ma'am. We aren't very formal here in the West."

"Will you call me Melanie?"

"My pleasure, ma'am." He walked to the oxen, looked them over, came back to the wagon, peered at the axle hubs to see if the wheels were properly greased, checked the leathers for wear or dry rot, crawled under the wagon to check the axles for cracks, came from under the heavy rig, and grunted with satisfaction. He gave Ned credit for everything being in almost perfect condition. "Hitch 'em up, Ned, I'll help. We're pullin' out for Hutchinson soon's you say we're ready."

"Yes, suh. No need for you to help, though. Figure I could do it in my sleep." His big smile said it all. He was pleased to have some of the load of protecting the women off his shoulders.

By the middle of the afternoon, Buckner figured they had put six or seven miles behind. Newton had long since dropped below a land swell. For miles, a rolling sea of grass, even now browning from the sun, bending with the wind, sighing, singing its song, standing straight with each slackening breeze, then again rippling in waves, the only moving thing in sight. Mixed with the ripening grass was the smell of dust, and the farther west they went, the heavier that scent would get.

Buckner dropped back from his lead position and rode alongside the wagon. "Ma'am, I'll not be spending much time back here. I'll scout ahead. Most likely not any Injuns close by, but I'd rather be sure. If we drive until dark, we ought to make the Little Arkansas. We'll take on water at that river. Might not be water again until we get to Hutchinson." He tipped his hat and rode ahead.

Not long after leaving, the small party dropped from his sight behind a slight rise. Another mile or so, and he cut tracks of unshod ponies, about ten of them he figured. They were headed north. Buckner shrugged. Nothing to worry about. Another mile, he again crossed the same sign. Then he saw them, but they saw him at the same time.

They kneed their horses in his direction, but didn't kick them into a run. He let out the breath he'd been holding. They'd be coming hell-for-leather if they meant him harm.

When they got close enough, he pegged them as being Osage, a tribe which had been friendly to Custer and Sheridan during the Battle of the Washita only five years before. But with an Indian you never knew. He kept his hand close to his handgun, they were that close now.

Their leader held his hand palm outward in the universal peace sign. Using signs, Buckner asked how far to water. Their leader signed back that he could reach it a little before sundown. Good, he thought, the wagon could make it by dark, or a little after. He asked if the party had crossed sign of anyone else. They answered, no. He reined his horse around and headed back.

At the wagon, he told them they wouldn't make camp for a while. He didn't want a dry camp. The oxen plodded on another five hours. They topped a rise before dropping to the river's floodplain bottom. Buckner stopped them and studied the trees, only a black line in the night. He looked for a flicker of firelight, an indication they wouldn't have the river alone. When satisfied they were here first, he motioned them ahead.

He led toward an oxbow where the river cut its path away from them. On this side there would be a cut-bank, on the other there should be a sandy beach. Although night would set in by the time they got there he wanted to camp on that beach. They would cross the stream in the dark. He worried about that only a moment. He'd find a ford before he led them into the sluggish water.

When the oxen stood up to their bellies in the river, Buckner let them drink their fill before signaling Ned to get them across. They reached the opposite bank without mishap. Then, when Ned went about setting up camp, Buckner nodded to himself with approval, mostly because the women stepped in and did their part. He then walked the bank gathering firewood.

He held the fire small, only large enough for cooking. No point in advertising their presence.

After supper, before sitting for coffee, he walked to the top of the bank and studied the horizon for sign of lightning. A riverbed was nowhere to be if it rained upstream. He watched several minutes, an occasional flash of heat lightning lit the sky, but nothing he worried about.

The four of them sat by the embers drinking coffee in silence. Finally, Buckner tossed the grounds from his cup, rinsed it in the river, picked up his bedroll, and started from the camp. He stopped, looked at Melanie, and said, "Miss, I don't want you to worry. I'll sleep away from the camp, be able to hear better an' see more that way. No need to set a watch tonight, I'll take care of that, for a while anyway. There'll come a time when we'll all have to take turns. 'Til then I'll take care of it."

She said, "Good night, Kurt."

He spread his blankets close to his picketed horse. The line-back dun stood watch for him most times when he thought horse-thieving Indians were no threat, and when he guessed danger was not too close. So it would again be tonight.

While lying, staring at the stars, his thoughts went to the girl. She was too beautiful to be real, and she impressed him with her backbone. Wanting to learn how to use weapons, and although raised as a lady, she did her share of driving the wagon, and in camp never waited for someone else to take care of any chore. He convinced himself his interest centered on her strength.

His thoughts shifted to the men following her, and he reminded himself he better sit her down and have her describe, in detail, the one she knew. Then he lay there soaking in the whisper of wind through the grass, the scent of baked soil and drying grass close to his cheek, and could think of nowhere else on earth he'd rather be.

After the war, he never considered going east when discharged. The West was where he belonged; the freedom, never depending on anyone but himself, the code of honor—and the swift, brutal justice a man carried in his holster. When he found those troubling the girl he would ask no lawman to help.

The next morning they were on the trail early, and the day was a repeat of the one before. But that night after supper, he took his coffee cup to where Melanie sat, and squatted in front of her. "Ma'am, I need you to tell me about the man following you. Need to know everything about him you can think of."

She stared at him a moment, blinked, frowned, then nodded. "All right. He's thin, with shoulders not nearly as nice and broad as yours." She blushed, apparently realizing she'd paid him a compliment, hesitated, then continued, "He's tall, about your height, and there any similarity ends. He's dirty, unshaven, sniffles continuously and wipes his nose on his sleeve every few seconds. His face is narrow, eyes close together, receding chin, bad teeth, and his nose is long, thin, and canted off to the side. At the top it flattens. It's probably been broken and never set. He has lank, greasy blond hair, looks like it's never been washed."

She sat there a moment, frowning, staring into the fire, then looked up. "The name he used back home was Paul Odom."

Buckner grinned. "Ma'am, if I could draw I couldn't have a better picture of 'im. Thanks." He picked up his bedroll and headed away from camp. He didn't ask what she knew that could get those following her hung. She'd tell him about that in her own good time.

About noon of the fourth day out of Newton, Buckner looked on the dark scraggly row of buildings making up Hutchinson's business district. "Ma'am, I'm gonna see if they have a decent hotel down yonder. If they do, I'll get a room for each of you so you can be comfortable while I'm gone."

"Gone? Where are you going?" Her voice sounded breathless, sort of scared.

Buckner studied her a moment. "Figure I better back-track. See can I come on any sign o' those men followin' you. If I cut their sign, I figure to ride into their camp in order to see what the other two look like."

Now she did look scared. "Won't that be dangerous, Kurt? Those are the kind of men who will rob you, given a chance."

He shook his head. "Don't figure to give 'em that chance, ma'am."

Melanie looked at him through a long silence. "Aren't you even a little nervous about meeting them alone?"

He cocked his mouth in a crooked grin. "If you only knew how often I've been scared, or nervous, ma'am, you'd fire me right now. Yes'm, reckon I know what fear is all about. I just pick the time to let it get ahold o' me."

She thought a moment, then looked at him and nodded. "All right, but get only two rooms. Mama Tilde and I'll share."

Buckner got the women situated in their rooms after arguing with Ned that he would scout the renegade's camp alone. He won that one, but lost when Ned insisted he would sleep in the wagon. "Ever'thing that little lady owns is in that there wagon, Mr. Kurt. I ain't lettin' nobody take nothin' b'longin' to her."

Kurt nodded. "I'll be back in a couple o' days, then we'll go shoppin'. Gonna make real shootists outta all o' you."

He'd never stripped the gear off his dun, so he climbed into the saddle and headed east within minutes after leaving the hotel.

Melanie watched Buckner from her room window. Every motion he made, to her thinking, was pure grace, and when he sat the saddle, he seemed to become part of his horse. She smiled. He was right handsome too, rugged features, black hair, and those steel-gray eyes seemed to look right through a person. She became aware that Mama Tilde was looking at her with a slight frown. "What's the trouble, Mama Tilde?"

"Trouble, little missy? That there man what just rode off is trouble—trouble for you."

"What on earth are you talking about? He's taking care of us, protecting us, and, I might add, in a very capable manner."

Tilde nodded. "You right, he doin' that all right, but you gotta remember, girl, I done raised you from a squallin', smelly little filly to a growed-up woman. Ain't never seen you look at a man like that." She busied herself hanging Melanie's dresses on a wall peg. "'Sides, that man's like some o' them wild horses we seen a few days ago. Ain't no woman gonna tame *him*."

Melanie went to Tilde and put her arms around her thin

shoulders. "Oh, Mama Tilde, I'm not interested in him *that* way. Besides, if I was, I wouldn't want to tame him. He's right nice the way he is."

Tilde stood back from her, arms crossed over her breasts. "See there? That's what I was talkin' 'bout, child. It's the way you look at 'im, the way you think 'bout 'im. Humph, like I said, that there man ain't gonna be nothin' but trouble."

Riding out of town, Buckner's thoughts centered on a different kind of trouble—gun trouble, man trouble. He figured he'd find those he looked for by noon the next day. It was late afternoon now and all he wanted to do was get out of town, put himself between the carpetbaggers and Melanie.

He made a dry camp that night and was on the trail again before daylight. About an hour after sunup, he walked his horse to a knoll, and sitting atop it searched the plains as far as he could see. No human form showed on the waving grass—but the fact he saw no riders meant nothing, they could be just over the next rise.

Every time he topped a rise he gave the distances a hard look. Then, soon before the sun reached its zenith, he saw what he thought might be them.

In the distance, appearing as only specks against the waving grass, were three riders. He reined toward them.

Buckner wanted to stay close only long enough to memorize what each looked like. They'd tracked Melanie's party with him as part of it since Newton, so now he rode fifty or so yards from the tracks he'd made before. The predators would know his horse tracks as well as he himself did. And after meeting with them, they'd know what he looked like. He didn't like the odds. In a shoot-out he figured he could get one, maybe two of them—but they'd get him too.

Approaching from opposite directions they closed pretty fast. About two o'clock, Buckner rode to them, keeping his hand close to his gun.

"Howdy, there aren't many on this trail. Good to see someone again."

The one in the lead, and from Melanie's description Buckner quickly tagged him as Paul Odom, said, "Where you headed, an' where you been?"

Blood rushed to Buckner's head; he tried to stop it but it didn't work. "Out here, mister, we don't ask a man those questions, so I have to say, it's none of your damned business." His fingers brushed the side of his holster, figuring he'd dumped the fat in the fire. Instead, Odom answered.

"You gotta 'scuse us, partner. We ain't used to them rules you got out here. Me an' my brothers, Abe, yonder on the gray mare, an' Sol there on the bay, are jest now gittin' into this country from the East."

Buckner sidled his horse away from them, nodded, and they rode on, looking only at the tracks made by the wagon and his horse headed west. He blew his breath out in a long gust. Someday he'd learn to keep his temper in tow. But now he'd know all of them when they met again. He continued in an easterly direction until they were out of sight, then in a roundabout route headed back to Hutchinson.

Buckner rode his horse hard to get back to town before Odom's bunch. He rode throughout the night, and reached Melanie's hotel about six o'clock the next morning. Thinking they might still be abed, he went to the dining room. He needed coffee and a good meal.

Before finding a table, he saw Melanie, Ned, and Tilde. "Ma'am, I found 'em. Know now what they all look like. I rode all night, figure they camped, so we should have all day to do our shoppin' 'fore they get here."

"You need sleep, Kurt. Make out a list and we'll do the shopping while you rest."

"Sleep anytime, ma'am. The first thing they'll do when they get here is look for the wagon, then they'll wait for you someplace the law won't bother 'em." He pulled out a chair and sat. "We'll eat first, buy what we need, and get on the trail. I'd rather be out where we can see." The waitress walked to their table.

When their breakfast came, they ate in silence. After his first cup of coffee, Buckner glanced at the three of them. "Don't hurry your breakfast, it'll be a while 'fore the stores open."

After their meal, they dallied over several cups of coffee before Buckner looked at his watch. "Time for buyin' that stuff we need." He stood.

In the general store, Buckner had each of them heft weapons, rifles and handguns, for weight. The women selected lighter guns. They each selected a Smith and Wesson .32. He thought that was sensible because the heavier guns would also kick harder when fired. He bought a Colt .44 for Ned. And he armed each of them with an 1873 Winchester .44-40 rifle.

On the trail he had checked the supplies, and now he replenished flour, sugar, coffee, and desiccated vegetables, a chunk of which, no larger than a man's hand, would swell enough to fill a vegetable bowl when wet. He loaded up on citric acid as a protection against scurvy, and other food-stuffs.

For clothing he requested the ladies to consider woolens, even though hot they would protect against the sun better, and the broad-brimmed felt hats he bought horrified the women, but he assured them they'd be happy they had them before long. Then knowing the bedding they had was good, he turned his attention to ammunition.

Finally satisfied they would be well fed, and able to protect themselves, Buckner had Ned pull the wagon to the back of the store. They packed their gear and put Hutchinson behind. The men who trailed them would make far better time on horseback than the oxen.

Melanie wanted to hurry, but Buckner cautioned her against haste for the animals' sakes. "Besides that, ma'am, there is no way we can go fast enough to stay ahead of 'em. We're gonna have to fight sooner or later, unless I can scare them into keepin' their distance. I figure to do that."

Without stopping, he frequently pointed out a rock, tuft of

grass, or cow pie, and had them fire at it. Without exception, they all needed individual instruction. The way it looked now, he was the only one who could hit the broad side of a barn—standing inside of it. The load sat heavier on his shoulders.

CHAPTER 3

BUCKNER STAYED IN the saddle from sunup until after sundown these days. The third day out of Hutchinson, they sat by their small buffalo chip fire drinking coffee. He'd had Ned sling a hammock under the wagon, and as they walked during the day they'd throw every dry chip they could find into it. Once they'd crossed a dry creekbed, where they found a few limbs and sticks washed down with some past rain. Melanie looked over the rim of her coffee cup at him. "Kurt, you're wearing yourself out. You won't do us any good dead." She took another sip of the hot liquid. "Why don't you leave a little later in the mornings, and come in sooner at night?"

He pushed his hat to the back of his head, frowned, and stared into the night surrounding them. "Ma'am, ahead of us are Indians, behind are men meaning you harm. If I can sight either o' them before they do us, it'll give us an edge. We're gonna need whatever advantage we can get. Ma'am, I don't dare slack off."

Melanie's smile looked as though she did it to cover the tears welling in her eyes. "I did you a great disservice asking you to take us to safety, didn't I, Kurt?"

He shook his head. "No, if I'd known the circumstances, you wouldn't have had to ask. But there was one thing I did know, an' I don't feel real good 'bout it even now. There are Indians out yonder, an' I hope I can keep y'all away from 'em."

"You talk like you know a great deal about the Indian. From your grammar, you sound like you've had more than a little schooling. How long have you been in the West?"

He stared at his cup a moment, then looked at her. "Been here all my life, but I attended Washington College in St. Louis a couple o' years. Went there from my father's ranch

23

in Texas, an' yes'm, I know quite a lot 'bout Indians. Fought the Comanche while I was growing up, then during the war I fought Apache, Kiowa, an' Yankees, then scouted for the bluecoats after the war." He smiled. "Now you know all 'bout me."

She locked eyes with his. "No, Kurt, I don't know nearly enough about you—but I will, given time."

He wondered what she meant by that last. They turned in early after cleaning up from supper. They'd have been in their blankets before now, except for Melanie staying up to keep supper warm for him.

Tired though he was, Buckner thought about the girl who had entrusted her safety to him. He didn't know how he had gained her trust, but there was no question about that. She *did* trust him implicitly. It made the burden even greater.

He turned on his side to see if it would help him stop thinking. A jagged streak of lightning cut the northwestern sky, throwing into sharp relief great, heavy buildups. He frowned, and focused his gaze hard in that direction, waiting for another flash to see the clouds better. Thunderstorms here on the plains could be as dangerous as anything nature threw at mankind.

The next flash showed angry, turbulent, gray-green masses close to the ground and reaching as high as he could see. He pushed out of the covers. Better safe than sorry.

Carrying his hastily rolled bedding, he woke Ned. "Get the oxen hitched. Rough weather on the way. B'lieve we still have time to get to a better place. I'll help in a minute."

Standing at the back of the wagon, he spoke quietly into the black maw. "Melanie, Mama Tilde, don't let us scare you. Ned and I are going to move the wagon, storm's gonna hit any minute now. Gonna lay my bedding in here at the back. I'll have Ned do the same, then I want you to close the back and front. No point in chancin' things gettin' soaked."

He found Ned at the front of the wagon, putting the animals in yokes. "Get your bedding and put it in the wagon, I'll finish up here."

While finishing the job Ned started, Buckner kept most of his attention on the clouds. Lightning flickered constantly now, and the storm closed on them faster than he liked. He needed more time. He'd seen a ravine about a quarter of a mile from where they camped. He wanted to get to it. He'd make up his mind what to do when he had a chance to gauge the storm better.

Ned joined him at the front of the team. "Ned, follow me. There's a ravine ahead. Don't go into it until I tell you. Leave the team hitched. We won't have time to mess around when I see what we have to do."

While heading for the gully, Buckner kept his eyes on the clouds. Lightning flashed in great jagged bolts, thunder a continuous crashing rumble, brimstone permeated the air. But he was glad for the light. Then, off to the side, a long, serpentine finger licked from the sky. His gut tightened, his hair roots tingled, and each hair stood on end. *Tornado*.

Ned brought the wagon to a stop almost on the brink of the ravine. "Hold 'em there, Ned. I'll tell you whether to go down the bank."

In the arroyo, danger from flash flood; here even more danger if the tornado headed toward them. The tornado thickened, blackened—and came to the ground. Rain pounded like wind-driven nails—then hail, about the size of small biscuits. "Get in the wagon, Ned. I'll handle the team."

Despite fear, Buckner kept his eyes glued to the angry black mass rolling along the ground. It looked like it would miss them. If it veered toward them he'd take the wagon into the ravine.

Again he thought of the three lives entrusted to his care, and figured they'd be better off lying flat on the ground if the twister hit them. "Ned, get the womenfolk outta the wagon. Lie down just over the brink of this gully—not in its bottom, but lower'n the surface o' this land we been ridin' on." He'd not taken his eyes from the roiling black mass. It looked like it would miss them.

The pound of hail deafened him, wind screamed like Comanche from hell and tore at his hair, his clothing. "Y'all get somethin' to cover your heads—somethin' hard, an' get in the ravine." He yelled at the top of his lungs, thinking the noise too great for them to hear. But they heard. Each emerged from the wagon bed holding cover over their heads. "Lie flat when you get over the bank." Again he was surprised they heard those instructions. Mama Tilde looked toward him and nodded.

Buckner's throat tightened until he had trouble sucking air to his lungs, his neck and shoulder muscles pulled at the back of his head such that he thought it would pull down into his chest. The smell of brimstone put a taste in his throat.

His eyes burned from staring at the constant explosions of light. Then, for the first time, he tracked the movement of the twister. If he'd been in its path, it would have grown, widened in his vision, but he'd not be able to see forward movement. From where he stood he saw the front edge of the boiling mass move toward him, but not at him. It looked to be heading barely to the side. He grinned, then laughed, knowing he must sound like an idiot, knowing his nerves let go with knowledge he'd done the right thing. His tight muscles relaxed, turned to water. Abruptly his throat opened to accept air. Hail still fell, but the stones got smaller by the second. In only a few moments, on the backside of the storm, rain fell in sheets, but danger passed them by.

"Come back to the wagon," he yelled.

A more bedraggled threesome he'd never seen. Clothes wet, muddy, clinging to their bodies, Melanie's hair stringing to her waist, all wide-eyed, staring at him—but they were the most beautiful people he'd ever seen.

Poor Tilde, so very thin, and now her soaked clothes accented her lack of flesh. He figured if he hadn't known she was there he'd have to look twice at the same spot to find her. His eyes locked on them, he laughed, laughed until tears ran down his cheeks.

"Laugh, damn you," Melanie stood with hands on hips, her chin thrust forward. "You're not so pretty yourself."

Buckner choked, gasped, controlled his laughter. "Ma'am, wet, muddy, face smudged, hair stringy, you're still the most beautiful woman I've ever seen."

"And you, Kurt Buckner, are the most magnificently brave and foolish man *I've* ever seen. You stood there in the path of that tornado, for some reason you and God alone know, trying to protect us."

"Ma'am, I stood there to see if I might be able to save the wagon. I was gonna wait'll the last minute and lead the oxen over the lip of the ravine, maybe save all your provisions."

"Oh, Kurt, our belongings are not worth you getting hurt. Don't ever do anything like that again."

"Yes'm." He said it but didn't mean it. If they'd lost the oxen, wagon, and its contents, they would have been as good as dead. But he wouldn't scare Melanie with that fact.

He pulled the heavy, silver watch from his pocket and glanced at it. "It's quarter of eleven, Melanie. You feel like cleanin' up and havin' coffee, or you want to get back to bed?"

"What do you think?"

"I think we should get to bed. Mornin's gonna be here 'fore we're ready for it."

Melanie nodded, and she and Tilde climbed to the back of the wagon. She smiled when she pulled the flap shut so she and Tilde could get out of their muddy clothes. Even though she'd told Kurt to call her Melanie, tonight was the first time he'd done so.

Mama Tilde's growling voice cut into her thoughts. "That man ain't nuthin' but trouble. I done told you what he was." She nodded. "Yeah, Lucifer wuz s'posed to be a sight for sore eyes, but I reckon if you stood Mr. Buckner alongside o' him Lucifer would a come out a mighty poor second. Mr. Buckner's 'bout the purtiest white man I ever done seen." She pulled her muddy, soggy dress over her head and put it in the pile she and Melanie would wash when they found a stream.

Melanie looked at Mama Tilde, not trying to hide her smile. Tilde looked at her and shook her head. "Child, I know what I'm gonna say ain't changin' yore mind one bit, but you gotta know that there is a wanderin' man. He ain't gonna set still for no woman, an' when he gets this here job done you hired him to do he's just gonna up an' ride on—an' he's gonna take yore heart with him."

Melanie pulled to her breast the only mother she'd known

since a small girl. "Oh, Mama Tilde, don't worry about me. I admire his strength, his courage, his loyalty—but I don't think of him the way you think."

"Humph. You ain't faced up to what you think of him. When you do, girl, you gonna surprise yoself, an' you gonna be the only what is surprised."

They finished undressing, put on dry gowns, and crawled between their blankets.

Melanie lay there thinking how her life had changed, and she thought of the man she'd given her trust.

If she'd ever had a doubt whether he had her welfare at heart, she had none now. When she'd peeked over the rim of that arroyo and seen him standing between her and harm, she almost died with fear for him. She'd come very close to climbing over the edge and going to stand at his side. She wondered, more than a little, if that wasn't where she belonged. Mama Tilde was wrong about one thing, she wasn't going to be surprised at any feeling she had for the tall, square-shouldered man. She just wasn't ready to pin down her feelings—yet. She again smiled. If Mama Tilde knew her thoughts, she'd pitch a fit. She went to sleep with that same smile on her lips.

A cloudless blue covered the heavens, washed clean and sparkling by the violent scrubbing the storm gave it. The grass took on a deeper green, the meadowlarks sang prettier, and a distant pronghorn bounded higher from the drenching of the night before. Melanie drank in the beauty surrounding her, and looked at Buckner. "It's awesome, Kurt. Anyone who's experienced a morning like this would have to fall in love with this country."

Mama Tilde grumbled under her breath, but Melanie heard her. "Be all right if the country wuz all a body gonna fall in love with."

Buckner returned her look, wary of what he thought he was beginning to see in her eyes. His free wandering ways were beginning to wear shackles. "Ma'am, it's true, this is a morning to hold close to your heart, but that rain's gonna make trackin' us mighty easy. We gonna leave ruts in this grass a blind man could follow." He looked at Ned. "Gonna ride out ahead, you keep a sharp lookout behind. If you see sign of anyone followin' fire a shot in the air. I'll come hightailin' it back."

"Yes, suh. You want I should shoot at anybody gettin' too close?"

"Three riders, yes. Don't take a chance. If they turn out to be friendly I'll square things with them."

Buckner forked his dun and headed west. While riding, he thought on ways to camouflage their trail, or a good place to turn north and maybe lose the predators following them. Regardless of his ideas, the tracks they were laying down, on dry ground, or mud, would still lead those following to their camp.

Movement broke his thoughts. He slitted his eyes and peered at the spot; another pronghorn bounded away. Satisfied no harm waited for them from that quarter, he nudged his gelding ahead. "Buckner," he muttered, "you're not thinkin' like you oughta. We can't outrun 'em, can't trick 'em, so that leaves only one alternative." He smiled, not feeling his face soften even a little bit. "That choice is what you should a been thinkin' all along."

Now he searched for Indians first, and second a ravine deep enough to hide the wagon. He rode another hour, keeping his eyes peeled for movement, and his ears tuned for a gunshot from the rear.

At the bottom of almost every swale, erosion cut through the thin topsoil, but not deep enough to pull the wagon into. He rode the shoulder of every rise, careful not to skyline himself and his horse. He rounded another of the rolling hills to see at its bottom a line of trees. That usually meant a stream. He hoped this stream had deep sides and most of the runoff from the rains of the night before had flowed on downstream.

Drawing closer to the line of cottonwoods and Russian olive trees, he searched for tracks, pony tracks. This would be a ready built place for an ambush. He picked up no sign, but didn't ignore the tightness in his chest, or his knotted stomach muscles. He rode just out of bow and arrow range while he scouted the area, counting on the fact if Indians were

there, with rifles, they would be poor shots with sorry
weapons, as was usually the case.

Buckner rode slowly, paralleling the stream. His gaze
picked the underbrush apart, twig by twig, leaf by leaf. The
only noise was the constant rustling of the cottonwood
leaves. He tested the air for smoke smell. What caused him
worry was the tightness of his muscles—and now, building
between his shoulder blades, a hard painful knot. Someone
had reached the stream before him.

As soon as he had the thought, something flashed from
the side. He dug heels into the dun, but not soon enough. An
arrow buried itself into his back muscles from the side.

Buckner reined the gelding hard toward the stream,
stretched low over its neck. He reached for his Winchester,
and pulled it from its scabbard at the same time he left his
horse's back at the tree line. He threw himself behind the
bole of a large cottonwood and lay still. The gelding ran
another twenty or thirty feet and stopped.

Buckner swept the area from where the arrow had come.
Then he looked at the dun standing in a shallow pool, ears
peaked, looking toward a bend in the creek to Buckner's
left. He gave that area most of his attention.

The arrow, after the first painful nauseating shock, sent
throbbing spasms through his back. Buckner put the pain
at the back of his mind. He figured there were no more than
two Indians set against him or they would have come
running by now. They had to know the arrow found its
mark. He waited, hardly daring to breathe.

Indians were known for their patience in situations like
this, while most white men would make some move that
would get them killed. Buckner had fought Indians all his
life, and adopted many of their ways. He lay still.

For over two hours, by Buckner's reckoning, he lay there,
not moving, dividing his attention between the bend in the
stream and the trees and steep banks to his back. Every time
he tensed his muscles the arrow lanced pain through him. If
the Indians had dipped the arrow point in rotten liver,
buffalo dung, or a myriad of other ways they knew to poison
it, he was in for some rough times, maybe death. But to lose

patience now was a sure way to bring about his last breath.

They were out there. He had never seen a warrior leave a fight without mutilating his victim, or taking his horse.

The sun reached its zenith and slipped toward the distant horizon. Buckner figured time now favored him. His attackers would make a move before dark. His horse still stood in the stream, water up to his fetlocks. Buckner wondered that he hadn't wandered off to graze. He glanced at the dun again, just as he swung his head to look to Buckner's right.

Buckner sensed a shape coming at him, swung his rifle and fired into the dark chest of the warrior who had already left his feet in a dive, knife held high for a swing at Buckner's body.

Buckner jacked another shell into the chamber and rolled to the side in time to avoid being hit by the falling Indian. He triggered another shot, this one to the head of the savage. His first shot would have killed the warrior, but not before he could kill Buckner. The second shot eliminated that chance.

Buckner twisted to look to his left. Another warrior splashed through the calf-deep water, an arrow nocked to his bowstring. Buckner put three shots in him before he could let the arrow fly. The Indian fell into the still waters, a red stain coloring the stream around him. Buckner still didn't move from the tree; there might be more of them.

He waited another hour, finally admitting to himself he had gotten the only ones in the area. They were probably a couple of hunters and had come on him by accident.

The sun, now only a half hour from the western horizon, urged him to get back to the three he was charged with caring for. He stood, taking care not to move the arrow more than he had to. The wound had stopped bleeding, but any movement shot pain through his back. Also he might start blood flowing again. He went to his horse, and headed for the wagon, hoping they had not had trouble. He glanced back at the high banks of the stream, satisfied he'd found the place to hide the Studebaker.

He rode into sight of their campfire a couple of hours after dark, and was surprised how quickly they learned.

None of them were in sight. "Hello the camp," he yelled. "It's Buckner. I'm riding in."

They appeared, not from the wagon, but from beyond the fringe of firelight. He nodded. They learned even faster than he thought.

When he swung from the saddle, stiff, sore, and very careful, Melanie ran to him.

"Oh, Kurt, you're hurt. Here, lie by the fire. Mama Tilde, get some rags. Ned, get one of those bottles of whisky Kurt insisted we buy, then fill the coffeepot and put it next to the fire."

Buckner walked to the fire and eased himself toward the ground. Before he could stretch out, Melanie stooped over him, holding his shoulders, tenderly letting him pick his most comfortable position.

CHAPTER 4

BUCKNER, STRETCHED OUT on his side, turned his head to look at Melanie, only to look deep into her eyes. He saw concern, tendering caring—but no fear. Even through the pain, pride in her tightened his throat; she was not just another spoiled, pampered Southern belle.

She said over her shoulder, "Ned, take Kurt's knife and cut this shirt away so I can see what damage this arrow's done."

"No, ma'am, don't cut this shirt off." His voice came out faint and wheezy, even to his ears. "I got only two more. I'll sew the hole up an' it'll be good as new."

"Kurt Buckner, you'll do as I say."

"No, ma'am. Let me tell you how to handle this. Reckon I've seen more o' this kind o' thing than you." He twisted to look as far back as he could to see the arrow shaft, groaned, grimaced, looked at her, then nodded. "All right, cut the shirt off. Then you gotta have Ned push the point through where he can grab the shaft, then break the fletch off. That way he can pull the shaft out." His face twisted in pain, though he tried not to show it. "After he gets the arrow out, I want you to clean the whole area, all the way through. Dip a rag in some o' that whisky an' push it through the hole with somethin'. Don't reckon those devils put poison on the head or I wouldn't have made it this far."

She stared at him, her face the color of cotton in the flickering firelight. "Kurt, you'll not be able to stand the pain. You'll pass out if I push a rag through that wound."

Not feeling any humor, he smiled, not moving a muscle for fear of causing another spasm of torture. "Ma'am, if you got any compassion in you at all, pray for me to do just that—pass out. Won't feel the hurt that way. Then, when I come to, I'll be wantin' a stiff drink o' that whisky, a good cup o' coffee, an' some o' that food I smell that's about to burn settin' by the fire."

Melanie's eyes widened, she whirled, took the hem of her skirt, and lifted the pot away from the coals. "Oh, thank goodness. I was trying to hold supper for you. I hope it's not ruined." Again she became all business. "Now, let's get you taken care of, and before we do anything I want you to take several big swallows of whisky. When you wake, you'll take another few swallows."

"Yes'm." Through the hurt, he couldn't help thinking this woman was *all* woman, the kind the right man could ride the river with. He took three healthy swallows of whisky, took another couple of mouthfuls, felt it burn all the way to his stomach, felt the arrow snap in Ned's huge hands—and in the middle of his groan, all went black.

He didn't know how long he'd been out, but when he swam out of the swirling darkness Melanie had wrapped a bandage around him and was tying it at his chest. "There," she said and patted the knot she'd made, "that ought to hold."

"Reckon it will, ma'am. How long I been out?"

Her eyes snapped from his chest to look into his. "About twenty minutes, Kurt. You ready for that drink now?"

"Yes'm, then while I'm eatin' y'all pack the wagon, hitch up, an' we're gonna ride a few more hours." He wanted to ask if the arrow went very deep, but figured it didn't. He thought it went from side to side not far under the skin. Anything worse, and he wouldn't have made it back.

"But you need to rest, Kurt, you . . ."

"No," he cut in, "I'm okay, an' we need to get the wagon hid 'fore those three coyotes catch up with us. We can't outrun 'em, so we'll pick our spot and fight."

"Can we find such a spot in the dark?"

He nodded. "Already found it. All we got to do is get to it. I figure when we disappear they'll muddle around tryin' to find us. When they do, we'll make 'em sorry." He took the bottle from her hands, tilted it, and swallowed until he was out of breath. Melanie had tied the bandage tight around him. It lessened the hurt when he moved.

He ate, then drank the coffee she had ready for him. When he finished eating Ned had the wagon ready to roll.

Only the rattle of trace chains and slap of harness broke the stillness. Buckner walked stiffly, favoring the raw wound in his back. He trudged along beside Ned and the lead oxen. He felt a little weak, but this was no time to baby himself. The dun trailed behind, tied to the tailgate. It was pushing three o'clock when they came on the stream.

Buckner made sure they were far upstream of where the afternoon's fight took place. They led the team into the creek, then by starlight walked farther upstream, staying in the water all the time, until the dim light showed sharp banks on either side with enough distance between the water's edge and the rise of the bank to park the wagon. He helped Melanie from the wagon bed, although she didn't put much weight on the hand he offered, while Ned lifted Mama Tilde.

"Ned an' I'll find firewood. Figure we can have a small fire an' coffee 'fore breakfast. Don't reckon those varmints trailin' us'll get here 'fore afternoon. We'll be ready for 'em."

Broken limbs and twigs were plentiful along the creek's edge, and before long they had as much fire burning as Buckner would allow. Sitting in comfortable silence, they drank coffee.

Buckner, after seeing how Melanie reacted to taking care of his wound, wasn't surprised that she seemed to be taking the coming confrontation with her enemies calmly. He studied her profile by the flickering firelight. She turned her head to look at him. "What's the matter, Kurt? I felt you staring at me."

"Just thinkin' you're one helluva woman, ma'am, if you'll pardon the expression. You've taken everything in stride, no backing off from anything."

She smiled, a quiet, pensive expression saddening her face. "Kurt, I was of an age to vividly remember the war. I learned a lot in those years, primarily, the weak don't survive. Whatever I am today is what circumstances made me."

Buckner stared into her eyes. "I reckon we can all say that, ma'am, and I say again, you're one helluva woman."

"Thank you, Kurt. I take that as a compliment."

"I meant it as such."

Silence again surrounded them until gray light showed in the east. Buckner stood and choked back a groan. His back had stiffened. He went to his saddle, pulled his Winchester from its scabbard, and slanted the three of them a look. "Check your weapons. Make sure they're clean and fully loaded. When they get here, hold your fire until I shoot. None of you are as good with your weapons yet as I want you to be, but you'll do. Shoot to kill. A wounded man is as dangerous as a healthy one."

The time between now and when Melanie's enemies showed up was the part Buckner hated. It gave them time to think, to worry, and time to let fear take hold of them. He found things for them to do, some were things that could have been put off, but if they were doing something it was less likely they'd dwell on the coming fight. He had Ned mend harness, Melanie and Mama Tilde washed clothes, he scouted the surrounding area, then walked downstream to find the warriors he'd killed the day before. Vultures already picked at the carcasses. He left them where they lay.

He went back to camp, picked places about twenty feet apart for each to take stations on, told them to continue what they were doing until he told them to get ready, but not to show themselves above the stream's bank. Then he took his station to watch.

Nothing indicated when their hunters would get this far, but by his figuring the wagon's speed, and the time it would take those on horseback to cover the same distance, he thought he wouldn't miss their arrival time by much. He didn't.

A hat's crown showed first, and as the rider climbed to the crest of the hill, more of him showed, then the other two rose above the hill's brow. Buckner slid down the bank, put his finger to his lips to signal silence, and motioned them to take stations. He almost had to laugh at Mama Tilde's fierce expression. She looked as though she welcomed the chance to fight.

From where Buckner lay at his downstream station, the only member of his party in sight was Melanie. He'd made sure he could keep his eyes on her all the way. The riders closed on them, seeming to take forever. Buckner wanted to get on with it, get rid of the vermin following them, then concentrate on getting his party across Indian lands.

The three rode close packed. All looked at the ground, following the muddy tracks.

The trail led them a distance downstream of where Buckner and his party waited. He slithered to the top of the bank to see what they'd do when they found the wagon tracks didn't appear on the opposite side of the stream.

They rode into the trees, time enough lapsed for them to cross the creek, then they returned to the side Buckner and his small party watched. They studied the tracks a moment, sat there and talked, then split, two going downstream, and one, not the leader, coming toward where Buckner lay. He looked toward Melanie and motioned her to lie flat.

Buckner heard the approaching rider splashing in the creekbed before he saw him. He hated to shoot a man from ambush, but he had three greenhorns to think about. Still he gave the man a chance—a very slim one.

"Over here, trash," Buckner said, his voice barely carrying the few feet separating him from the rider.

The squat, heavily muscled man Buckner remembered as the one called Abe jerked as though shot, looked toward Buckner in time to catch the slug that knocked him from the saddle. He hit the ground, groped for his side gun, but never got hold of it. Buckner jacked another shell into the chamber and fired into the man's head. Half of his face disappeared in a spray of red and gray. Buckner blew a hard breath through his nose to rid himself of the acrid stench of gun smoke. He spun to look at Melanie. "Stay where you are. Keep the others here. I'm goin' after the other two." She opened her mouth as though to say something. He motioned her to silence and turned his attention downstream.

He worked his way down the creek's edge, tree to tree, each time stopping long enough to search ahead. He favored his wound, but not enough that it caused him to make noise. His stomach rolled with fear for the woman he'd left behind. If the renegades got him, the two darkies would never be able to protect her. Odom, the one she seemed to fear most, was out there somewhere. He again stopped behind the bole of a large cottonwood; a Russian olive's branches and leaves would hide him but wouldn't stop a bullet. He again searched ahead—and saw movement, only a shadow flit to a tree about two hundred yards downstream.

They had left their horses, at least one of them had. Buckner stayed where he was. Waited. Soon the shadow moved from behind the tree, ran to another and crouched behind it. Buckner drew a bead on the tree, but his eyes were busy, searching for the other gunman. The one behind the tree wasn't Odom.

The man ahead of him had never learned patience. He stayed behind the tree only long enough to take a quick glance at what might lie ahead, then darted for another tree. Buckner's bullet caught him in mid-stride. He fell and squirmed back to the tree he'd left.

Buckner knew as soon as he fired he'd shot too fast. Another shadow joined the one Buckner shot, but didn't expose enough of himself for Buckner to get off a shot. He'd probably drag his partner to safety.

"Damn!" Buckner reached in his pocket and shoved fresh loads into the magazine. He kept his eyes on the cottonwood, but it shielded any movement behind it. After a long while, he heard running horses.

He darted from the trees and saw two men racing away, one leaning over the horse's neck, holding to the saddle horn. They took the extra horse with them. Buckner raised his rifle, took careful aim, fired, but knew when he did the range was too great. Odom and his brother headed back the way they'd come.

Buckner slid down the creek bank, went to the man he'd killed, gathered his guns and what money he had on him, then motioned Melanie to get Ned and Mama Tilde and come to the fire. When they got there he looked tiredly at them. "They're gone for now. Figure they'll go off, lick their wounds, an' hit us another day. You notice they went back the way they come? That's so they won't lose us. Our tracks'll lead 'em to us again." He looked at the coffeepot still sitting by the coals. "Relax. That coffee should be 'bout thick as mud, so let's enjoy a cup of it."

While they drank, Buckner studied each of them, and wished he hadn't. They were like children. They put their trust in him fully. There was no indication they thought he might not be able to get the job done, and with that they showed no fear. Thank God they didn't know how scared he was, or what Indians could do to a person before killing them, or what they did to mutilate an enemy's body after death. It was time they had another lesson in marksmanship.

"Soon's we finish our coffee, we're gonna do some more shootin'. Last night made me aware y'all have to protect yourselves without me helpin', so you're gonna learn to shoot with the best of 'em."

Melanie stood. "I'm going to look at your wound first. You've done nothing to give it a chance to start healing."

"Aw now, ma'am, it'll be all right. Wait'll in the mornin'."

She shook her head. "I'll look at it now." Buckner sighed. He was learning that to argue with her was futile.

After looking at the wound and pronouncing it red and irritated, but good enough until the morrow, she picked up her rifle.

Buckner set up a target and had them face it. He had his choice of putting his arms around one of them to demonstrate how to hold their rifle. He chose Melanie.

Standing behind her, holding the stock to her shoulder, and holding her hand under his to the barrel, he fired a couple of shots with her, then had her try it alone. When she missed, he repeated the action. The third time, she said under her breath, so only he could hear, "I think you're getting too much enjoyment out of this, Kurt Buckner." Even though there was a smile in her voice, he felt himself turn fiery red. He stepped back.

"Sorry, ma'am. Reckon I can show Ned, or Mama Tilde, an' you can watch."

The smile in her voice turned into a full-throated laugh. "Don't you dare, Kurt. I do believe I'm having as much fun with this as you are." She hoisted her rifle to her shoulder in an exaggerated erroneous position and smiled over her shoulder at him.

He frowned. "No. We won't use ammunition for a while. We'll dry-fire until each of you know how to hold, aim, and squeeze off a round."

The three of them dry-fired rifles and pistols until late in the afternoon. It was only after he was satisfied with their progress Buckner let them load and fire at the target. By sundown, he grunted his satisfaction. "That's enough for one day. You're all doing better'n I expected." He looked at Mama Tilde. "That rifle is bigger'n you, but you handle it like a two-hundred-pound man." He swept them all with a glance. "Let's clean up. Figure our stomachs need fillin'." He glanced at Melanie, who obviously waited for a word of praise. "Reckon I'm gonna have to give *you* some more lessons from scratch." He got the reaction he wanted. She blushed prettily to the roots of her hair. Buckner hid a grin, picked up a few pieces of wood, and stoked the fire.

Every fifteen or twenty minutes during the afternoon Buckner had walked to the top of the bank and searched the swells of the surrounding hills for sign of strangers.

After supper, he told them he and Ned would take turns standing watch; he didn't expect the two renegades back yet, but there was always the chance for Indians. They soon crawled into their blankets.

Long into the night, Buckner thought of Melanie, her strength, her beauty, the feelings he felt stirring in his chest. He denied those feelings, fought them, while only a few feet away, in the wagon, Mama Tilde talked to Melanie about *her* feelings.

"I tell you, child, you wuz actin' like a brazen hussy with that there man, lettin' him snuggle up close to you learnin' you how to use that gun, an'—an' you wuz invitin' him to keep on doin' it long after you knew 'zacktly whut to do."

She slipped another petticoat over her head. As soon as her mouth came clear again, she continued. "Now, little missy, I didn't raise you up like that. I brung you up to act like a lady, an' you ain't doin' it. Now you got that man actin' the same way, sayin' he gonna start you to learnin' all over again. You don't need no more teachin' with that gun. You jest need practice, an' if he puts his arms around you tomorrow I'm gonna whop 'im a good one 'crost his haid."

Melanie tried to choke back a giggle, but it came out anyway. "Oh, Mama Tilde, we were just having fun with each other. I think you don't want *any* man to pay much attention to me. I'm a grown woman, honey. I know you mean well, but I'm not going to do anything to make you ashamed of me."

After several more minutes of grumping, Mama Tilde pulled the covers up to her chin, looked at Melanie, grinned, and said, "Reckon if I wuz a young lady I'd take a second look at that man myself. He shore is pretty, ain't he."

Melanie giggled again. "Mama Tilde, he's about the handsomest man I've ever seen. To top that off, he's the *most man* I've ever seen." She pulled her cover up, turned on her side, and snuggled down with her thoughts of the tall, square-shouldered man. He had some rough edges, and had more self-confidence than any man she'd known—but maybe that was what drew her to him. She smiled into the dark, pulled her blankets up under her chin, and closed her eyes.

Chapter 5

THE NEXT MORNING, Melanie dressed his wound before breakfast and checked for signs of festering. "It looks good, Kurt. Do you always heal this easily?"

Buckner put on his most solemn face. "Well now, ma'am, I'll tell you my secret. First off, I live a mighty clean life; second, it's the good brand o' whisky I drink. It heals things almost faster'n they stop bleedin'. And third, I always try to get shot where there's a beautiful woman to give me tender care. Amazin' what a healin' influence a beautiful woman can be when she places her hands on me." He looked at her, all wide-eyed innocence. "You reckon that's what folks mean when they talk about placin' of the hands?"

She stood back from him, hands on hips. "Kurt Buckner, that's outright sacrilege. It's a wonder a bolt of lightning doesn't strike you."

With an amused expression, Buckner looked at her a moment. "Ma'am reckon just 'bout everything has happened to me *except* a lightning strike. Also, you're gonna find I'm not what many would call a religious man." He reached for his coffee cup. "An', ma'am, you're the only *beautiful* woman I've ever known. Yeah, I've seen a few I'd call downright pretty, but none who could hold a candle to you." He filled his coffee cup. "That you can take as a compliment too." He went to his bedding, placed his cup on the ground beside it, and rolled his blanket tight around his belongings for storage behind his saddle.

When he had his bedroll tight enough to satisfy him, he sat there on his knees, frowning. What the devil was the matter with him? He wasn't given to loose banter with women, nor was he known to give idle compliments. Usually, if he spoke to a woman, it was to offer a wish for a good day. He shook his head. This wasn't loose banter, or idle compliments. He had meant every word—and it worried him. He'd better get these folks where they were going—soon, or those endless trails over the next hill would be over for him. He tied his bedroll to the back of his saddle and went to the fire. Breakfast was ready.

He didn't talk much during the meal, and when he'd finished eating he threw his hull on the dun, cinched it down, and climbed aboard. The gelding offered a couple of halfhearted bucks as though he knew it was expected of him. "Ned, keep a sharp eye toward the rear. I'll be out in front. You women keep your rifles close." He kneed the dun toward the limitless west, and the last thing he heard was Melanie's "Please be careful, Kurt."

All day, he rode a half circle in front of the heavy Studebaker's course, looking for sign. He thought on what action to take if he crossed Indian sign. He'd fight only if he couldn't avoid it.

He would keep his party below the crest of every hill, keep them out of sight, if possible. If he could spot a war party before they saw him, he thought with careful maneuvering he could get his charges across this territory and on to Dodge safely. He'd find out Melanie's plans from there.

About four o'clock, the sun still high, he figured his party had made about fifteen miles; they'd make close to twenty before the sun set. He rode about two miles ahead of them. Then he saw the Indians, six of them. They obviously saw him at the same time and kneed their horses in his direction.

Buckner swallowed the brassy taste of fear, but more welled into his throat. When they were close enough, he recognized the lead warrior—Yellow Tail; he'd fought with and against him many times.

"Buckner, what you do out here? Where the so-jurs, they behind you?"

Buckner thought to try and lie himself out of this, but figured it would be futile. "No soldiers, Yellow Tail. I travel with two women and a man. They're behind me. What you do here?"

"This Kiowa land. Belong here. What *you* do here?"

"I take women an' man to mountains, then I, alone, will

cross the hot sands on the other side of the mountains, there's no water there, then I gotta cross more big mountains, an' finally I'll get to the great waters." Buckner nodded, then continued, "Yeah, this's your land. I only want to cross it in peace. You're not painted for war, you look for somethin'?"

Yellow Tail eyed him a moment. His warriors pulled abreast each other in a line, but left the wiry little warrior out in front. Yellow Tail nodded. "Look for two warriors, my warriors. They been gone two suns."

Buckner thought on his words a moment. The two warriors the Kiowa party looked for were surely the ones he'd killed. How could he get out of this? He decided the only way was to lie, and hope.

"Yellow Tail, three men been chasin' me an' my woman. I come on your warriors about the time those three were in a fight with them. I joined up with your men. The three chasin' us killed both o' them. I killed one of the three. The other two ran." Buckner pointed toward the east. "They go toward the morning sun, but will come back. They want to kill my woman."

The wiry warrior studied Buckner a moment. The tall man hardly dared breathe; he wanted to swallow the bile in his throat, but the Kiowa would notice that small thing and know it was fear. Finally Yellow Tail spoke. "Many times you fight with the Kiowa against our enemies." A slight smile broke his solemn countenance. "And, Buckner, when Kiowa got no enemies to fight, you fight *us*."

The smile told Buckner he could breathe again, for now. He grinned. "That's the way with men, brave chief." He spread his hands. "What would life be without a good fight?"

Yellow Tail motioned his men to ride on, and before urging his pony ahead, said, "Cross Kiowa land in peace, Buckner. We not bother you."

When he looked only at their ponies' rumps, Buckner blew his breath out through puffed cheeks. Now the only things he had to worry about were Comanche and Arapaho. Maybe Yellow Tail would catch the remaining two of

Melanie's enemies and save him the trouble of killing them. He reined his horse toward the wagon.

He figured when Yellow Tail found his warriors and the dead white man, he'd believe his story because the white man had been killed with a bullet.

While covering the distance, he tuned his ears for shots, hoping Ned, Melanie, or certainly Mama Tilde would not fire at Yellow Tail's party and bring on a fight. When he rode to the Studebaker without hearing shots, he knew the Kiowa had stayed out of sight.

Ned walked alongside the pair of lead steers, while Melanie and Mama Tilde sat in the box. Buckner reined the gelding to ride alongside. "Y'all see anything?"

Melanie shook her head. "Only rolling hills and distance, Kurt."

He grinned. "Count your blessings, ma'am. Usually, out here anything you see other than those things you mentioned is not good."

They rode another four hours. Kurt again wanted to camp in a ravine where they could have a fire. He found what he wanted. The only water sat in low places in stagnant pools, enough for the oxen. He figured for coffee and washing up they'd use water from the barrels tied to the side of the wagon.

After supper, sitting with their usual cup of coffee, Kurt looked at Melanie. "Figure you can trust me enough now to tell me what you know about the men chasing you. You know what I mean, the thing that can get 'em hung."

"Oh, Kurt, it's not that I haven't trusted you. I—I'm just so ashamed of the cowardly way I handled it." She stared into her cup a few moments, then looked him in the eye. She sighed. "I'll tell you now. I hope you'll not think less of me."

He narrowed his lids. "Ma'am, I reckon there's very little on this earth that would make me think less o' you. Now, I'm not pushin', but if you feel like talkin' 'bout it, tell me the story. It might give me an edge sometime when I need it."

She stared into the fire a few moments, stood, poured a

cup of coffee, sat, and gave him a straight-on look. She nodded. "It was a cold day, a light powdering of snow lay on the countryside, and I rode over to see my good friend, Nellie Bryson. Her husband, Orrin, was mayor of the village close to our plantation.

"I didn't want to bother the stable boy, get him out in the cold, so I rode straight to the barn, put my horse in a stall, and was about to head for the house when horses rode up. Normally, I would have gone outside to see who the company was, but for some reason I held back, but looked around the edge of the door to see them. It was Odom and two others. I couldn't see the two. Their backs were to me.

"Odom hailed the house, yelling for Bryson to come outside, they wanted to talk with him.

"Bryson walked into the yard, and the next thing I knew they were arguing. Odom hit Orrin, knocked him down. That's when Nellie ran from the house with nothing but a broom for a weapon. She hit one of the other two on the head and shoulders with it, then started after Odom. The third man swung at Nellie, knocked her to the ground, and pulled a gun. Odom also drew a weapon and they both fired into Orrin. I found out later those two shots killed him.

"Then Odom went and stood over Nellie, reached down and ripped her dress off. The three of them took turns violating my dear friend, and—and I did nothing."

Tears streaked her cheeks, then she sobbed. "I let them do their evil thing, Kurt, and didn't even try to stop them." She lowered her face into her hands and sobbed until her shoulders shook. Buckner wanted to console her, but had never been faced with a woman crying her heart out. He didn't know what to do.

Finally she looked up. "I had no gun, or I might have tried to protect her. After they slaked their animal lust on poor Nellie, they rode off. I was scared to death. I didn't know where to run, or who to notify. I mounted Beauty, my pet mare, and ran for home. That's Beauty tied to the tailgate, along with another prize mare. The stallion back there is a thoroughbred. I think if I ever find safety, they'll make a start on a horse herd.

"I hadn't gotten far when I saw one of the three had tarried behind, I suppose to see if anyone followed. He saw me as soon as I saw him.

"For the first time in my life, I put the spurs to Beauty. I almost ran her to death, but I got home ahead of the man pursuing me. I ran in the house, took the Greener, double-barreled twelve-gauge off the wall, loaded it, and ran him off.

"It was coming on to dusk by then. Ned, Mama Tilde, and I packed our things. I knew if we stayed there we'd never be safe. They couldn't let me live, knowing I'd seen them commit their evil deed. I took only a few of my most prized possessions, and I took the money I'd sworn to use only to save the plantation, and we left. We've managed to stay ahead of them until now."

"Where was the law all this time?"

"Kurt, the law in our village belonged to the likes of Odom. They were all carpetbaggers. They came to town in the same bunch, and literally took over. I had no idea how to reach the Army, and the large towns were too far away to make a run for, so we headed west." She gazed into her empty cup, and almost in a whisper said, "You must think I'm the most contemptible woman alive for leaving my friends like that."

Buckner stood, walked around the fire, stooped, took her chin between his thumb and forefinger, and lifted her face so he could look her in the eyes. "Ma'am, reckon in the same situation, with nothing at hand to fight with, I'd a done the same, anyone would. Now, you quit blamin' yourself for somethin' not of your makin'." He cocked her head a little to the side. "Now you dry your eyes an' give me one o' those pretty smiles I've seen so often."

While Melanie washed her face at the side of the wagon, Buckner went to his bedroll, poured himself a stiff jolt of whisky, turned to again sit by the fire, frowned and looked at Ned. "'Scuse me, Ned. You want a drink? For that matter, would either o' you ladies like a toddy?"

"I don't know about either of them, Kurt, but you could pour me just a bit in my cup."

Ned cleared his throat, and looked at Mama Tilde. She stared daggers at him, daring him to accept. He glanced at Buckner, then looked at the ground and mumbled, "Don't reckon I better, Mr. Kurt, my stomach's been givin' me a little trouble lately." Then he grinned, a smile that showed snow-white teeth. "An' besides, reckon if I took that drink my stomach would get a lot worse, 'specially after Tilde got through beatin' on it."

Mama Tilde rocked back on her skinny backsides, slapped her thighs, and laughed. "Aw, git outta here, man. You go on an' have a drink with Mr. Kurt. I ain't gonna, though. Somebody in this here bunch has gotta keep good sense about 'em."

Buckner sweetened Melanie's coffee, poured Ned a healthy shot, and again sat by the fire, thinking. Finally, he looked at the three of them. "Don't know who's carryin' the badge in Dodge these days. Don't know if the telegraph has reached there yet, but if it has, I'll try to get the marshal to verify your story. If he can do that before Odom and his man get there, we'll show that trash what Western justice is all about. He ought to look mighty fine dancin' from a cottonwood limb."

"Kurt, I don't want either of them to hang."

Surprised, Buckner looked at her. "Don't you want them punished?"

If he hadn't seen it he wouldn't have believed it. Those beautiful eyes were hard as agates. "Mr. Buckner, hanging is too swift, too easy. I want them to hurt as bad as they made Nellie hurt."

He stared into her icy eyes a long moment—a very long moment. "Ma'am, if that's what you want, I better take care o' them myself. Reckon I know how to get it done to satisfy you."

She nodded, never softening. "You do that, Mr. Buckner, and I'll be mighty beholden to you."

Damn, he thought, I want to be awful careful never to make an enemy of that woman. She's got a hard streak in her like railroad iron. Then, he smiled to himself, but she sure can be soft and feminine the rest of the time.

Another four days passed before they topped a rise and saw Dodge City spread below them. Buckner studied it a moment, surprised, wondering if he'd taken them to the right town. Dodge had grown. From the distance, he picked out Front Street, the jail, and several other buildings he recognized. He led his charges into town.

After getting the three settled in the hotel, Buckner looked up the town marshal. "Hear you're havin' ever'body check their guns on comin' into town, Marshal." At the marshal's nod, Buckner continued, "I need to keep my weapons." The lawman opened his mouth to protest, but Buckner cut him off. "You take my weapons, an' you're gonna cause a young woman and her two companions to get killed. You don't have the time or the men to protect her." Then he told the marshal the story Melanie had told him.

The lawman stared thoughtfully at his scarred old desk, then with a jerk of his head, said, "That'll do it." He reached in his top drawer and pulled out a badge. "Cain't pay you nothin' for wearin' this, but it'll give me an excuse for you keepin' your guns." He grinned. "Hell, you done been doin' law work anyway, bringin' in them lawbreakers."

Buckner pinned on the badge. "Won't do anything to shame this badge, Marshal, just want to take care o' those who trust me to do so."

Despite wearing the badge, Buckner saddled up every morning and rode out of town. He wanted to meet Odom and his partner outside of the marshal's jurisdiction if possible. In town, he'd have to kill them, or put them in jail. That wouldn't satisfy Melanie, or him. Out here, he thought to take them prisoner and deal with them according to Melanie's wishes. He covered as much territory east of town as one man could.

Sitting atop a knoll, a week after arriving in Dodge, Buckner scanned every hilltop, every stretch of open prairie. The two horsemen he looked for were nowhere in sight. He glanced at the sun and guess five o'clock was close on him. He headed back to town. They'd wasted enough time.

He thought to cross Raton Pass, go through the Cimarron

Canyon, and look at that country south of Red River, although he'd heard the town of Red River harbored every hard case in the west at one time or another. He shrugged; they wouldn't be any tougher than those he'd faced in the past.

He still had in mind to scout the land for a good place to raise horses. A herd of the hammerheaded wild mustangs would be a start, but he'd like to get a good stallion to upgrade them. From his musings, he looked up and found himself on the outskirts of Dodge. "Have to watch getting lost in thought," he grunted.

CHAPTER 6

As soon as he hit town, Buckner headed for the hotel. "Ma'am, you reckon you're rested enough to hit the trail again? Don't figure Odom an' his pal are comin' in town. I been watchin' our back trail for the last week, an' haven't seen sign o' them. Fact is, I reckon they holed up somewhere to get the one healed up—or Yellow Tail took care of our troubles for us, but I'm not bankin' on that."

Melanie smiled. "Kurt, I must be part Gypsy. I've been ready to go since the second day."

"Good, I'll tell Ned. In the mornin', we're gonna have to replenish our provisions." He stepped toward the door. "At supper we'll need to talk about where you want to go from here."

She seemed to square her shoulders and brace herself at his words. "Are you anxious to finish with us and leave, Kurt?"

He studied what to say next. He had other things to do, but he'd agreed to see them safely wherever they decided to stop running, and by his thinking, he'd agreed to make sure Odom didn't harm them. "No, ma'am, but we can't wander aimlessly about in these western lands. I have some ideas about places you'd like. We'll talk about it at supper. You think on it 'til then."

Buckner went from Melanie's room to the barbershop, got a haircut and a bath, thought to go by the marshal's office and turn in the badge, again changed his mind, and decided to keep it until morning. He went to the saloon. He wanted a drink, and to play a few hands of poker. The Longbranch had always been his favorite watering hole.

He had one drink and was nursing his second one when he heard a ruckus toward the back of the room. He squinted to see better, not believing his eyes. Sneed, the dirty, mouthy man he'd had trouble with in Newton was up to his old

51

tricks, drunk, gambling, and causing trouble. Buckner wondered how he'd gotten in town without his seeing him. He shrugged. It didn't make any difference, he was here. Buckner stepped toward the door. He'd find a poker game somewhere else.

"Hey, bounty hunter, come on back an' sit in on this here game. Maybe I can catch you bottom-dealin' this time."

Buckner stopped, turned toward the filthy runt. He'd gone quiet inside. A cold clarity fitted itself to his brain. He'd taken all off this scum he figured to take. With having to check your guns in this town, he figured he'd whip hell out of the trash and leave him lying on the floor with the rest of the filth. Then, through habit, he glanced at Sneed's holster. *It had a gun in it.*

"Sneed, give me your gun, and we'll forget those words."

The little man looked him up and down. "Ah. See you done got yourself a badge since I seen you last. Well, big lawman, come take this here 44 off'n me—if you can."

Buckner didn't want to kill the man, didn't want to take advantage of the favor the marshal had done him, but how was he to get out of this without a killing? "Sneed, your only problem is, you got a big mouth. Take the gun off an' I'll go someplace else to do my drinkin'. We won't have any trouble that way, an' you can stay here an' enjoy your game."

Sneed sneered. "Scared, big man? You don't have Hickok backin' you here. You gotta fight your own battles. Draw, damn you!"

Buckner thought if he turned his back and walked away, he might avoid this fight—but knew better.

He twisted toward the batwings, but kept his eyes on Sneed while doing so.

"Damn you!" Sneed yelled. His hand flashed toward his gun. He was fast, a lot faster than Bucker had figured.

Buckner threw himself to the side. His Colt came into his hand almost by magic. It belched once—twice. Sneed staggered back, two holes in his chest. He caught his balance, stepped toward Buckner, and brought his gun up to fire. Buckner thumbed off another shot. It took the small gunman in the face, tearing it apart. Sneed stumbled again, his reflexes triggered off another shot that went into the ceiling, then he fell like a wet rag at Buckner's feet. The tall man stared through the powder smoke at the lump of meat that had only moments before been a man—of sorts. He shucked spent shells from his Colt and shoved fresh ones into the cylinder. The silence was complete, he could hear every shell click into its seat, then noise erupted around him. Several men at once announced they'd seen the whole thing. One told Buckner he thought he was a gone gozling when he turned his back. Others commented on his gun-quick. A couple of others gazed at the corpse a moment, then ran for the door to get rid of their supper. A graying, grizzled, United States deputy marshal stood at Buckner's shoulder. "I saw it, son. I was afeared when you turned your back, he'd kill you." He nodded. "It was self-defense, all right. Fact is, I never seen a draw faster'n your'n, but I do know you drew after he started his."

"Thank you, sir, but I really never took my eyes off him. He did exactly what I figured he'd do. Any man that predictable isn't gonna live long."

Buckner walked to the bar, had another drink, and brought a couple of bottles to take with him. For me, one would a been enough, he thought, but looks like Melanie's gonna have a toddy with me 'bout every night.

He went from the Longbranch to the marshal's office and turned in his badge. "Thanks, Marshal. I'd a been a dead man if you hadn't let me keep my gun. Thanks again." He tipped his hat and left.

He'd lost his desire to play poker, so he went to his room, stashed the bottles, and went to the dining room.

He sat there drinking coffee until Melanie, Ned, and Mama Tilde came in.

After eating, he again brought up the subject of where they were going. "Thought maybe you might have an idea of what you want to do, an' where you want to do it."

She looked lost. "Kurt, I have no idea where I want to go. I don't know anything about this country. I thought to raise horses, but I'm going to need a lot more than a couple of brood mares and one stallion. I'm going to need men. I'll need to build a house. Oh," she shook her head, "I don't know. All I've thought of so far is escaping Odom. I have to do a lot more planning." She turned those blue eyes on him. "Will you help me plan the things I must do, Kurt?" He felt those imaginary shackles tighten, and the long trails become a mite shorter.

He wanted to say, "No, ma'am. I'll deliver you to wherever you say, an' then I'm takin' off." Instead, he heard himself saying, "Why sure, ma'am. Reckon we can figure out somethin' together."

Well, hell. He couldn't go off and leave a poor defenseless female out in this wilderness all alone. Her smile made him feel a little better.

"Well, ma'am, I been thinkin' o' horse ranchin' myself for a spell now. I can take you to the country I been thinkin' 'bout settlin' in."

For some reason, at that very moment, Mama Tilde groaned, buried her face in her hands, and said something Buckner understood as, "Lord help my poor little girl, the devil done got 'er."

He shook his head, naaahh, he must have misunderstood. Those words wouldn't make any sense at all.

Melanie glanced at Tilde with a strange expression, grimaced, and looked at Buckner. "Tell me about this place."

"I figure to head outta here, stay on the Old Santa Fe Trail, right alongside the Arkansas to Bent's Fort. There, we'll stay on the trail, but we leave the Arkansas, may have a few dry days ahead of us. Then we'll cross the Purgatoire at Trinidad. Outta there we go over Raton Pass, down to Cimarron Canyon, through it to Eagle's Nest. Everything north, south, east, an' west outta Eagle's Nest is the kind o' country I been lookin' for. Course, if you'd rather, we'll go to Walsenburg and take it from there."

Melanie shook her head before he had the words out. "No, Kurt, we'll do as you say."

Again, Mama Tilde growled, "Ain't got no mind o' her own no more, just does what *he* says. Like I told 'er, trouble's sittin' slap dab in her lap, an' she ain't doin' nothin' to git rid o' it."

Buckner frowned. "Mama Tilde, somethin' botherin you? Aren't you feelin' well?"

Tilde looked at him, her face bland as baby food. "Nah, suh. I wuz jest sort a singin' a song to myself, one we use to sing back home. Didn't know you could hear."

He nodded and turned his attention back to Melanie. "We'll buy the things we need in the mornin' an' head out. Get a good night's sleep." He stood, frowned. "If we're gonna go down that way, we might hook up with a wagon train outta here. There's still quite a few of them. Of course, some are takin' the Cimarron Cutoff, but it's drier'n a cowboy who's been ridin' fence for a month. Anyway it won't take us to where we need to turn off for the canyon. We could put the wagon on a railcar, but the railroad only got to Dodge last year. They're still a long way this side o' Trinidad. We wouldn't gain anything that way.

"A couple days ago I saw a group o' wagons snakin' their way toward Dodge. If they'll let us join 'em 'til we cut off toward Cimarron Canyon, we won't have to worry so much 'bout redskins." He took another sip of his coffee. "Fact is, we'll kill two birds with one stone; the Odoms'll know we joined up with a train, but they won't dare attack you while you're with it. They'll have to wait until we get to Bent's Fort, or Trinidad, or after we cut loose from the train down below Raton." He talked while he thought through the problem. He frowned. "The only problem with that is they're gonna know where we're goin' long's we're with the train and'll be able to get ahead o' us." He shrugged. "We'll worry 'bout that when the time comes."

Melanie agreed. They talked only a moment longer before going to their rooms.

Buckner argued with himself half the night as to why he'd promised to take Melanie to the very place he'd thought to start his horse ranch. "Well, hell," he muttered, "there's room for two ranches there, an' I can help 'er get started." With that thought, he turned on his side and went to sleep.

At breakfast, Buckner told Melanie to do what shopping she needed. He intended to ride out east of town and see if the wagon train's arrival was imminent. He handed Ned a list of things he needed.

He'd only topped one hill when he saw what he looked for, but by his figuring it would take the wagons until noon to get to Dodge.

He watched a moment, thinking to go back to the hotel and await their arrival, then thought he might as well ride out to meet them, see the wagon boss, and if it was agreeable he could get back to town and have his party ready to go by the time the westward bound immigrants reached Dodge. He kneed his horse toward the wagons rolling in four parallel columns.

The four columns told Buckner the wagon boss was an old hand at trailing west. Riding parallel like they were accomplished several things, not least of which was the ease to circle up for defense.

It took him an hour to reach the foremost wagon, a Conestoga. A tired-looking, middle-aged man held the straps. His wife, weathered, old before her time, rode at his side. Buckner tipped his hat. "Howdy. Where y'all headed?"

"California—if we ever make it."

"You got a lot o' dry miles ahead o' you, but you'll get there. Where might I find the wagon boss?"

"Just rode toward the end o' the train. Ride on back. He's a tall man, wearin' one o' them big hats, black, like the one you got on. He's ridin' an Appaloosa gelding, only horse like it in the train."

Buckner again tipped his hat and rode toward the last wagon. He hadn't reached the end when he met the man he looked for coming toward him. The closer he got, the more certain he was that he knew him. He grinned. "Carraway, you old sunuvagun, still herdin' pilgrims to the promised land?" Before giving the old man time to answer, Buckner cocked his head to the side and raked Carraway with a look from head to toe. "Damned if I don't believe you're gettin' fat. I only gotta look once to see you."

Carraway, tall, gangly, looking like he wore skin only to

hold his bones together, smiled. "Buckner, what you doin' out here all alone?"

Buckner reined the dun around to ride alongside. "Hell, man, I'm not alone now. I'm with you, but you lose any weight at all, *then* I'll be alone."

"Uh-oh, you treatin' me friendly with no more insults than that, you want somethin'."

Buckner nodded. "You got that right, you dried up old hunk o' rawhide. I got a woman an' her two companions I'm tryin' to get to Eagle's Nest. We'd like to hook up with your outfit to where we cut off for Cimarron Canyon."

Carraway frowned. "Fine by me, but you know I got to get the okay from the people in the train. Fact is, I ain't seen nothin' but greenhorns, 'cept for my scout, since we left Independence. I shore ain't gonna say no. We can use yore gun."

"How long 'fore you can let me know?"

Carraway squinted into the distance, chewed on his huge cud of tobacco a couple of times, then looked at Buckner. "Figure to have an answer by supper tonight. We'll pull the wagons to that field other side o' the Santa Fe tracks." He rolled his cud to a more comfortable position. "Figure you'll git a 'come on in' from them. They'll have new blood to argue with."

Buckner nodded, tipped his hat, and kneed his horse toward town.

He was even with the general store when he saw Ned come out the door. He tied the gelding to the hitching rail and stepped to the boardwalk. "Miss Melanie with you?"

"Yes, suh. She's in yonder looking at stuff she done looked at ever' day since we got here." He pushed his hat to the back of his head. "Mr. Kurt, the only women I ever knowed wuz Miss Melanie an' Tilde. Now what I want to know is, do all women got somethin' missin' in their haid that makes 'em got to look at ever'thing in a store ten times, an' each time they look at it, they gotta *touch* it, *smell it, ooh an' ahh over it*, then they kind of sniffle, give it a look like 'what in the world would a body make somethin' like that for,' then they walk off. But they come right back the next day an' do the same thing."

Buckner could see Ned's patience was at its limits, but couldn't let him get away without rubbing salt in his wound. He put on his most serious face. "Ned, I don't rightly know, maybe it's the same sickness makes us do that very same thing when we're lookin' for a woman, 'cept we usually only take two or three times to make up our minds."

"Humph, if we had a ounce o' brains, we'd tuck our tails an' run like the devil. Leave 'em all to drive each other crazy."

Buckner laughed and slapped Ned on the back. "Yeah, an' then we'd go crazy with wantin' 'em." He went in the store, found Melanie, and told her not to get in a hurry, they'd wait for the decision of those in the wagon train. From there he went to the Studebaker. He placed their provisions for easy riding, tied them down, greased the axle hubs, tightened the big wheel bolts, checked the harness, inspected the animals for sores, and when satisfied all was trail-ready, he went back to the hotel and sat on the bench in front of the store. From there, he watched Carraway bring the train in soon after noon, and park them in the same formation as they'd had while rolling.

While the men took care of the stock, the women, in groups of five or six, walked toward the business district. Buckner grinned to himself, thinking there was enough looking, touching, and mind changing in any one group of them to put poor Ned in the nuthouse.

He whiled away the afternoon, talking with loiterers in front of the store, drank coffee in the cafe, played poker, and finally stood and walked toward the wagons.

Carraway met him when he walked up. "They're agreed y'all can join up with us. Don't reckon I ever had a doubt they'd say yes."

"Good. How much you gonna charge us for that short distance?"

Carraway grinned. "Now don't start talkin' like y'all ain't gonna be with us no further than that there livery barn yonder. That's a fur piece you gonna be usin' my protection an' trail savvy. You be needin' both, *you* still bein' wet behind the ears."

"Why dang you, Bill Carraway." Buckner rose to the bait. "I'm half your age and twice as trail-wise. I—I . . ." He stopped in mid-sentence, studied the old man a moment, then laughed. "You old bag o' bones, you did it to me again." Through slitted lids, he looked hard at Carraway. "How much it gonna cost us?"

"Well, we talked it over, an' after my convincin' 'em you wuz one ring-tailed Texas bad man with a gun, an' knowed Injuns better'n any man I ever seen, they said if you'd help scout, it wouldn't cost you nothin'."

Buckner nodded. "I owe you, Carraway." Then he shook his head. "Yep, I owe you, an' wish I didn't. Know dang well you gonna get to me good 'fore we leave the train."

Carraway grabbed his hat by the brim, swung it from his head, and slapped his knee with it, laughing like he'd heard the funniest joke ever. "You right, Buckner. I'll git you."

CHAPTER 7

 · ——————— ·

BUCKNER AGAIN FOUND Melanie, this time in the cafe. "All set. We join 'em, an' I pay for the priviledge by helpin' scout. We got one of the best wagon bosses there is, I've known 'im a long time."

"If you have faith in him, Kurt, I know he's all right."

Although Melanie appeared to have all the faith in the world he could protect her against any odds, Buckner felt a ton of weight come off his shoulders. Getting across Comanche and Arapaho lands weighed heavy on him. Riding with the wagon train increased their safety a hundredfold.

He looked up. Ned and Tilde walked to the table. "Ned, after we eat, drive the wagon to that train, an' park it where Mr. Carraway, the wagon boss, wants it. We do what he says until we leave 'em the other side o' Raton Pass."

"He ain't gonna have no trouble from me, Mr. Kurt."

"Good, I wasn't sayin' he would, Ned, just wanted you to know that in a wagon train there's only one boss, an' I won't be it."

They ordered, and when the waitress brought their food, Buckner looked at Melanie. "We better get you outta the hotel and your stuff in the wagon 'fore Ned takes it down yonder. We'll sleep at the train tonight. Don't want to miss leavin' with it, but I sort of think Carraway'll stay here a couple o' days, let the womenfolk rest a bit 'fore headin' out again."

They did as Buckner thought. The wagon boss gave them three days to rest and get their equipment in shape. During that time, Melanie, Ned, and Tilde got to know their traveling companions.

The train included Southerners and Northerners, many who had fought in the War Between the States, and,

Buckner thought, some among them had been in the same battles, only on different sides. He looked at Carraway. "You have any trouble with Rebel an' Yankee sentiment among these people?"

Carraway gave Buckner a straight-on stare. "Podnuh, how long you knowed me?" He nodded. "Long time, huh? You know how I run a train. Ain't gonna stand for no trouble. For the most part, most o' these here people already thinkin' o' themselves as Californios. They're tryin' to put the war behind 'em, but we got two men, neither o' them married, what would be troublemakers if I give 'em half a chance."

Buckner raised an eyebrow. "Somehow, I don't figure you give 'em that much chance. Bet if we pinned 'em down, neither o' them fought on either side."

"You're probably right, son. Now, reckon you better git some sleep. I want these wagons rollin' by first light, an' you gonna be out ahead o' us a ways."

Buckner hitched his gun belt to a more comfortable position. "You gonna keep 'em on the north side o' the river?"

Carraway nodded. "Yep. Ain't gonna ford the river 'til we pass Bent's Fort."

"Been meanin' to ask you, Carraway, anything still goin' on at Bent's place?"

"Don't know, son. Last time I wuz by there, it wuz being used as a stage station. Might be all shut down by now. We'll know when we get there."

The next morning when Buckner rolled out of his blankets, Melanie was already up and had fixed breakfast for him.

"Ma'am, there was no need for you to do this. You need your rest."

She cast him a slight smile. "Kurt, when a man's going out to try and keep us safe, the least I can do is be sure he's properly fed. Now you eat and drink your coffee. I'll catch a few winks after you leave."

While eating, he couldn't help thinking how nice it was

for a woman to concern herself enough to take care of a man
when his job would keep him from fixing himself something. The shackles of captivity tightened.

By the time the sun topped the horizon, Buckner was two
or three miles out ahead of the train. He studied the terrain,
trying to figure where he would come at the train if he was
a Comanche. Normally, they roamed to the south of the
Arkansas, but in his experience a Comanche went wherever
he wanted, whenever he wanted. He kept a sharp eye on the
south side of the river, but didn't neglect the side he rode on.

Several times during the day, he crossed the stream, rode
to the brow of the highest hill, and searched for sign of
riders. About three o'clock he came onto pony tracks, about
thirty of them by his best guess. That big a party must be
wearing war paint.

From the saddle he gazed at the tracks, climbed down,
and took a closer look. While on the ground, he pulled a few
blades of grass, so dry and brittle they broke off in his
fingers. Finally satisfied, he climbed back in the saddle. The
sign he'd read said the party passed this way over a week
before. "Hope we don't get any closer to 'em than that," he
muttered. The last time he'd seen Comanche up close and
personal, the Kwahadi had insisted he be their guest, until
he managed to steal a pony and hightail it outta there with
about twenty howling warriors on his tail.

He again crossed the Arkansas, thinking how dry the
grass was. Any little spark from a campfire, or a lightning
strike, would start a prairie fire. Also, it was not uncommon
for the Plains Indians to deliberately start a fire to trap deer.
"Well, no sense in me borrowing trouble. Got enough
without that." Buckner rode until the sun edged below the
horizon, not until then did he turn his horse toward the train.

It was after nine o'clock when he climbed from his rig
alongside the fire where Carraway hunkered sipping a cup
of coffee. "All's quiet. Grass is mighty dry, though. Caution
your people to be careful with fire." At the thin man's nod,
Buckner turned toward Melanie's wagon. She had supper
ready for him.

"Gonna have a drink first." He glanced questioningly at her. "Have one with me?"

She smiled and nodded. "Looks like that's the only excuse I have to sit and talk with you."

"Never figured you needed an excuse. Sit. I'll pour us each a belt." His gaze swept the area. "Ned an' Tilde already turned in?"

"An hour ago."

He poured their drink, and they sat there quietly sipping it. Buckner felt himself relax with the whisky warmth working its way to his stomach. He started to ask if any riders had joined the train since morning, thinking if there were it might be Odom, but he knew she would have told him *that* news right off. After a while he felt her looking at him.

"Kurt, do you look for us to have trouble? You stayed out so long after dark I was getting concerned about you."

He looked over the rim of his cup at her. "Ma'am, the things can happen are countless, an' most o' them bad. No, ma'am, I don't look for us to have trouble, but I dang sure better keep my eyes open for it. Nothin' for you to worry 'bout, though." He grinned. "You're in good hands. Carraway knew what he was doin' when he asked me to scout for this train. The other scout's a good man, but he hasn't had the experience at it I've had."

Melanie smiled in that quiet way she had. "I wasn't worried about us back here in the wagons. I was worried about *you*. Your confidence might cause you to take chances."

"Nope, that's the edge experience gives a man. I know when to take chances, mostly when I have to."

They sat there awhile longer, then Melanie asked, "You ever been married, Kurt?"

He studied the small swallow of whisky in the bottom of his cup a moment, thought to have another shot, and decided against it. He wondered where this conversation could lead, and braced against it. "No, ma'am, never been. Never stayed still long enough. Reckon someday, if I ever settle down, I might feel the need."

"But you can't ride these hills, alone, forever. Do you never think of going home? You said your father has a ranch down in Texas. Who'll run it when he gets too old?"

Buckner shrugged. He felt on safer ground, now that the talk was off the subject of marriage. "My brother Karl always wanted it, and he doesn't get itchy feet much, so he can have it. If I ever have a ranch, it'll be one I build with my own hands."

She nodded. "I can understand that. I've never experienced building something on my own, but I imagine it would be a wonderful feeling." She looked at his cup. "Going to have another before you eat?"

"Nope, this's enough."

Melanie dished up his supper, poured coffee, hesitated, then poured herself a cup. "I shouldn't do this, probably won't sleep a wink."

In the middle of his meal, Buckner cast her a glance. "It's not that I don't appreciate it, ma'am, but you stay in your blankets in the mornin'. No need to fix me breakfast."

She smiled. "I wouldn't think of it, Kurt. Breakfast will be ready when you are."

Buckner turned in soon after supper. Saddle-up time would be here before he knew it, and he was tired. Despite his fatigue, he lay awake, thinking about the talk Melanie laid on him while he had his drink. "Why goldang it, she might nigh ruined the taste o' good whisky," he growled to himself. "It's not as though I haven't been lookin' at 'er. Lordy, have I ever. She's just too danged beautiful, too danged nice to me, too danged trusting, too—too. Oh, hell. Too everything. And to top it off, she's a strong woman. The kind who'd put her shoulder to a load right 'longside her man."

He thought to find Carraway in the morning and negotiate paying for Melanie to stay in the train under its protection, then he'd just flat out ride off—no, he'd kick that line-back dun into a fast run and get gone fast as all getout. But, come daylight, he rode well out in front of the train, his eyes peeled for danger. Again, he left the train with a full stomach.

He crossed pony sign twice that morning. Each set of tracks were several days old. That afternoon it rained, not enough to do the grass any good, but enough to wipe out the ability to judge the age of any tracks he might find, unless they were made after the rain. About four o'clock, he shot an eight-point buck, tied it across his horse's rump, and headed for camp. He'd still have daylight left when he got there.

Still about a mile from the lead wagons, he topped a hill, abruptly reined the dun around, and dropped below the brow. He ground-reined the gelding, came out of the saddle, and snaked his way back to the top. Two warriors lay just under the ridge of the next swell, looking the opposite direction. Buckner had not a doubt they had the wagon train in full sight, and if he let them alone they'd leave, and come back with a good-sized war party.

The Indians' ponies stood at the bottom of the swale between him and them. He drew a bend on the horse nearest him, shook his head, and took his rifle sights off the pony. He'd kill a horse only as a last resort. He studied the warriors lying across from him, absorbed in the sight ahead of them, and wondered how close he could get before they became aware of him. He decided to find out. His grin didn't reflect humor, he did it to cover fear.

You're a fool, Buckner, he thought. You could stay there behind that hill and shoot them both before they knew you were there.

His stomach muscles tightened, a knot formed in his throat, a brassy taste choked him. He eased toward them with no more sound than the wind. Scared, yeah, but times like this made life worth living.

He held his Winchester at the ready in case either of them turned and saw him. He got to their horses, passed them, and it was then one of the mustangs snorted and stomped his hooves. Buckner ran toward his quarry. The Indian to Buckner's right twisted, brought his rifle around, fired, but his shot went toward the heavens. Buckner's shot tore into his chest; he staggered, came on on rubbery legs, bent at the waist, falling. Buckner fired again. His second shot took the warrior through his right eye. Buckner shifted his Winchester to his left hand, drew his side gun, thumbed off a shot, missed, and slipped his thumb off the hammer a second time.

He never saw where that shot went. A sledgehammer hit him alongside his head. The world turned a brilliant, shimmering red. He tried to get off a third shot, but couldn't make his thumb work right. All went black.

From total darkness, Buckner tried to swim out of the deep, weightless void. His arms weighed a ton. He tried to move his legs under him. They wouldn't do what he wanted. He had to get going, get out of whatever kept him from doing his job. He had to warn Carraway.

He opened his eyes a slit. Red again shimmered and danced in front of him. He opened his eyes wider. A fire flickered in his ring of vision. He closed his eyes again, not wanting to look around, knowing he'd see the red, cruel faces of Comanche. He'd failed Melanie, and Carraway.

The inside of his head felt like he'd been on a tequila drunk. All the demons of hell beat a tattoo both inside and outside his skull.

He tried to move his hands, certain they would be tied. They weren't. He tried his legs. Bonds didn't hinder their movement either. He again opened his eyes. He lay in the middle of a circle of wagons. Carraway sat on the ground staring at him. Melanie stood there, her face pale. She stepped toward him, but the wagon boss stuck out his arm, keeping her away. "Leave him alone, girl. Let 'im get his bearings. He's liable to come at you swingin' 'fore he knows where he is."

"Mr. Carraway, he's hurt—bad maybe. He needs me."

"Miss Corbin, if he wuz hurt bad, I'd be right there with you, fixin' 'im up, but he ain't, so leave 'im be."

"Damn, Carraway, let the woman take care o' me. You just jealous 'cause nobody would fix you if you were hurt."

Melanie's eyes widened, Carraway smirked, shifted his chew from one side of his jaws to the other, and looked at Melanie. "See what I mean, ma'am? He's sneaky. Bet he's been a-layin' there playin' possum, tryin' to get some attention."

Before the thin man finished his sentence, Buckner remembered why his head hurt so bad. "Carraway, there were two Comanche 'longside that hill. I know I got one, but I figure the one who shot me got away. Remember firin' at 'im. Think I missed."

The wagon master shook his head. "Naw, you got 'em both, boy. We heard shots, then ever'thing went quiet. It was then I rode out to see what was goin' on. Found you a-layin' at the feet o' one. The other was stretched out a little farther up the hill, both dead." He squinted at Buckner. "Reckon you are back to the world enough for Miss Melanie to dress that scratch you got 'longside yore head?"

Buckner tried to stand, got as far as his knees, then all went dark again.

When he came out of it the next time, tender fingers swabbed at the side of his head, and Melanie was crooning words any man would like to hear from a beautiful woman. "Oh, you poor dear. I don't know what I'd do if I lost you. You're the sweetest, bravest man who ever lived. I can't believe anyone would think of you as a cold, uncaring man. I'm going to make you well if there is any way in this world to do it."

Next, the cut alongside his head burned like she'd stuck a branding iron to it. He smelled whisky. "Ma'am, you're not wastin' my good whisky on that gash, are you? 'Sides, I'm all right now." He tried to sit up. She placed her hand flat on his chest.

"You're not going anywhere right now, Kurt Buckner. You're going to let me fix this wound, bandage it, give you a healthy drink of this whisky, then I'll let you go back to our wagon, but I'm going to help you. You'll have to lean on me."

It wasn't until then he became aware most in the train stood in a circle around him, watching Melanie administer to his sore head. "Ma'am, if you think I'd let all these people see me leanin' on a tiny slip of a girl like you, you must've taken a hit on the head worse than I did."

"Kurt Buckner, I'm no slip of a girl. Just because you stand a whole head taller than me doesn't make me small and dainty. You're a big man—well not so big sideways, but tall and well-built."

"Why, thank you, ma'am. Didn't know you'd noticed what a fine figure of a man I am." He felt pleasure at seeing his sarcasm make her blush.

She finished taking care of his wound, and despite his protests helped him to his feet. He stood still, wavering a bit, trying to get his equilibrium. When finally he thought he could make it without help, he stepped toward Melanie's wagon, staggered, and felt her arm go around his waist. He didn't fight it this time.

When Ned saw them coming, he hurried and took Buckner's other side. They got him to their fire, helped him to slowly sit, then Melanie went to get his cup. She gripped the bottle in her left hand after using some of its contents to disinfect his scalp.

Being careful to pour only a small amount in the cup, she looked past the cup into his eyes. "Ma'am, that's not a man-sized drink. Pour a drink into that cup."

"Kurt, it might not be good for you. You have a pretty bad concussion."

"Get your cup an' have one with me. I'll drink it slow."

They were in the middle of their drink when Carraway walked up. "Buckner, take it easy tomorrow. One man can handle it."

"Sit down, Carraway. Have a drink while I tell you how it's gonna be."

"Uh-oh, yore ears are gitten longer, boy. Much more an' you'll look like the stubborn mule you act like."

"Mule or not, Mr. Wagon Boss, I'm goin' out in the mornin'. Comanche gonna be all over these hills. You don't need a damned greenhorn out yonder. You need me."

CHAPTER 8

SEVERAL TIMES DURING the night, Buckner woke. He'd turned on his side and rested his head on the raw, throbbing head wound, hurting enough to bring him out of a sound sleep. When finally it again wakened him, he smelled frying bacon and the aroma of coffee brewing. Melanie had stoked the fire and sat at its side turning strips of bacon in the skillet.

He sat up, groaned, and sat still, letting the world stop spinning. He'd not had such a headache since one night in Juárez; a Mexican hit him alongside his head with a full bottle of tequila, breaking the bottle, and not doing his head much good either. A terrible waste of good tequila.

"You just lie back down, Kurt. You're not riding today. The horse's jolting might start your head to bleeding inside. It'd kill you."

He squeezed his eyes tight shut a moment, then squinted at her. "Ma'am, if I don't go out yonder, I might not be the only dead jasper round here." He nodded toward the coffeepot. "If that mud's fit to drink yet, I sure could use a cup."

A worried frown marring her forehead, she poured him a full cup. "I wish you wouldn't do this, Kurt. Let someone else take the risk today."

"No, ma'am. I'm the one to do it."

She dished him a plate full of beans, put four strips of crisp, thick sliced bacon with the rind still on at the side of his plate, along with a couple of hot flaky biscuits. He slanted her a teasing look. "Lordy day, ma'am, don't see how a woman who cooks like this can stay single. Looks like some lucky man would a grabbed you up a long time ago." The words hardly out of his mouth, he wondered why he'd said such a danged fool thing.

She cut him a piercing gaze. "Kurt, it's only recently I ever met a man who I'd let grab me up, as you say."

Oh, Lordy, those shackles tightened a few more links. As good as the breakfast was, Buckner ate in a hurry. He had to get on the trail—besides, he didn't trust himself to sit here by the fire with the most beautiful woman in the world. He was hell-bound to let his big mouth get him into a lifetime of staying in one place. He swallowed the last bite, stood, squeezed back the dizziness, thanked her for again sacrificing her sleep in order to feed him, and saddled the gelding.

When he rode from camp, the only sounds in the early morning darkness were the swishing of his horse's hooves through the dry grass.

Careful not to skyline himself, he rode the shoulders of every hill, studying the rim of the next one before riding to circle it.

As soon as the Comanche figured the two scouts they'd sent out were not coming back, they'd be hell-bent to find the cause, and Buckner gave them only until about high noon to accomplish that goal.

The sun about two hours high, Buckner rounded a rocky outcrop—and faced a young warrior, not a horse's length ahead of him, painted for war. He didn't even think of his handgun. A shot would warn the whole Comanche Nation. His hand swept to the back of his belt and pulled his Bowie knife in one fluid motion.

The young buck didn't hesitate. He opened his mouth to utter a warning cry when Buckner kneed the dun into the side of his pony. The warrior fell off the opposite side of his horse.

Buckner left his gelding in a leap, hit the ground, crawled between the legs of the Indian's pony, and fell on top of the man, trying to get his knife into action. Any cry from the Comanche would bring the war party down on him.

The warrior squirmed from under Buckner, bounded to his feet, and unsheathed his blade. The sport of hand-to-hand combat apparently overcame his desire to warn his fellow tribesmen.

They circled one another, looking for an advantage. A rock rolled under Buckner's right foot. He staggered. The warrior swung his blade and caught Buckner's left arm. Only a scratch. The Indian swung again.

Buckner caught the knife blade against his own. They stood there, each straining against the strength of the other. Buckner stared into the black, emotionless eyes a moment, then pushed with his left hand. The Comanche stumbled back a step.

Buckner followed, swung his own blade, missed, and faded back. The warrior followed—too quick. Buckner stopped abruptly, and stuck his knife straight out, felt it slide off of something and slant downward. He walked in on the Comanche, pushing his knife to the hilt in the man's stomach, below his ribs.

The Indian's mouth formed a round "O"; his eyes widened. Buckner pulled his knife out, grabbed the buck around the head, and ran his blade across the Indian's throat. A gusher of blood sprayed onto his sleeve.

A shrill yell sounded in the swale between the two hills. Another warrior sat his horse there, looking straight at Buckner. The war party would have no doubt where he was now. Buckner sheathed his knife, ran to the gelding, and pulled his Winchester. Hanging off the side of his horse, the warrior bore down on him.

He jacked a shell into the chamber and fired without taking aim. His bullet caught the Comanche in the shoulder. He let out another shrill yell. Buckner jacked another shell into the chamber and fired. This shot knocked the Indian off his pony. Buckner toed the stirrup and swung to the saddle. He had to get to the wagons.

Yells, sounding like the whole Comanche Nation, tore through the beat of his gelding's hooves. He glanced over his shoulder. No less than forty warriors, not over a quarter of a mile behind, ran their horses belly to the ground.

Buckner seldom pout spurs to the dun, but he did now, and the horse added a surge of speed. The Comanche were adding shots to the hell they were raising. No bullet came

close enough for him to hear it, but Buckner worried that
one of them would get lucky.

Another glance. He thought he'd gained on them. Using
his reins as a whip, he swung them from side to side in front
of his saddle. The gelding pulled more speed from somewhere.

When Buckner thought he was within gunshot hearing of
the wagon train, he pulled his .44 and began firing evenly
spaced shots, one every fifty or so yards. He had to give
Carraway time to circle up. The sound of his shots might
reach the wagons before the sound of the Indians, that much
edge might make a difference.

If this chase lasted much longer, Buckner feared he might
kill his horse—and he would die too.

He topped a hill. Below, Carraway directed the last
wagon into a tight circle, leaving a slight space for Buckner
to ride through.

The gelding jumped a wagon tongue. Buckner reined him
to a stop, hit the ground running, pulling his Winchester
when he left the saddle. Rifles already fired from between
every wagon around him. He spotted Melanie's team and
headed for it.

He went belly down and crawled under the wagon to her
side. "Lie flat. Don't want you gettin' hurt."

She stared at him a moment. Her eyes took in the
blood-soaked sleeve. "Me get hurt? *You're* already hurt."
She reached for his shirtsleeve.

"Comanche blood. Not mine." He brought his rifle in line
with one of the warriors streaming past outside the ring of
wagons, led him a little, squeezed off a shot, and nodded,
satisfied when the buck threw up his hands and fell off the
back of his pony. He pushed Melanie to the ground. "Stay
down, dammit. There's enough o' us to take care o' them
'thout you gettin' your head blown off."

He jacked another shell into the chamber, sighted at the
next warrior to come under his gun, and emptied the saddle.
Looked like that war party was getting thinned down pretty
fast. The Comanche made one more circle around the train
when the leader signaled them to withdraw.

Melanie pounded her fist on the dry earth. "We whipped them, whipped them good, Kurt," she said, and grabbed him around the neck. She pulled him to her and kissed him smack on the mouth. She drew back, her eyes wide, shocked. "Oh—oh, Kurt, what must you think of me?"

He touched his fingers to his lips. Even though he knew the excitement of battle had caused her to kiss him, it had been one he'd not soon forget. With the taste of maiden honey on his mouth, he smiled. "Ma'am, don't worry 'bout it. I know the thrill o' winnin' made you do it. We often do strange things after a good fight. Some cry, some laugh, an' well, ma'am, now I reckon I found out at least one pretty lady kisses." He still smiled even though the shackles tightened around him until they began to hurt, only he didn't seem to mind as much as he had in the past. He held out his hand to her. "Come. Let's see how we fared in this fight."

They crawled from beneath the wagon in time to see people come from under almost every vehicle, but Buckner's vision blurred. Each person seemed to split, becoming two, then three forms, then they slipped back together to become a single person. He shook his head, and the pain in it brought him to the verge of heaving. He squeezed his eyelids together, opened his eyes wide, felt himself falling, tried to shove his hands out to keep from hitting the ground hard, then all around him went away.

When he came to, he was in a wagon. He figured it was Melanie's Studebaker. She sat by his side, and Mama Tilde was talking. "I tell you, child, that man yonder's like the wind. You ain't gonna put a bridle on him, ain't nobody ever gonna do that. You done let yoreself get all bogged down in mush over him, an' all it's gonna do is break yore heart."

Buckner felt low as a snail's belly, lying there listening to them, knowing they thought him still unconscious—but he wanted to hear how Melanie would answer Tilde.

"Mama Tilde, I don't want to put a bridle on him, that would be a crime. He wouldn't be the same man if a woman tied him down. Besides that, let's say I *am* all bogged down in mush over him, and I'm not saying that I am, let's suppose if he does break my heart there's one thing I can always remember."

"What's that, chile?"

"*That*, Mama Tilde, is that it took one helluva man to do it."

"Wash yo mouth out, girl. I ain't never heard you talk such before. I didn't raise you up talkin' like that."

Melanie giggled, and Buckner, through slitted eyes, watched her hug her arms to her breasts. "You know what, Mama Tilde? Soon's that fight was over, I pulled Kurt to me and kissed him right on the mouth. I know it was excitement that caused me to do it, but if I'd known it was that good I'd a done it sooner."

Mama Tilde reached over and tucked the blanket up around Buckner's shoulders. She looked at Melanie. "Girl, you a woman now, an' you gonna find ever' time a woman gets kissed it's either from excitement before, or brings on a whole lot of excitement afterward—or maybe along with it. It's that excitement gets a woman in all sorts o' trouble."

"I never kissed a man before, except out behind the stables one day, I let Jed Caldwell brush my cheek with his lips, but *that* wasn't a kiss. I don't think the one today was either, but I know if it's Kurt Buckner doing it, I'm sure willing to find out what a real one is like. That one today caused some stirrings inside me."

"Hush yo mouth, girl. You talkin' like a sho-nuff hussy."

"Don't care, Mama Tilde. That's the way I feel, and I'm not gonna fight it."

Buckner felt shame he'd lain there and played possum listening to their conversation. He felt sneaky and dirty from doing it. That was the kind of talk a mother and daughter had, and he shouldn't have heard any part of it—but he couldn't lie here and listen to more. He groaned, turned on his side, and groaned again.

"Oh, Mama Tilde, I think he's waking up. This time I'm putting my foot down. He's not going to do a thing until I think he's able to."

"Humph, that'll be the day, child. That man gonna always do what he figures he's called on to do."

Buckner tried to sit up, but felt both Melanie and Mama Tilde push him back in the blankets. "Don't know what happened out there. Looked like everything doubled up on me, then I went blank."

"Told you that concussion would give you trouble if you didn't take care."

Carraway stuck his head in the back of the wagon. "How's he doin', ma'am? It hadn't a been for him, them devils would a hit us 'fore we wuz ready. We'd a lost some people."

"Carraway, you skinny old goat, I figure I led those Comanche right back here to the train. Hadn't a been for me, you might not have had a fight at all."

The wagon boss stuck his head farther into the opening. "You awake, huh? Nah, they'd a found us in pretty short time after you had a fight with their scouts." He cocked his head to the side. "You did tangle with their scouts, didn't you? Figure you got that cut along yore arm from some-body's knife."

Buckner sat up despite the protests of Mama Tilde and Melanie. "Yeah, I tangled with two o' them. One I managed to keep quiet. We fought with knives. The other's yell could be heard all the way back to that canyon they hide in. Had to shoot 'im. That brought the whole bunch down on me. Had to run."

"Anybody would a run, son, with a bunch o' Kwahadi Comanche comin' at 'im. You get some rest now. You done yore part."

Buckner threw a leg over the tailgate to get out. Mama Tilde and Melanie raised more hell than he thought two women could, but he got out anyway.

"Gonna sleep on the ground like I always do. Not gonna push you ladies outta your sleepin' space." Despite his words, he wished he could stay in the wagon. His head felt like it would explode. It didn't take him long to find his place under the Studebaker where Ned spread his blankets. He crawled in, pulled the blankets up, and went to sleep— or passed out.

When he awoke, sometime during the night, Melanie sat

by his side. "What you doin' up, sittin' here by me? You ought to be in bed gettin' some sleep. Gonna be a long day again tomorrow."

"Kurt, you haven't eaten, and you need your strength. You feel like a cup of coffee and a plate of stew?"

"Yes'm, reckon I do, but you get back into your blankets, I'll dish me up somethin'."

"You'll do no such. You lie still, I'll be right back."

Before he ate, he and Melanie shared a small drink of whisky in a cup of coffee. After eating, and before she'd leave him, he promised her he'd sleep late and give his head a chance to stop hurting. Only then did she crawl from under the wagon.

He lay there long into the night, staring at the underside of the wagon, knowing she lay only a few feet above him. He couldn't get his mind off her, and even though it'd been sneaky to have listened to her conversation in the wagon, he was glad he'd heard it. He smiled to himself. Maybe, just maybe, if she wasn't going to throw a rope around him and keep him tied tight to one place, having a woman like her would be kinda nice. He went to sleep smiling, thinking thoughts of her she would have been shocked to know.

He did sleep late the next morning. The sun had already tinted the horizon when he opened his eyes. Feeling guilty, he crawled from under the wagon. He had to get going, had to keep Melanie safe for reasons he was reluctant to admit.

CHAPTER 9

"WHERE DO YOU think you're going, Kurt Buckner?"

"Goin' out an' do the job I'm gettin' paid to do. Try to keep you an' this wagon train safe."

"You have more than earned any money you might make out of this, Kurt." She locked gazes with him, her face hopeful. "Is money the only reason you're so determined to keep us safe?"

He lowered his eyes to stare at the ground, then again looked at her. "Ma'am, reckon when I take on a job I give it everything I got. But, to answer your question; no, ma'am, money isn't the only reason I'm tryin' to keep y'all safe. There is another reason I'm doin' it now, an' I'm not gonna talk about what my reason is."

She put her hands firmly on her hips, stamped her foot, and pinned him with a look he hoped not to see very often. "Kurt Buckner, you're the most stubborn, secretive, arrogant man I've ever known." She spun toward the fire. "Come on. I'll feed you so you can go out and get yourself killed."

For some reason, when she acted like this, those shackles he'd begun to feel comfortable with tightened enough to make him squirm. He went to the fire, dished his own plate of food, and poured his coffee. He ate in an uncomfortable silence, saddled his horse, and rode out.

Melanie watched his broad back disappear around the crest of the same hill he'd come across the evening before, chased by Comanche. Tears threatened to overflow. The lump in her throat was so large it hurt. Why had she treated him like she had? She answered that question for herself. She was in love with him. She had come close to admitting it to herself several times before, but now she faced it squarely.

77

In the lavishly furnished ballrooms of Virginia, or at the fine dinners she'd attended, of the many men who'd showered her with attention, none of them had taken hold of her like the rough-cut man who rode from her sight. Mama Tilde walked to her side.

"That look you givin' that man who jest rode away tells me you done made up yore mind. I done lost my little girl. Lordy hep you, little missy, you gonna have a mighty rough road to ride."

"Yeah, but, Mama Tilde, if I can capture him, it's going to be a wild, gloriously beautiful road I'll be happy to hit the bumps on."

Tilde looked at her, tears in her eyes. "Girl, reckon wuz I a young lady with fire still flowin' in my body, I'd grab that man an' hang on for the ride o' my life. Bless you, little one." She put her arms around Melanie and held on as though she knew she'd lost her.

"Well now, seems the lil' ole Southern woman takes care of her slaves like one of the family." Melanie turned quickly to see who had so crudely spoken.

Lonnie Bledsole, one of the men Carraway said he thought might be trouble, leered at her. His eyes traveled from her head to her feet, stopped, and lingered on her breasts for an uncomfortable moment.

Melanie felt as though he'd undressed her with that look. Her back stiffened. "Suh," she drawled her words out in the manner he seemed to expect, "this lady *is* paht of mah family, 'cept she didn't borned me." Her eyes narrowed and she felt as though they spit flame. "Now, you blue-bellied trash, get out of my sight, and—and, if you ever look at me like that again I'll kill you. Remember those words, for I never meant anything more in my life."

He sneered. "You counting on that Johnny Reb to come to your defense? You know, the one everybody thinks is a big hero."

Carraway walked up. "This man troubling you, ma'am?"

Still so angry she could spit, Melanie turned her eyes on the wagon master. "Mr. Carraway, anytime I can't handle trash like this, I'll yell."

A fourth party broke into the conversation. "Little brother, sounds like you done raised the hackles on this nigger lover." It was Tilden, Lonnie's brother.

"Bledsole, where I come from we don't stick 'mister' before the name of cow dung, so I repeat, Bledsole, the hero of this train will not need to help me, but if he does, you'd both better tell Mr. Carraway here what you want to be buried in. If I tell him about this incident, you won't have time later."

Tilden, the tall one of the two, grasped his brother's shoulder. "C'mon, Lonnie, we don't talk with slave owners. We done beat 'em in a sure-nuff war. That was all the talking we needed to do." His eyes widened in mock horror. "Besides that, she sounded mighty dangerous. She might even shoot you."

"There isn't any *might* about it, blue belly. Now get out of my sight."

Carraway stepped forward. "You said you whipped the South. What outfit were you in during that war?"

They both stammered a moment, then Lonnie said, "We was in Mr. Grant's army, cain't recollect the 'zact name of the outfit."

"Bledsole, you're a damned liar. No man forgets the name of his outfit. You nor your brother wore a uniform. Now here's somethin' you can take to the bank, if I ever catch you near this lady again, she ain't gonna kill you—I am."

They again tried to bluster their way out. Tilden said, "You right. We didn't neither o' us wear a uniform. We wuz spies."

Carraway's eyes didn't waver. "Again you're a damned liar. There are honorable men in this train who fought, some for the South, some for the North, an' you two ain't fit to ride with none o' 'em. I should oughta kick you outta the train, let the Comanche get you, but I'm gonna wait and watch this little lady, or the hero, as you call 'im, kill you. Get back to your wagon and stay there."

Melanie watched them a moment when they walked away, then looked at Carraway. "Thank you, sir. I didn't have my gun with me or I probably would have shot them."

Carraway nodded. "No thanks needed, but I'm tellin' you here an' now, you carry that gun with you all the time. I don't like the looks o' that pair. We're gonna have trouble with 'em before much longer. If you tell Buckner 'bout what happened, we'll have that trouble tonight."

"I don't intend to tell him, Mr. Carraway. He might get hurt, and I don't want that on my conscience."

Carraway smiled. "Ma'am, that's one thing you ain't gotta worry 'bout. Ten like them two ain't gonna ever hurt Kurt Buckner. It'll take real men to brace him." He tipped his hat and headed toward his wagon.

Melanie put her arm around Mama Tilde's shoulders. "That was a nasty scene, Mama Tilde. I'm sorry about the things he said."

"Don't you worry yore haid 'bout it another minute, missy." She stood back from Melanie. "You do like Mr. Carraway done said. You put that gun Mr. Kurt got you in yore reticule. Don't you even go to the bushes to relieve yoreself 'thout it." She took on that fierce look Melanie had seen only once or twice before. "I'm tellin' you right now, child, I'm gonna have mine with me. Not that I gotta worry 'bout a man gettin' smart with me, but I might have a chance to use it on one o' them two."

Melanie again squeezed the old woman's shoulders.

After all in the train had eaten, put their fires out, and cleaned the area of trash, Carraway led them off toward the distant horizon.

Like the days behind them, the sun beat down mercilessly. Dust rose from animal hooves and wagon wheels. It crept inside clothes, under hats, into wagons. During their nooning, even the food tasted of grit. For the hundredth time, Melanie looked at the surrounding hills, hoping to see Kurt, but knowing he'd probably be gone until after dark.

Before they'd headed out, Carraway looked at the ashes of every fire, personally making certain there was no chance one might flare up. He had told them several times, individually and collectively, they'd voluntarily experience ten Comanche raids rather than one prairie fire. Watching him, Melanie thought he had scared everyone in the train. She'd have to ask Kurt about that when she saw him.

That afternoon, they made camp earlier than usual, close to the banks of the Arkansas. Carraway called them together. "Want you men to all stand watch, loaded guns. Yore women take what time they need to wash clothes, wash themselves, whatever. You men're smellin' like a bunch o' goats, so you wash, an' I mean yore whole body after the womenfolk. Yore women will stand watch while you scrub up." He waved his arm in a circle. "They might be Comanche or Arapaho behind any one o' them hills. Ain't tryin' to scare you, just tell you like it is. If they's a sign o' any redskins, the one who sees 'em fire a shot in the air. At the sound of a shot every danged one o' you get back inside the circle. Got that?" At their nods, he said, "All right. Women first, get at it."

This far up the Arkansas, water had settled in pools. The women chose the sumps that satisfied them, and scrubbed clothes first, then themselves. Each had brought a complete change, so when they finished, they were clean from the skin out. The girl children went with their mothers, the boys waited for their fathers.

Melanie and Tilde both carried their reticules on their arms when they went to the river, each of them heavy with the weight of the handguns inside. Melanie watched while Tilde washed, then Tilde took her turn making sure no one came near. Melanie's fear she might be molested by the Bledsoles only sharpened her resolve to keep a close watch. She smiled to herself, thinking how nice she'd smell when Kurt came back.

She frowned, wondering why he never smelled of stale sweat, then she smiled. She'd noticed several times his shirt and jeans were wrinkled, as though they'd been wet and worn while they dried. And they were free of dust when he returned at the end of those days. "Sneaky, Kurt Buckner, real sneaky," she mumbled. "You're the only one in camp who's been clean. Wonder how you stood the rest of us?" She attacked her clothes with increased vigor.

She was back in camp and had supper ready when Kurt rode in. He stripped his horse, hobbled him, came to the fire, and took the cup of coffee Melanie handed him. He squatted by the fire and glanced around. "Notice y'all had a chance to clean things up a mite. Wonder you can stand me. Haven't had a chance to get in the river all day."

"Yeah, but you've been bathing on a regular basis, while we've had to wait for Mr. Carraway to give us permission."

He grinned. "Ma'am, that's one thing 'bout me you gonna learn, I stay as clean as events and availability of water'll let me."

Melanie nodded. "When I thought about it, I was certain that despite Indians and any other danger, you were sneaking a bath on a regular basis." She placed her hands on her hips. "Did you know, Kurt, people even in the highest social circles back East seldom take baths. They just cover up the dirt and perspiration with sweet-smelling perfumes. They seem to think bathing is not healthy." She pinned him with a look. "Kurt Buckner, *I'm* not one that subscribes to that belief."

He felt his face flush. "No, ma'am, never figured you was one o' that kind." He wondered how to get away from discussing this subject. Why, it was downright indecent to be talking about bathing with a young woman. Then he thought how nice she smelled, and figured it was good to know she too stayed as clean as possible. She saved him further embarrassment by handing him a full plate of food. At the same time she changed the subject.

"How's your head, does it still hurt or cause you dizziness?"

Buckner swallowed and shook his head. "Still sore, but I'm doin' fine. Everything go all right here today?"

She hesitated, then said, "Yes, Kurt, everything went well."

He wondered at her hesitancy. "You sure? You weren't very fast in answering."

She looked him straight in his eyes. "No, Kurt, everything

was not all right, but I don't want you involved. I'll take care of it."

"Melanie, when you hired me, keeping you safe was part of the bargain. Now you tell me what happened."

"No. You have enough to worry about. Now eat your supper. If it ever happens again, I promise I'll tell you." She stared at him a moment with no give in her look. He nodded.

"All right—this time. But whatever it is that bothered you better not happen again, or I'll tear this wagon train apart."

"I know, Kurt, I know you will. It won't happen again."

Buckner ate, chewing his food slowly, wondering what could have disturbed Melanie. The longer he thought on it, the angrier he became.

When he finished the food Melanie brought him, she took the mess tin from his hands and filled it again. When he took it from her hands, he shook his head. "Ma'am, you keep feedin' me like this and I'll be fat enough to butcher by the time we get where we're goin'."

Melanie opened her eyes wide. "Heavens to Betsy, what a thoughtless woman I've turned into, turning a nice slender man into a waddling monstrosity." Then she smiled. "As hard as you work, Kurt, I can't believe you'll ever put on weight. Fact is, I think you've lost weight on this trip."

He ate his second plate of food without tasting it, still mulling over Melanie's problem. Finished, he stood, told Melanie what a fine cook she was, went to the river, washed his gear, and went looking for Carraway. He found him squatted at the fire by his wagon. "Old-timer, Miss Corbin had trouble of some kind today, what was it?"

Carraway slanted him a look across his shoulder. "You ask her?"

Buckner nodded. "Yeah, she wouldn't tell me. Said she could handle it herself."

The wagon boss puffed his pipe a couple times, staring at Buckner. He took the pipe from his mouth, spit into the fire, and said, "Reckon if she wanted you to know, she'd a told you. Leave it alone, Buckner, I ain't lettin' nothin' happen to that young lady."

Buckner, his face feeling stiff as dry leather, speared Carraway a look that had no give in it. "Tell you somethin', boss, anything happens to Miss Corbin I'll tear this train apart, wagon by wagon, person by person."

Carraway's look raked him from head to toe. "Son, if I thought they wuz anything 'bout to happen to her, anything she or I couldn't handle, I'd a come to you. You wouldn't a had to look me up."

Buckner felt some of the angry fire drain from his head, and at the same time shame took its place for having braced his old friend. He shook his head. "Sorry, Carraway. Reckon I got worried 'bout not bein' able to be in two places at once. Know you'll watch out for her."

Carraway's face softened. "Looks like you're beginnin' to think on her as your woman, son. Good luck. She's got a lot o' iron in her."

Buckner returned Carraway's look, then scruffed his boot toe in the dust, staring at the pattern he'd made. "Don't reckon I'm ready to talk about that, old friend. You just keep a sharp eye on her when I'm not around."

The wagon boss grinned. "Ain't nobody gonna get more lookin' after than that lady. Now don't you worry none. Get on back to your bedroll, get some sleep. Gonna be 'nother hard day tomorrow."

Buckner took his time about getting to his blankets. Was he beginning to think of Melanie as his woman? He didn't think so. But on the other hand he had to settle down sometime, and there had never been anyone that caused him to feel about them the way she did, like shackles were tightening around him, or emotions that caused him to feel he had to deny them.

He shrugged. There were still a lot of mountains he wanted to see the other side of. And he never thought his final destination was all that important, it was the points along the way that made life worthwhile.

Back at the wagon, a sense of disappointment flooded him when he saw the circle of firelight didn't embrace

Melanie's beautiful form. Well, hell, she *was* a mighty fine-looking woman.

He stashed his mess gear, crawled between his blankets, and watched heat lightning paint the far horizon with flickers of orange-red. He wished rain would come.

CHAPTER 10

THE NEXT MORNING, Buckner and Melanie sat next to each other by the fire, Buckner eating, and Melanie making sure his plate was full as long as he wanted more. The sun was yet an hour or so from ending the dark hours. She stood, filled each of their cups, and again sat by his side.

Finished eating, Buckner packed his pipe, lighted it, and sat puffing on it quietly.

"Kurt, I believe there's a cloud cover, you suppose we'll get rain?"

He glanced at the sky. "Maybe, but not right soon. Those clouds are high and mighty thin. They do indicate moisture comin' in, though. The next couple of days'll still be dry."

Melanie folded her arms across her breasts. "Rain'll make for harder travel, but I'll welcome it. I feel dry to the bone. Be nice to snuggle down in my blankets and listen to raindrops softly beat on the canvas."

"I want it for a different reason. I want this grass to take a good soakin', get real wet before lightnin' or some Comanche can set fire to it." He looked over the rim of his cup and smiled. "Mud will make for hard goin', but I'm willin'." His face hardened. "Melanie, I don't want you goin' anywhere without your handgun. If anybody bothers you, shoot, don't bluff, shoot and shoot to kill." He pinned her with his eyes. "You understand? Bluffing'll get you hurt." Then, under his breath, he said, "I don't think I could stand that."

She nodded. "I'll do as you say, Kurt." Her face glowed. He had called her Melanie again, and even though she was not meant to hear his last words, she had. Cloudy though the sky was, and the sun not yet risen, it shone as brightly as at noontime for her.

Kurt stood and went to his horse he'd saddled before

sitting to eat. Melanie watched the swing of his shoulders, the quiet confidence he exuded, and wanted to go to him, ask him to be careful, let him hold her close. Instead, she looked at him and said, her voice soft, "Take care today, Kurt. I'll have supper ready when you get back."

He hadn't gone from sight before she stood, picked up her reticule, stepped toward the wagon, and changed her mind. It was only a short time before the camp stirred. She thought to take care of her personal needs while she still had privacy.

Melanie walked softly toward the riverbank. Dry grass crinkled and crackled under her feet, a faint smell of wood smoke from fires still smoldering from the night before came to her, a cool breeze caressed her face and arms. She breathed deeply, savoring the moment.

She stopped behind a bush, glanced toward the wagons to ensure she was alone, took care of her need, and walked to a large pool. Still a few feet from the water, she unbuttoned her blouse and pulled it down to the tops of her breasts and down her arms. She squatted, dipped her hand into the water in order to splash her face and shoulders. A sound she couldn't identify came from somewhere behind her. She drew her hand from the pool, pulled her reticule in front, stuck her hand into its wide maw, and grasped the cool steel of her revolver. The sound again—closer. Then a rush of footsteps.

A callous hand circled her head and closed over her mouth. The stench of an unwashed body assaulted her. Another arm reached around and cupped a breast. She fought, twisted, and looked into the eyes of Tilden Bledsole.

"Don't fight so hard, little lady. You an' me's gonna have a little fun." The hand cupping her breast turned loose and grabbed at the front of her dress. She kicked, glad for once Buckner had made them wear hard-soled men's boots. Her foot hit his shin. Bledsole danced on one foot, kept his grip on her and her dress, but loosened his arms enough for her to twist farther in his grip. She faced him now. The course material of her blouse ripped down the front. She brought a knee into his groin. Bledsole groaned, but kept hold of her.

Melanie let the reticule drop from her hand. In the other she gripped her .32. She pressed it to his chest and pulled the trigger. He staggered back. She closed on him again, put the barrel to his chest, pulled the trigger again, moved the revolver to point upward under his chin, and pulled the trigger again. She stepped back.

Bledsole's eyes popped from his head, the top of his skull had disappeared. Melanie stared at him, stared at what she had done to another human being. Her stomach churned. She swallowed a couple of times to rid herself of the nausea. But her only thought was that Kurt would be proud of her. She pulled her blouse together, holding it with her left hand, her right still held the small handgun. Footsteps, many of them, came toward her.

The first to reach her was Lonnie Bledsole. "What you doin', woman?" He looked at the body of his brother, lying half in the pool. "Damn you, you killed my brother." He made a move toward her. Melanie calmly raised her revolver to point at his chest.

"You take another step closer to me, and I'll send you to hell right alongside your brother."

Bledsole stopped. In the dim light his face turned the color of biscuit dough. "Now, now, young lady, be calm. I ain't gonna hurt you."

"That's probably the only true statement you ever made, white trash, you *ain't* gonna hurt me."

Carraway, his slim body a lance out of the darkness, barreled into the side of Bledsole, knocked him down, then kicked him in the side. Without waiting for the man to roll to his stomach and regain his feet, the wagon boss landed atop the troublemaker. His fists like shots from a Gatling gun pummeled Bledsole's filthy face; his nose flattened, his right eye disappeared in a spurt of blood from a gash above it. His lips split against rotten front teeth. Then Carraway wrapped his fingers around the throat of the man, already senseless.

Hands dragged Carraway off. Someone said, "Carraway, you 'bout done killed 'im, stop for now. We'll take care of him."

Horse hooves pounded the earth, slid to a stop within the circle of men. Buckner left his horse in one smooth motion. He went to Melanie, stared at her hand holding her blouse together, then into her eyes. "What happened?"

She tried to steady her voice, but the one word came out thin and reedy, "Bledsole."

Buckner's look shifted from her to the body lying half in the water, then he looked at the circle of men. "Who killed 'im?"

Sturdivant from wagon number three nodded toward Melanie. "Miss Corbin had 'im on the ground by the time we could get here. She wuz 'bout to put his brother down when Carraway entered the fight." Buckner glanced at the sodden mass the wagon boss had left on the ground at Melanie's feet.

He walked to Lonnie Bledsole, grabbed his shirtfront, and pulled him to his feet. He looked for a gun belt at Bledsole's side. There wasn't one. "I'm gonna walk you to your wagon. I'm gonna watch you strap on your gun. Then I'm gonna give you a chance to get it in your hand. Whether you do or not, I'm gonna kill you." His rage clouded any chance for reasonable thought. He twisted the man in his grasp and caught him by the scruff of his neck. "Walk." His glance flicked across the circle of men. "Get back to your wagons." A glance at Melanie showed him she still stood grasping the front of her blouse. "Come, Melanie. I'll walk you to your wagon. You can change while I take care of this garbage."

Buckner stopped at the rear of Melanie's wagon long enough to watch her climb into it, and then shoved Bledsole toward his rig. About ten feet before he pushed Lonnie to the rear of his wagon, a group of men walked to stand in front of him. One of them said, "Buckner, we can't let you do this. We decided we'll have a trial, in a civilized manner, to determine what to do with Bledsole there."

Buckner let his gaze travel slowly, from one man to another until he'd looked each one in the eye. "Gonna tell you how this works, men. There's not enough o' you to stop me from what I intend doin' with this trash. Now, if you don't want to get hurt, stand aside." He stared at them until one by one they lowered their gazes and stepped from his path. The slight break the men caused let his brain begin to function. He pushed Bledsole another step toward his wagon, stopped, and twisted the man to face him.

"Changed my mind. You don't get a gun. You get nothin'. You're leavin' this train with only the clothes on your back. We'll wait until full daylight, then I'm taking you out ahead of us about a mile or so an' cut you loose—walkin'. If you can make it to Bent's Fort you're home free—unless those at the fort kill you, and if you're still there when we get there, I'll tell 'em what you an' your brother tried to do, and they probably will decorate a cottonwood with you, if I don't."

Bledsole stared stupidly at Buckner a moment. "You cain't do this, Buckner. It ain't human. Them Comanche'll kill me 'fore I get two hours from here." He turned his look on the men of the train. "You cain't let him do this to me. I paid for the right to travel with you."

Bob Reed, standing in front of the group, spoke up. "He's right, Buckner. And if he merits punishment, we'll decide what his punishment will be, or we'll take him to a settlement where he can stand trial."

"Wrong on both counts, Reed." Buckner's words dropped in front of the men like ice shards. "A shyster might get him off free. Right now I'm the judge, jury, and executioner. Stand out of my way."

He walked Bledsole to outside the circle of wagons. "Sit." The stubby man bent his knees and squatted. Buckner kicked his feet from under him. He fell to his side, staring at Buckner, his eyes wide, terror an alive thing in their depths. His mouth worked, trying to say something. No words came. He tried again.

"Buckner, I ain't done nothin' to yore woman, my brother wuz the one an' he's dead. Don't do this to me."

Buckner gazed down at the man. "You and your brother were cut from the same cloth. You're leavin'. Don't try to come back or I'll shoot your legs from under you and leave you lay there in the dry grass." He glanced at the eastern horizon; a sliver of sun edged above it. He yelled over his shoulder, "Carraway, bring my horse." He waited until he felt his horse's reins placed in his hands and said thanks without looking at the wagon boss.

"Stand and start walkin'. You try to turn around an' I'll run my horse over you. Walk."

"Afoot like this, I might get snake-bit."

Buckner grinned, his mouth felt stiff and his eyes cold, but he grinned. "Bledsole, I can't think of many things I'd like more. You staggerin' around out here with your leg swollen, turnin' black, hurtin', an' fear of the Comanche eatin' your guts." He nodded. "Yeah, now that's a right nice thought." He wiped the smile from his face. "Keep movin'."

While following, Buckner searched every arroyo, swale, and hill for sign of Indians, and nudged Bledsole ahead with his boot toe when he showed sign of slowing.

The sun stood at high noon, a pale oval above the thin clouds, when Buckner decided to leave Lonnie. He rode to the front and looked down. "You're learnin' a lesson you should've gotten at your mama's knee, if you ever had a mother. Here in this country, the West, we don't treat our womenfolk like nothin' but ladies. Even the saloon girls we protect, and cherish. You're gettin' your lesson the hard way, an' it will never do you any good. You won't live to profit by it. See you in hell, white trash." Bledsole opened his mouth to say something, but Buckner didn't hear him; he rode ahead, still using care not to skyline himself. He didn't want the Comanche doing to him what he hoped they'd do to the man he left behind.

While riding, he tried to gauge when they would reach Bent's Fort. After mulling it over a few moments, he figured the train might take another three days. He crossed pony tracks twice during the afternoon, one group of them made only a short while before he rode across them. "Might need a little more care," he grunted, then shrugged; he always used all the care a man could. If he hadn't he would have lost his hair to some Indian a long time ago.

His thoughts centered on Melanie. He pushed her from his mind. Then he thought of the Odoms still behind them, and got rid of those thoughts too. Out here, the only thoughts he dared allow himself were those affecting the safety of those in the wagons.

He kept glancing toward the northwest, hoping against hope to sight rain clouds. He had turned back toward the wagon when he sighted a small herd of buffalo, fourteen in the bunch. He reached for his Winchester; the people in the train could use fresh meat. Then he thought better of it. Those Comanche might hear the shot.

He made a slight circle to avoid meeting Bledsole, if he had lasted long enough to still be tracking west. The band that made the fresh pony tracks might have found him by now.

The sun was low on the horizon when he tested the air—wood smoke, the wagons were not far ahead. Another few minutes and he topped a swell to see the wagons circled up, cookfires flickering and dancing inside the circle, one fire by each wagon, and women and children busily working at their chores, the men visiting in a group toward the center of the encampment. Buckner knew he'd be confronted with stone-faced glances, accusing him of being inhuman. He sighed. Unless those in the train settled in a town somewhere, they'd learn this was a hard land, you did what you had to do to prevent the lawless from taking over. He rode into the circle of firelight and headed for Melanie's wagon.

As soon as she saw him, she came to him, stopped and looked at him. "You're a hard man, Kurt Buckner, but thanks for taking care of me. How did you get there so fast this morning? I thought you'd be a goodly distance ahead of the wagons by the time Bledsole attacked me."

He slanted her a look across the couple of feet separating them. "Ma'am, seems like you took care of yourself, right well."

"Yes, Kurt, but I killed a man in doing so. I'm not yet sure how I feel about that."

His eyes held hers. "Ma'am, if you hadn't shot him, you'd be the one dead. Feel good about it, woman. I'm proud of you, not many could have done as you did—his brother won't be botherin' you either."

"You kill him, Kurt?"

He shook his head. "No, ma'am. But he won't last long yonder where I left him. Didn't want to kill 'im. The Comanche'll take care of that." He glanced at the fire, saw supper was about ready, and asked, "Reckon you can keep that food from spoilin' for a few more minutes? I need to clean up, an' I want to face the men who think I took care of Bledsole in a high-handed way."

A slight smile crinkled the corners of Melanie's lips. "You don't back off from anything, do you, Kurt?" Then, without waiting for an answer, she said, "Supper will hold until you take care of whatever trouble it is you're expecting. Go ahead, I'll just set it to the side of the fire."

Buckner glanced at Ned. "Take care o' my horse, Ned?"

Ned nodded. "No trouble atall, Mr. Kurt. He'll be all took care of time you git back to eat with us."

Before he got to the group of men, Buckner heard voices raised in anger. "We don't need a man in our midst who takes the law into his own hands. Need to drive 'im outta here," someone said.

Then Carraway's voice lifted above the din. "I'm gonna tell you men somethin'. Ain't a damn one o' you—or all o' you together, for that matter—big enough to drive Mr. Buckner nowhere. Long's I'm boss o' this here outfit, Buckner stays."

The group parted, made a lane through its middle for Buckner. He stopped in the middle of the bunch. "Seems like I'm the topic of conversation here. If you've got somethin' to say about me, or to me, say it, but I'll tell you right now I take my orders from Carraway. He hired me, an' he's the only one'll fire me."

Carraway stepped to Buckner's side. "Before this here gets outta hand, I'm gonna tell you men somethin'. The young man who wuz scoutin' for us 'fore Buckner is good, but they ain't none bettern' the man standin' by my side." He chewed on the wad of tobacco, shifted it to the other jaw, spit into a nearby fire, and looked at them. "Kurt Buckner's done saved yore bacon more'n once since he took over as head scout. Warn't fer him a good many o' these here wagons would be burned-out hulls behind us somewhere. A lot o' you men standin' here would be lookin' at the underside o' a pile o' grass. Yore womenfolk, many of them, would be Comanche slaves—or dead. Now I'm tellin' you, long's I'm in charge, he stays." He stepped from the group, then turned back. "Buckner's a hard man, but if you gonna survive out here, that's the way you gotta be." He stomped off.

CHAPTER 11

・ ━━━━━━━━━ ・

BUCKNER'S GAZE FOLLOWED the thin form until it broke clear of the bunch of men, then he turned his attention back to them. "Gonna tell you somethin'. None o' you is qualified to tell me how to do my job, so don't try. Somethin' else, you hired yourselves one of the best wagon bosses you'll find anywhere. You better let him run things 'til you get somewhere safe, like in a town where you can lose yourselves among all the other sheep." He frowned, stared at the ground a moment, then directed his look at all of them. "That man I took outta here this mornin' was alive when I left 'im, but don't any o' you figure to see him still breathin' the next time you see 'im. That's the way I want it. Now don't interfere with the way *I do my job—ever again.*"

He gave each of them a hard look, held their gazes until each of them lowered his eyes to look at the ground, then he spun on his heel and went to Melanie's wagon.

"Trouble, Kurt?" She handed him a cup of coffee. "Drink this while I dish up." She picked up his plate. "I heard part of it. I want you to know I'm not one of those who think you're too hard." She smiled. "But then I've known you long enough to know under that tough armor is a rather soft, caring man."

He studied her a moment. "Melanie, don't say that too loud, you'll ruin my reputation." She laughed, a full-throated, deep-chested laugh that brought a smile to his face. He sobered. "Long's you don't think I'm some sort o' monster, ma'am, reckon I can stand what the others think."

She placed her hand on his arm. "Thank you, Kurt, I'm happy you think highly of my opinion." His arm tingled all the way to his chest. The shackles tightened another link.

"'Fore you fill that plate, reckon we got time for a drink?" He looked across her shoulder at Ned. "Thanks for takin' care of my horse, an' if Mama Tilde will let you, come have a drink with us."

"Reckon y'all done made me a orphan. Ain't never gonna offer *me* one o' them devil's potions." Mama Tilde's voice came from the dark interior of the wagon.

Buckner stared wide-eyed at Melanie, only to see her eyes as wide as his, but her look also accompanied a knowing smile. He wondered what secret he'd missed out on.

They had their drink and ate, Mama Tilde included. The four of them sitting closer, talking in low tones. Buckner thought any family could not be more close than they were.

After supper, Buckner and Ned went to the river to wash the pots, pans, and plates, while Melanie banked the fire. She looked at Mama Tilde and smiled. "What you grinnin' at, chile? You know somethin' I don't?"

Melanie shook her head. "Mama Tilde, I don't know anything you don't, but I think I just realized something you didn't want me to know."

"I ain't keepin' no secrets from you, little missy. What you think I don't want you to know?"

"I think you're beginning to think Kurt is quite a man."

"That ain't no secret. I done told you, only I don't want you gitten yoreself hurt. What makes you think I done changed my mind?"

"When you sat with him and had a drink with him, I believe you were letting me know you think he could make me happy after all."

Mama Tilde looked into the fire and smiled. "You jest gitten too gosh danged smart, little missy. I knowed all along he could do *that*, but I wuz worried 'bout for how long. Now seems like when that there man takes on a job he stays with it. Ain't gonna worry 'bout you no more."

Melanie pulled Tilde's spare little frame to her and held her tight.

"Turn me loose 'fore you squash me, honey. Now let's get to bed. Lordy day, the sun'll be up in a few more hours."

Melanie went to sleep at peace with the world. She made up her mind with Mama Tilde's approval of Kurt to somehow make him see her more as a woman rather than the object of a job—but how was she to do that?

Buckner, lying under the wagon, stared at its underside. That woman, only a few feet from him up there in the wagon, was the kind to ride the river with. She was strong, could take care of herself, and when her man had a job to do she didn't stand in his way. He jerked wide-awake. *Her man?* What was he doing thinking of himself as *her man?* He didn't belong to her, nor she to him—but that time they spent by the fire with Ned and Tilde had been one of the nicest he'd spent in a long time. He smiled into the dark, despite feeling the shackles tighten a little more.

Morning came, dark, sultry, the leaden skies hanging low, but not giving up their moisture, and the sun beating on cloud tops would probably cause them to hold the rain until late afternoon—if then. The longer rain held off, the tighter Buckner's chest became. He threw his blankets back and crawled from them.

After making up his bedroll, he saddled the dun, went to the fire, ate, and rode out. The only person to wish him a good morning besides his own party was Carraway. Buckner's face hardened. Despite their opinion of him, he'd do his job.

Two hours from camp, he peered downhill toward a flock of vultures. They worried at a chunk of carrion, hopped off a ways, then went back to pecking and pulling at it. Long before he rode to them and scared them off he knew what they had under their beaks. Bledsole hadn't made it very far.

He sat the dun and stared at what the Comanche had left of the stumpy man. They'd dismembered him, and there was enough left of his head to see he'd been scalped.

Buckner thought to bury what was left. His stomach churned. Bile boiled in his throat. The smell alone made him squeamish. He reined his horse around the grisly mess and rode on. He hated for the women and children to see what the Comanche could do to a person, but, he shrugged, they came to this country, they might as well learn what it was really like.

Another hour, he reined to a stop, slitted his eyes, and

peered toward the northeast. A fresh breeze fanned his cheek. Hope swelled his chest, he wanted to shout. A thin gray cloud hung close to the ground. Rain, it was finally raining off in the distance. The hope died, his throat tightened. A reddish-orange stream danced at ground level under the smoke cloud.

He wheeled the dun on his back legs, put spurs to him, and raced toward the wagons. The fire should take another hour to reach them—and it would take him at least a half hour to get back to the train. It would be close, maybe too close.

The dun carried him to the front of the lead wagons. Buckner pulled him to a stop and motioned toward the river. "Get your rigs in the river, slosh water on the canvas. Move! No time to waste." His shout rose above the clank of harness and yells of the wagoners. He wheeled his gelding and raced toward the rear. At each wagon, he waved them toward the sparse stream. "Fire! Break away and get your wagon in any pool of water. Slosh water on the canvas."

He met Carraway about halfway of the train's length. "Fire!" He needed to say only the one word, Carraway took over from there.

Buckner pushed his horse toward the rear of the train. Melanie was back there. Before he reached them they had taken their cue from the leaders.

Ned popped his whip over the backs of the oxen, but the teams needed no force. They seemed to sense the need. The tough animals began to trot then turn toward the river.

Words were useless now. Billowing clouds of smoke climbed high into the air. A wall of white heat pushed toward the frantic emigrants. The teamsters urged their families to get on the ground and run for whatever water they could find while they whipped their teams toward the stream.

Ahead of the fire, burning ash filtered on humans, animals and canvas. Acrid, throat-parching smoke filled the air. Buckner ran the gelding to the opposite side of the team Ned tried to get even more speed from. He fired his six-gun into the ground at the oxen's feet, wishing he could pick them up and carry them.

Upstream two wagons heeled over and fell on their sides; another one, its canvas too dry to fight off smoldering ash, burst into flame. The women who had left their seats on the wagons came back from the river carrying buckets of water, threw the contents onto dry canvas, and went back for more.

The air, thicker now, made breathing hard. Buckner led Melanie's team into a pool about a foot deep, then lifted Melanie and Mama Tilde from the big Studebaker. "Wet your clothing and pull it up around your face. Breathe through it." He and Ned grabbed buckets, filled them, and threw the contents on the wagon's cover. A glance along the riverbed showed Buckner the other members of the train were doing the same.

Three more wagons began to burn. Several member of the train rushed to help try to save them. They managed to save only one.

What had been a wall of flame now weakened, burned lower, but still threatened both man and animals alike. Cinders were a hazard. Haggard, worn, tired, the settlers continued to throw water to the tops of their wagons, trying to save all they had left of their previous life, and what they hoped would help them begin anew. It began to rain.

Softly at first, a few sprinkles, then harder, then a steady downpour. Men, women, and children of the train turned their faces to the heavens and let the cool drops wash over them. Some simply dropped to their knees, then sat in the pools they had found.

Buckner studied them a moment, then noticed a thin stream begin to flow down the bed that had only moments ago been dry except for the sumps. He yelled at Melanie and Tilde, "Get on the bank. Move it." He looked for Ned and found him sitting under the nose of the lead steer. "Ned, get the team and wagon outta here. Now! Hurry."

He mounted the dun and raced along the length of people and wagons. "Get your belongin's to the bank. Do it now. You haven't much time." Many of them looked at him through tired, pain-filled eyes. Some stared with looks of resistance to any order he might give. Some gazed at him with built-up hate from the morning before, brought on by the fact he had shown them up for being small in a world of men.

"Damn you, all o' you," he yelled. "Get off your butts and make a move. You gonna drown if you stay here." They still glared at him with a "to hell with you" look.

He pulled his handgun and fired it into the water at the side of men and animals. "Get movin', damn you." Their eyes spewed hate—and fear, but fear was what prompted them to carry out his orders. Carraway pulled up alongside.

"You thinkin' what I'm thinkin', Buckner?"

"Carraway, you're thinkin' what I'm knowin'. A wall o' water could come down this bed any time now. We gotta make these damn fools get outta here." They rode in opposite directions, coaxing, bullying, begging the people to save themselves. The bullying had the best effect.

Buckner heard it first, then saw the wall of water rolling, roiling, tearing down the almost dry watercourse. All but one wagon sat high on the bank out of harm's way. Oxen dragged that remaining vehicle from the middle of the stream. The lead steers of the slow team made it to the edge of the cut-bank, dug hooves into the now muddy incline. Hooves dug in but would not hold. The steers slipped, went to their knees—and tons of water grabbed the wagon, carried it downstream, and pulled the oxen with it.

Shelton, owner of the wagon, scrambled the remaining few feet up the bank, turned and watched his life savings carried away. His wife and children were on the bank above him. He turned angry, accusing eyes on Buckner.

"You done that to me, Buckner. You caused me to lose my team and wagon. You run me into that there river without no cause. I'd a been all right if I'd stayed on the bank. You done it to get even for me buckin' you on takin' that Bledsole man outta here to die."

Buckner looked at him straight-on, held his gaze, spit at his feet, turned and went to Melanie. "You an' Tilde all right, ma'am? Ned's over yonder helpin' those folks with the four kids. He's okay."

Melanie wiped the back of her hand across her smudged and blackened face, sighed, and smiled weakly. "Yes, Kurt, we're fine, thanks to you and Mr. Carraway."

"Get in the wagon outta this rain. If it slackens a bit I'll build a fire. Thank goodness we have the hammock almost full o' firewood an' chips."

"There are many who don't, Kurt. We'll have to share with them."

Anger swelled his throat. He wanted to deny anyone the fruits of Melanie and Tilde's labor. They had walked miles beside the wagon, picking up buffalo chips and throwing them in the hammock slung under the wagon bed. Then when they'd gotten close enough to the river they'd picked up driftwood and put it in with the chips. There were those who gathered only enough to satisfy their needs for the day. He frowned, pulled his pipe from his pocket, swallowed, nodded, and said, "Reckon you're right, ma'am. Dumb an' lazy as some o' them are, reckon we gotta share." He kneed his horse toward where he'd last seen Carraway.

"By my count, boss, we lost five wagons, four to fire, an' one to water. Don't believe we lost any people."

Carraway nodded. "Jest took a count, ain't nobody missin', thanks to you."

Buckner smiled, knowing it was bitter. "There's a bunch o' these folks thinkin' to blame me for their wagons burnin', and the one who lost his rig to the water already blamed me for *that*." He shook his head. "Don't think a man can win. We're damned if we don't and damned if we do."

Carraway pulled a sodden plug of tobacco from his pocket, offered Buckner a chew, and when he declined bit off a healthy mouthful, got it settled in his jaw, and squinted down the line of wagons. "Son, you an' me, we're sorta like lawmen in these frontier towns. People hide under our coattails as long as we're needed, then want to be rid o' us soon's they feel safe. They're shamed because they feel they cain't stack up with us as men. When they don't need us no longer their shame turns to hate."

A trickle of rain ran between Buckner's shoulder blades. He shivered. "Tell you somethin', they don't want to rid themselves o' me any more'n I want to be rid o' them." He again glanced down the line of wagons. "Gonna circle up an' make camp now?"

Carraway chewed his cud a couple of times, spit, and nodded. "Might's well. Make sure all the livestock's inside the circle. This'd be a good time for the Comanche to hit us again. Don't look for a fight, but they'd sure like to have our horses."

Buckner nodded. "I'll pass the word, an' I'll keep watch tonight."

Carraway spit again. "I'll spell you 'bout midnight."

CHAPTER 12

⬩ ─────── ⬩

BACK AT THE wagon, Buckner hunkered under the wagon until the rain slackened, then crawled from under it, bringing an arm load of firewood with him.

He started the fire while Melanie readied the pot for coffee and sat it at the edge where there would soon be coals. While waiting for the blaze to grow, she gave to others who needed wood. Buckner went to the river's edge and cleaned up. He brought a bucket of water back with him for the women to wash themselves, poured himself a cup of coffee, and stared into the fire, wondering where and what the Odoms were doing. Trouble from that quarter still hovered over them.

Finished with his coffee, and supper not yet ready, Buckner figured he might use the time to tell the people to make sure their livestock were safely inside the circle.

Amid sullen, often hostile stares he carried his message from one wagon to another. Several men stood in a group, talking. When he told them to secure their horses, a man, huge, dirty, and mean, looked at Buckner and sneered. "You tryin' to prove to the wagon master he still needs you?" Buckner knew the man as Clanton, a troublemaker.

He only stared at the man and turned away.

"What's the matter, big brave Indian fighter, you scared? Why don't you take a swing at me?"

Buckner stopped, trying to smother the white heat burning in his head. He pierced Clanton with a look. "Clanton, gonna tell you somethin', the day I leave this train, I'm gonna whip your butt, fists, knives, or guns. No man— ever—has questioned my guts. You won't either after I get through with you, but for right now these people need my gun and knowledge in order to survive. I'll not jeopardize their safety to shut your big mouth." He nodded. "Remem-

103

ber that. The day I leave, we meet, an' think about it, big mouth, your wife may find some use for you if I let you live. Right now I'm figurin' on killin' you." He walked away, still trying to swallow his anger, and a little ashamed he'd let the brutish lout push him into a war of words. He should have ended it right there with a fist to Clanton's gut.

Melanie had supper ready when he walked to the fire. She brought him a plate of food, handed it to him, and stood gazing at his face. "What's the matter, Kurt? You're pale. Are you sick?"

He stared back at her, then slowly shook his head. "No, ma'am, I'm not sick. I'm tryin' for all I'm worth to swallow a big mad that's sittin' right in the middle of my gut. I'm tryin' to convince myself these sheep in this train are worth stickin' my neck out for—an' I'm not makin' much progress."

She took his plate from his hands, set it on the ground to his side, walked around him, grasped his shoulder muscles, and with strong fingers kneaded the ropy cords until the tightness began to ease. His eyes closed, he leaned his head back into the motion of her fingers and felt the anger flow from him. About to open his eyes, he felt soft lips touch his forehead. He went from white heat anger to a soft, protective feeling in his chest. Hell, it was his job to feel this way about her, wasn't it? He hired on to do the job.

Only a moment longer and Melanie released his shoulders, picked up his plate and handed it to him. "Eat your supper, Kurt." She smiled. "Feel better now?"

He nodded. "Never had anything like that done to me before. Yes, ma'am, I feel a lot better." He'd not touched his food. "You s'pose you could keep this warm while we have a drink?"

She looked him in the eye. "Kurt, I will do anything you ask of me." Abruptly she looked away, took his stew back to the pot, dumped it in, and went to the wagon for a bottle. They broke their routine, on this night they had two drinks, and Melanie sat close enough Buckner had to use special care their shoulders didn't touch.

After eating, Melanie climbed to the wagon bed, and

Buckner spread his groundsheet on the soggy soil under the wagon. He'd promised Carraway he'd stand the first watch, so every quarter hour, he crawled from beneath the big Studebaker and walked around the outer perimeter of the circle, then he went back to his blankets and relaxed until time for another round.

About one o'clock he thought to wake Carraway, shrugged, and figured to let him sleep a little longer. A sound, not one of night animals, or camp noises, broke his thoughts. He strained to catch more of the slight noise.

Faintly, sounds as of cloth tearing, yet not tearing, but those noises a heavy cloth would give off if being cut—and they came from above his head, from the side of the wagon on the outside of the circle. Buckner pulled his Bowie knife from the sheath he'd removed from his belt when he lay down. He rolled to his knees, crawled to a wheel, and squatted behind it searching for what made the noise. A kicking, thumping inside the wagon, then bare, dark legs, looking almost black in the night, reached for the ground followed by a short muscular torso. Arms stretched into the hole cut in the side of the canvas. The face above the ropy-muscled shoulders showed white streaks. War paint.

The warrior stood within a yard of Buckner. Melanie's head showed in the hole, her mouth covered with the Indian's hand. She squirmed, trying to break loose, but the Comanche's corded muscles bunched, strained to keep hold of the girl. Buckner launched himself at the warrior, his Bowie knife stuck straight out in front of him.

A second before his blade found its mark the Comanche twisted to drag Melanie to the ground. The Bowie slipped along the Indian's ribs. He loosened his hold on Melanie and faced Buckner. He'd pulled his knife. Buckner yelled at the top of his voice, "Indians!" hoping to waken the camp, but never taking his eyes off the short Comanche. He moved around the Indian in a circle, away from the knife.

The warrior swung his blade; Buckner caught it against his own and closed, chest to chest, with the lean-muscled body. The smell of rancid grease from the Indian's slick body caused him to hold his breath a moment.

Strength strained against strength. Buckner won. He threw the Comanche back, freeing his knife hand. He followed, looking for an opening. The Indian swung his knife first. A streak of fire traveled across Buckner's ribs. He sucked breath against the pain, and at the same moment felt a warm gush of blood soak his shirt.

He'd better make short work of his adversary or loss of blood would make short work of *him*. But if he got careless, he wouldn't have to wait for bleeding to weaken him. Buckner sliced again and felt a tug on his knife. He'd scored a hit. But the warrior never backed off.

The Indian raised his knife for a downward slice. Buckner threw his hand up, grabbed the other's wrist, stepped in close, swung his blade toward the Comanche's exposed neck, and felt his blade bite deep. The wrist he held lost its strength. Blood gushed in spurts, his heart pumping the life from the brave warrior. He stood, arms at his side, staring at Buckner. He tried desperately to bring his knife up with what strength he had left. Then he fell at Buckner's feet. Not until then was Buckner aware the camp had wakened.

Yells and shots broke the night's stillness around the encampment. His yell had sounded the alarm. He walked to Melanie, her head and shoulders sticking from the hole the Indian had cut. She held to the side of the wagon, staring at Buckner.

"You're hurt. Bad?"

"Damn my hurts, woman. Did he hurt *you*?"

She shook her head. "Only my pride, Kurt. I should have been able to take care of myself better."

"The hell you should. That's what you got me for." His voice sounded harsh even to his ears.

The camp noise subsided to a steady drum of voices. If there had been other Comanche, they were now gone.

Melanie pulled back into the wagon, and in only a moment climbed from the back followed by Tilde. Ned crawled from under the wagon rubbing sleep from his eyes. The attack had lasted only a moment.

Holding strips of cloth, Melanie came to Buckner. "Let me look at your side. It's still bleeding."

"I better check the rest of the people first, then if you would, I'd appreciate you wrapping it for me." He glanced at the groups of people in small clusters gathered in the circle. "Be back in a few minutes." He held his elbow tight to his side to stanch the flow of blood.

Carraway met him before he could question anyone. "That you what yelled 'Indians'?" At Buckner's nod, Carraway looked at the blood on his shirt. "What happened?"

"Comanche tried to steal Miss Melanie. Carraway, those Comanche must have been awful close to scout us enough to know what wagon Miss Melanie slept in. Almost had 'er when I stopped 'im. We lose anybody?"

"Ain't checked yet." He turned to walk beside Buckner. "They'll be them what'll try to blame you fer this raid."

Bucker grimaced, then chuckled. "Wouldn't doubt it. They've laid 'bout ever'thing else at my door." He shook his head. "Old-timer, you can't imagine how happy I'm gonna be to shed the dust o' this bunch. You figured your only troublemakers were those Bledsole brothers. Carraway, you got a lot more pot stirrers in your company than those two, an' to top it off, most o' them are whiners. Damned few of them stop to think, with a little more effort on their part to use their heads, they might avoid most o' their bad luck."

They talked with three groups and found they'd lost seven horses, no cattle, and none of the people hurt. A man stepped from the fourth group when they walked up. Buckner knew only one man that big—Clanton.

"Well, the big hero shows up after we done lost our horses an' runs them Injuns off. Where wuz you when we got attacked, Injun fighter?"

He knew better, but he'd had enough of the bigmouthed lout. The man's stench alone angered Buckner. A red haze swam in back of his eyes. Pain stabbed his side. He pushed it out of his mind. He didn't try to control the surge of raw emotion that threatened to boil his stomach. Without a word he stepped toward the man who easily outweighed him by forty pounds. He swung from his boot tops; his fist caught Clanton flush on the jaw and sent him to the ground.

He waited for Clanton to regain his feet, and heard Carraway, from the side, say, "Don't a damn one o' you touch a gun, or try to join in. You do an' I'll blow a hole in you big'nuff to drive a Conestoga through."

Buckner didn't dare let the man get in a good punch. Hurting like he was from the slice on his ribs, a hard punch would finish him.

The brute climbed to his feet, shook his head, and charged. Again Buckner set his feet and swung from low at his side. His fist went into Clanton's gut up to his wrist. The big man's breath pushed between his lips like a gigantic belch, but his club of a fist caught Buckner on the shoulder. Buckner's left pumped into the brute's face and opened a cut above his right eye. Buckner followed the left with another right to Clanton's heart. The huge man stopped dead in his tracks, his eyes wide, his mouth rounded, sucking air like a fish out of water. Another left to the big man's face, a right to his gut, and he went down, flat on his back. He rolled to his knees, tried to get up but couldn't.

A couple of the men stepped in to help him up. "Don't a damned one o' you touch 'im. Figure Buckner ain't through yet." Carraway's hard, knife-like words cut across the crowd. They stepped back.

Clanton sat there, swaying on his knees, trying to straighten his legs enough to climb to his feet. Buckner stared at him a moment, stepped toward him, and swung his right foot. His sharp-toed boot caught the big man under his chin. Blood spewed even while he catapulted backward and landed on his shoulders.

Buckner's brain began to clear. The red haze thinned behind his eyes. His gaze stabbed at the body lying on the ground. No movement, and hardly a discernible breath. Buckner wondered if he'd broken the brute's neck—and didn't care one way or the other. He swung his eyes to sweep the group surrounding him.

"Gonna tell you nice folks somethin'." His chest rose and fell with deep breaths, more from the cooling anger than from the exertion of the fight. Each breath sent piercing lances of pain through him. The bleeding flowed steadily down his side. He again looked at each of them. "I don't really give a damn for any of you," his words hammered them. "Don't care if the Comanche tear your gutless souls to hell. There's not a one of you I've noticed who is worth me stickin' my neck out for, but I made an agreement with Carraway to see you safe as far as I travel with you. So far I've done it." He sucked in a deep breath, trying to cool his temper even more, but feeling the taste of bile in the back of his throat, and smelling the collective stench of fear in those he faced. Their smell fed fuel to his anger. "When I cut loose from you, you're gonna be deep in Jicarilla Apache country, an' frankly, at that point I don't give a damn if Carraway is the only one who gets through, you're not the kind to settle this new land." He turned on his heel and walked toward Melanie's wagon.

She watched the tall, high-shouldered man approach, walking stiffly, holding his right arm close to his side. She'd seen his fight with Clanton from a distance and wondered then how he could fight like he did with a knife slice in his side. He stopped directly in front of her, smiled, his face looking stiff as old leather. "Sure could use a drink while you fix up my side." His words were hardly clear of his mouth when he leaned forward, put out an arm to balance himself, then fell into her arms.

She caught him around his chest, feeling his entire weight sag against her. Before she could fall, Ned put his shoulder and arms between them and eased Buckner to the ground.

"Git them rags you wuz gonna fix this here cut with, girl. An' bring that whisky he asked you for. We gotta take care o' this man. Seems like he's the only one round here fightin' for us." Ned's words were strong, and loud enough for the settlers to hear.

Melanie hurried toward the wagon. In only a moment she gathered what she needed for dressings, went back, and knelt beside him. He stirred, opened his eyes, and recognition slowly showed in his look. "What did I do, pass out like some weak-kneed pilgrim?"

Melanie swallowed the fear in her throat. "Kurt, a lesser

man would never have made it as far as you did. Lie still while I fix your side, then I'll pour your drink."

"'Preciate it if you do it in reverse order."

She gazed at him a moment, went to the wagon, and poured him a drink. Then she went about dressing his wound, thinking all the while how good she was getting at the task. Spending time around him, she would probably get even better with all the trouble he was so adept at getting himself into. A tender swelling came behind her breasts. Oh, what she'd give for the opportunity to take care of him the rest of her life—but he'd not shown one whit of interest in her like a man would a woman. She smiled to herself. She'd take what she could get.

Later, sitting by the fire, each sipping a drink, hers coffee laced with just a tad of whisky, Buckner's second drink straight bourbon, Melanie looked over the rim of her cup at him. "Kurt, I heard the way you flayed those people after the fight." She frowned. "You were pretty hard on them. They're scared, Kurt. Some strike out at something, anything, to relieve the tension."

His eyes avoided hers, then locked onto her gaze. "Yes'm, reckon I was." He sipped his whisky, his look still on her. "Fact is, ma'am, I was terrified at seeing you in the grasp of that Comanch'." He smiled. "Reckon all o' us had the same reason for actin' like we did—but I'm glad I whipped Clanton. I'd do it again, right now, if I was up to it. He's a bigmouthed troublemaker. I haven't heard the last outta him. Next time I'll kill 'im."

Her heart felt like a huge fist squeezed it. She breathed in the scents of the prairie along with a faint breath of wood smoke, trying to let the peace and quiet of the moment relax her fear for him. It didn't work. "Can't you just let it go, Kurt? He might kill you, you know."

He took another swallow of his drink, grimaced at the strong bite of it, and shook his head. "Ma'am, I'll let it go if he will, but if he brings it to me, then what will happen will happen." He shrugged. "That's the way it is, ma'am."

He looked to the sky. Melanie's look followed his and

saw a few stars peeking through the broken clouds. "Looks like it'll be a pretty day tomorrow."

Buckner nodded. "Yes'm, only it's already tomorrow. Sun'll be up soon an' I gotta be ready to ride. Don't figure we're gonna have any more Indian trouble right away, though."

"You're in no shape to go out again this soon, Kurt. Why not rest today? You just said there shouldn't be trouble."

"Only way I'll know for sure is to take a look. Better do that." He turned his cup up, drained it, picked up his rifle, checked the magazine, and went to saddle his horse.

CHAPTER 13

BUCKNER RODE ACROSS scorched earth, leaning into his side to keep from opening the wound which now sent stabbing pain coursing through his chest.

Blackened grass pushed against the sodden ground. Buckner's eyes searched only for pony tracks, the worry of fire gone. Yesterday's fire would, in little over a week, bring from the ground tender shots that by first snow would be a sea of green. Grass that would again feed the buffalo, deer, and antelope.

Wind, after the rain, had shifted to the northwest, lowering temperatures, but the rain had made it more humid. Sweat trickled between Buckner's shoulder blades, rivulets ran down his face. Down his thighs his jeans were wet.

He pushed his hat off his forehead and mopped his brow for at least the fiftieth time since mid-morning. Now, a couple of hours past noon, Buckner topped a rise and looked down on Bent's Fort.

Built in a rectangle, the fort stood in the middle of a flat plain. The adobe bricks were stacked two stories high, with a bastion at two of the opposite corners. It had been built and used by the Bent brothers and Ceran St. Vrain as a trading post to trade with trappers, the Comanche, Arapaho, and Cheyenne. When they abandoned it, the structure had fallen into disrepair, and had intermittently been used for other purposes, the latest being as a stagecoach station.

From his vantage point Buckner saw tiny, doll-like figures moving about inside the fort's walls. The sign of life answered the question in his mind whether going by there would be a waste of time. He glanced to the north side of the adobe walls looking for the corral. It still stood where he remembered it, snug against the side of the fortress. The immigrants would have a place to keep their livestock while resting a day or so in the security of the high, thick walls.

The promise of friendly faces inside those walls pulled Buckner to ride down and visit awhile. Instead he reined his horse in the direction of the wagon train and the people who felt only animosity toward him. He thought there might be no more than four people in the train he could count as friends, but those four were worth any hundreds of others.

By mid-afternoon, Buckner had seen no pony tracks, no wildlife, only desolation. Animals had probably crossed the river to range where the fire had not devastated all vegetation. The Comanche had experienced the firepower of the settlers, and as a result he thought they'd stay south of the river and wouldn't make trouble unless they could muster a large force.

Night had settled in when he rode into the circle. Fires broke the darkness. People moved about, some preparing supper, some through with their meal and cleaning up, some visiting. Buckner stopped to see Carraway.

"Topped a hill outside o' Bent's place 'bout two o'clock. Didn't ride down, but saw plenty o' people down there. Reckon the stage station's still operatin', or some other kind o' business. Figure you'll want to stop there."

Carraway nodded. "When you figure we'll get there?"

Buckner pushed his hat to the back of his head and frowned. "Reckon we can have our noonin' there day after tomorrow."

"'Bout when I figured." Carraway chomped down on his tobacco a couple of times, spit, and waved his hand toward Melanie's Studebaker. "Go git yoreself some supper." He grinned. "Reckon a day off'll give yore ribs a chance to heal a little. The rest'll be good for you. You need it more'n the rest o' us."

Buckner kneed the dun toward the wagon, and there, climbed from his horse and handed the reins to Ned who stood, a worried frown creasing his forehead. "You all right, Mistuh Kurt? Yore side givin' you a fit?"

Buckner sighed and nodded. "Hurtin' pretty good, Ned.

Thanks for askin'." Before he could seek Melanie out, she walked to his side and held out a cup.

"This might ease the hurt in your side, Kurt. Take your time drinking it. I'll keep your supper warm. We've already eaten or I'd join you in a drink."

"Well, dang it, if I'd a known you wouldn't have one with me after you'd eaten I'd a hurried a little more." He smiled to show he was joking, took the cup from her hands and sat, leaning against the aft wheel of the Studebaker. He packed and lighted his pipe before taking a taste of the bourbon. Melanie busied herself at the back of the wagon a moment and walked to sit beside him. She held a cup of coffee laced with a little whisky.

She slanted him a devilish look. "Couldn't stand the thought of a man drinking alone. Now take your time."

Sitting there, a beautiful woman at his side, a drink in his hands with no movement of his horse to wrack his side with pain, the hurt dulled to a steady throb. Moments like this made life worth living.

His cup still half full, Buckner became aware that a man walked to their fire and stood, hat in hand. "Mr. Buckner?"

Buckner's nerves tightened. This was probably more trouble. He speared the man with a hard look. "I'm listenin'." His voice was no softer than his look.

The man shuffled his feet, studied the pattern he'd made in the soft earth, then returned Buckner's look straight-on. "Sir, I just come to tell you, there's many on this train who are mighty beholden to you for all you've done for us. We know how dangerous it must be out yonder all by your lonesome, makin' sure we don't ride into harm's way." He twisted to walk away, turned back, and said, "They ain't many in this train who don't feel the way I do, only they ain't the ones who always mouth off. Jest want to let you know we appreciate what you've done, an' you've paid for it with your blood. Thank you, sir. I'm Bob Lee if'n you ever feel the need for a friend."

Before he could walk off, Buckner stopped him. "Mr. Lee, a man always needs friends, seems I do more than most." He smiled. "Much obliged for your words, sir."

Lee nodded and walked to his own wagon. Buckner turned his look from the slim settler to Melanie in time to see her lower her lids over tears that flooded her eyes. "Times like this, I feel mighty humble." His words came out soft as silk. Somehow, his hurt felt better, and saddle-weary bones relaxed.

"I'm so glad he brought you those words, Kurt, I think you needed them. It's so difficult to do a job when it's not appreciated."

Buckner wasn't surprised at her understanding. She was there with help or gentle words every time he needed his spirits bolstered. Before taking another swallow of his drink, he looked down his shoulder and studied her. Pretty women were a dime a dozen, but there were few who had looks, strength, and compassion. She had them all. Also, she probably had the capacity to love with every bit of her body and heart. He'd never known another like her—and most likely never would again.

Why didn't he reach out to her, let her know how much he enjoyed the moments they had together? He decided he needed time to think on it, time to figure whether she'd meant it when she told Mama Tilde she didn't want to change him. He'd give it some thought.

Buckner and Melanie finished their drinks, she fed him, he helped clean up the dishes and camp area despite her protests he needed to rest, and they turned in.

He lay in his blankets, thinking back to the reason Melanie hired him. The two remaining Odom brothers were out there somewhere if the Indians or fire hadn't taken care of them, and Buckner never counted on luck to solve his problems.

Horseback, they were certain to make better time than the train. He gave them credit for having better sense than to go into towns that could be reached by telegraph where the wagons stopped. Buckner didn't know whether Bent's Fort had telegraph, but felt sure the wires hadn't reached Trinidad because the railroad still had a distance to go before reaching that town. Before sleep took him, he decided to scout both the fort and the town when they got that far, before letting Melanie roam the streets.

The next day was as uneventful as the one just past. Buckner made certain there were no Indians in the area, then crossed the Arkansas to see if he might run on to a buffalo. Fresh meat would be a treat, and he figured if he drew the attention of Comanche party he could outrun them to the fort, or the wagons, whichever was closest at the time.

The dun was glad to get off the scorched earth and showed it by taking a mouthful of the first grass they came upon. Buckner's gaze alternately searched the ground for pony tracks and the surrounding swales and rises for sign of the huge humpbacked beasts. Even then, he almost rode upon a band of Comanche.

He rounded the shoulder of a small hill, reined the gelding around, and slipped out of sight. Eleven warriors by his count, and a twelfth one rode away from the bunch— and away from Buckner. They had two buffalo on the ground. The one riding away would be going to bring the women and children to skin, dress, and haul the meat away.

Buckner backed the dun a couple of steps and turned him toward the river. Fresh meat would wait until another day.

Back at the camp that night, he told Carraway what he'd seen, then he ate and went to bed.

The next morning the settlers were up and tending the day's chores by the time Melanie had his breakfast ready. They were usually asleep when Buckner rode out, but today was different. The camp was abuzz with voices. The word had spread they would be at Bent's Fort by noon. The weary travelers were ready for a break in the tedium, ready to take time to wash clothes, ready to visit with those they didn't see every day, and ready to be free of the spine-jolting bumping of their wagons rolling across the plains. Buckner wanted to look the place over to see if the Odoms were there, or had been there.

Like every other morning, he left the train to range ahead of it. He figured to ride into the fort and see who might be there before returning to the settlers.

On his ride out, he saw no sign of danger. Two hours after

sunrise, he rode around the north side of the fort, skirted the corral, counted the horses inside, and from their numbers figured the stronghold was now being used as a stage stop.

He circled to the west side and entered the adobe walls through the gate. The courtyard was busy with Mexican laborers stacking boxes of cargo along the walk. There were a few Cheyenne men sitting against the walls of the fort, some asleep, and some just watching the comings and goings within the walls.

Buckner figured travelers would be gathered around a whisky keg, so taking a chance the bar was still where the Bents had located it, he headed for the southwest corner of the building. When he saw men stacked three deep along a rough pine slab, he knew he was right.

Two men opened a place for him. The tall, broad-shouldered one said, "Welcome, stranger, step up an' wet yore whistle."

The other, a slim dangerous-looking man, grinned. "Hell that ain't no stranger, that's Kurt Buckner. You're liable to see 'im anywhere in this country." He knocked back the drink sitting in front of him and looked at Buckner. "Have a drink, old friend, long's you ain't lookin' for me."

Buckner smiled. "Billy, reckon I got enough trouble without huntin' up more. I ain't lookin' for you."

Bill Bonney sobered. "Glad of that. Never wanted to have to draw against you—figured I might lose." He motioned the bartender to set up a round, then introduced the big man next to him. "Meet Quint Cantrell, Buckner. Figure he can beat either one o' us."

Buckner shook Cantrell's hand. "I'll take Billy's word for it, Cantrell. Heard 'bout you. Glad to know you."

Cantrell smiled. "Don't believe everything you hear, Buckner. I ain't about to try an' prove nothin' anyway."

Billy squinted into his drink, sipped it, then locked gazes with Buckner. "What brings you out here this time?"

Buckner sipped his drink, shuddered when the raw whisky burned its way to his stomach, pulled his pipe from his vest and began packing it. "Scoutin' for Carraway. He's herdin' another bunch o' pilgrims to California."

They talked awhile longer until Buckner found the two had been at the fort several days. He thought he could ask about the Odoms without raising suspicion. He bought a round of drinks, then, looking at Billy asked, "You seen a couple o' riders, one of 'em built sorta like you, Billy, but dirty, nose got broke somewhere an' he's always wipin' it on his shirtsleeve?"

"You lookin' for 'em?"

Buckner studied on how to answer Bonney's question a moment. He nodded. "Figure to put a few leaks in their sorry carcasses. They figure to kill a lady I hired out to protect," he grinned, "though there are times I wonder if she needs anybody to stand between her an' trouble. She's one helluva woman."

Cantrell frowned. "Sounds like she means more to you than just a few dollars."

The grin left Buckner's face. He stared into his empty glass a moment, nodded, and looked at the wide-shouldered man. "Cantrell, I been wonderin' 'bout that myself. But I got a lot more o' this country to see 'fore I get corralled." He ordered another round. "Back to my question, you seen the two men I'm lookin' for?"

Billy answered, "They left here two days ago, said somethin' 'bout headin' for Trinidad, wanted to beat a wagon train there. Figure it's the same train you're scoutin' for."

Unconsciously, Buckner settled his .44 in its holster. "You can bet your last dime on that, Kid." He glanced around the room. "Need to find who's in charge here and find where Carraway can park the wagons."

"Name's Clem Best." Billy nodded toward a short, bookish-looking man. "That's him over yonder."

CHAPTER 14

THE BLOND, DIRTY man wiped his nose on his shirtsleeve, kneed his horse onto the trail, and looked at his brother Sol. "You reckon they'll remember us back yonder?" He sniffled again, wiped his nose, and without thinking about it nudged his horse to a faster pace. "Wanna get away from there. Them two men, what was their names, Bonney an' Cantrell? Hell, them two looked like they'd jest as soon kill you as look at you."

Sol Odom frowned. "Stop wipin' yore damned nose all the time. Yeah, the big one looked right bad to me, but that slim quiet one seemed like sort of a mamma's boy. Don't think he'd be much in a fight. His name was Bonney, some called 'im Billy, but most o' them called 'im the Kid. He wasn't old 'nuff to be very bad."

Paul nodded. "Think you're right." They rode in silence awhile. Paul mulled over what they came out here to do. The Corbin woman's plantation was theirs for the taking, but not if she lived to testify against them.

As though reading his mind, Sol said, "Why don't we turn back an' leave that woman alone? Hell, she ain't never gonna go back to Virginia. We scared the hell outta her."

Paul sniffed again, looked at his right sleeve, saw it was dirty and greasy, and wiped his nose on his left sleeve. He nodded. "We scared 'er all right, but she's been in a few towns what had the telegraph. She might a sent a message back, or she might a told the law what she seen. Any way you look at it we gotta get rid o' her. That way they ain't gonna be no witnesses, an' with no witnesses we're off free with all them acres o' Rebel land. Hell, Sol, we can live right highfalutin. Them folks been lookin' down their noses at us like we wuz trash." He looked over his shoulder to their back trail, still uneasy about the two men at the fort,

"We'll show them snooty bastards soon's we get to be their neighbors."

"What's the name o' that town we goin' to?"

"Trinidad." He sniffed again, but this time ignored the need to wipe his nose. "Been thinkin' we might get a shot at our gal, or maybe use a knife on 'er if we sorta stay outta sight. Ain't had no chance to do nothin' since she joined up with that wagon train. Maybe they'll take a rest in Trinidad an' we can get to her without nobody knowin' we're around." He rolled a cigarette, put a light to it, and again twisted to scan their backtrail.

Sol pulled his horse close and took the cigarette from Paul's hand, took a couple of drags, and handed it back. "Been wonderin'. Who you suppose that was killed Abe back yonder at that creek? It shore as hell wasn't her nigger what done that shootin'."

"Never got a look at 'im. I wuz goin' the same way as you, downstream, remember?"

A worried frown creased Sol's forehead. He nodded. "Yeah, I remember, but I sure do wish we knew who he was."

"Yeah, me too."

They rode quietly. Paul pondered who the girl might have gotten to ride with them, then he settled in to figure out how to get to her once they got to Trinidad. He gave it up as impossible to figure out until he saw the lay of the town and what the people in the train did once they got there. They might have to wait until they got to Las Vegas, in the New Mexico Territory, to take care of her.

His thoughts shifted from the girl to Indians. He'd heard tell there were dangerous Comanche out here. He grunted. Probably rumors started by those who wanted to keep all this land for themselves. He scanned the land ahead. Hell, from what he'd seen, he didn't know what anybody would want with any of it. The grass grew in tufts, trees grew only where there was a river or creek, towns were hundreds of miles apart. He snorted and wiped his nose. If they gave him every acre of it he figured he'd give it back. His thoughts again turned to the identity of the man with the Corbin woman.

Satisfied the two he searched for were not at Bent's Fort, and also thinking there was no danger to the settlers before they could catch up with him for their nooning, Buckner decided to wait for them here and show Carraway where the station master said to park the wagons. He thought to unsaddle the dun, but decided to wait until after he'd talked with the wagon boss. He squatted against the adobe wall, pulled his hat brim down in front of his eyes, and smiled to himself—he might be squatted next to a warrior that in some past time he'd fought, and might again. He sat there, sweating, nodded, and soon slept.

Cracking whips, harness rattling, teamsters yelling brought Buckner awake. He opened one eyelid a slit and glanced up the trail. Another half hour the settlers would park their wagons and stream through the fort's gate. He mounted the dun and rode to meet Carraway.

Still a distance from the wagons, Buckner held one arm over his head, waved it in the direction of the fort, and in a circular motion toward the west side indicated where the wagons were to park. He grunted. He might as well ride out and tell the wagon boss the station master said to keep the gate area clear for unloading supplies.

An hour later, most of the vehicles were parked and the settlers had begun unharnessing the animals when Ned and Melanie, one on each side of their team, reached their spot. Buckner walked over to help Ned with loosening their animals and herding them to the corral. "You an' Tilde go on inside where it's cool. Ned and I'll take care of things out here."

Melanie took Tilde's arm, frowned, and looked at Buckner. "Better not. I'll get our fire started and put dinner on to cook first."

He shook his head. "Go on inside. I'll cook up somethin', if you aren't afraid to eat my fixin's."

They argued a moment about who would do the cooking, but Buckner prevailed. After getting everything going the way he wanted he left Ned to watch the food so it wouldn't burn. He went to find Melanie.

She and Tilde sat at a table drinking sarsaparilla. On his way to her table, Cantrell caught his elbow. Grinning, he stared into Buckner's eyes. "That pretty lady sittin' yonder the one you hired on to keep her from gettin' killed?" Buckner nodded, and Cantrell, his grin widening, said, "Tell you somethin', Buckner. You ain't thought on it yet, but I got a notion your wanderin' days has jest about done come to a stop." He laughed a good belly laugh. "Yep, you done been roped, throwed, an' hawg-tied. You jest don't know it yet."

Buckner felt his face turn red. "Hell, Cantrell, Billy didn't tell me you were a nosy bastard." He grinned, shrugged, stepped toward the table, then said over his shoulder, "I'm not takin' bets either way." Cantrell grabbed his sides and guffawed.

Frowning, Melanie looked up at him. "What was that all about?"

Buckner again felt like his face was on fire. "Nothin'. That guy, Cantrell, just figures himself a real funny dude. Messin' in my business." Before seating himself, he glanced at their drinks. "Want another sarsaparilla? Gonna get myself a man's drink." When they declined his offer, he got his drink and sat. He took a swallow of the almost straight alcohol, shivered, and looked at Melanie. "You ever hear of Billy the Kid?" At her nod, he said, "Want to meet 'im? He's a right nice youngster."

"Kurt Buckner, are you kidding? A known outlaw wouldn't be here with all these law-abiding people."

Buckner smiled and looked over his shoulder. "Hey, Billy, Cantrell, y'all come over, want you to meet a friend o' mine."

They sauntered over and Buckner introduced them. Billy smiled, along with Cantrell. "Ma'am, looks like Buckner's been tellin' you what an awful man I am, judgin' by the way you're starin' at me. Don't believe a word of it, he don't never tell the truth."

"No, Mr. Bonney, Kurt hasn't told me anything. I read all

about you in the Eastern papers. Looking at you, I'm inclined to not believe a word of it."

"Like everything else, ma'am, they's some truth, an' a whole lot o' hawgwash in the stories they tell about me." He reached for his Bull Durham sack and looked a question at her. She nodded. He twirled his smoke, lighted it, then gestured toward both Cantrell and Buckner. "Now, you take either o' these hombres, if stories, true stories were written about us, them two would put me in the shade." He smiled again. "I'm a right nice man 'longside o' them, Miss Corbin."

Melanie's eyes and lips crinkled at the corners. "I'm inclined to believe you, Mr. Bonney. Fact is, I think the three of you are nice men."

Carraway, who had walked up behind her, chuckled. "Beggin' yore pardon, ma'am, an' all due respect, if I wuz gonna have to go into a fight an' somebody give me a choice of twenty-five men to take with me, or them three, I'd take the three." He shoved his hat back on his head with his thumb. "But you're right 'bout one thing, ain't a one o' them what ain't right nice—if you don't prod 'em."

Melanie's eyes widened in awe. Buckner thought she was overdoing it a little when she said, her voice dripping Southern accent, "Well, mah goodness, you'd never know to look at them they weren't complete gentlemen." She tilted her head to look at Carraway. "La de dah, I still think they're nice men."

Carraway and Buckner roared with laughter. Carraway said, "Little miss, what these men don't know is that you're more dangerous than all three of them put together."

Melanie, still using her accent, said, "Now, why would you say that, suh? To a frail little thing like me. I do believe you've hurt my feelin's."

Buckner just stood there shaking his head, a slight smile creasing the corners of his mouth. "Men, if you're gonna believe anybody here, believe what Carraway told you. That woman sittin' there could charm one o' these prairie rattlers while she swung it around to snap its head off. I gotta watch 'er every minute."

They talked, every once in a while teasing Melanie, when Billy punched Cantrell in the ribs. "Gonna go out yonder an' see if I know any o' them people, wanna come?" Cantrell nodded and they left.

Buckner felt Melanie studying him and looked at her. "What's the matter?"

She smiled and shook her head. "Nothing, Kurt. I was just thinking what terrible mistakes people make in judging others. To look at those two, or you for example, most would think what nice-looking, gentlemanly men you are."

"You sayin' we aren't gentlemen?" His eyes crinkling at the corners indicated he wasn't serious.

"Oh, heavens to Betsy, Kurt, no, I'm not saying that. Well, what I mean is, there are few who would guess that according to Carraway you might be three of the most dangerous men in this country."

Buckner frowned. "Melanie, there are those who would say that, but they'd be wrong. Around the bend in the trail there's always someone who can top the ladder ahead of you." He took a swallow of his drink and smiled. "But Carraway's right about one thing, if I had my druthers, I'd rather have those two at my side as much as any others I know."

They talked awhile, finished their drinks, and Buckner stood. "Better get back to the wagon, see how that haunch of venison's doing."

"Where'd you get venison? I thought you said it might be too dangerous to fire a shot, the Comanche might hear you."

"Bought it here from the station agent. Figured he'd have fresh meat and he did."

Melanie and Tilde went with him. Buckner took Ned a drink from the bar.

They ate, and when they were just about through cleaning up, a loud voice sounded across the camp. "Y'all gather around. We're 'bout to have ourselves a meetin'." The voice sounded like Clanton's.

Strange, Buckner thought. Carraway didn't say anything about a meeting. He looked at Melanie. "Know what this is all about?"

"No, but we better find out, it might affect us." She looked at Tilde. "You and Ned come on."

When the four of them walked to the crowd gathering at the front of the train, there were but a few stragglers still coming in. Tom Clanton stood at the front of the crowd. "Y'all take a seat anywhere so you can hear. I done called this meetin' cause we got trouble in this here train an' we got to do somethin' 'bout it."

Carraway walked to Clanton's side. "What kind of trouble you talkin' 'bout, Clanton, an' why ain't I heard about it?"

Clanton twisted to gaze at the wagon boss, his look belligerent, threatening. "You ain't heered about it, Mr. Wagon Master, 'cause you're part o' the trouble. The other part is that there scout you seem to think is so god-awful good."

Carraway stepped to the side, looked out over the crowd, nodded and said, "All right, let's hear what kind o' trouble Clanton's tryin' to start now."

Shock showed on Clanton's face, he obviously had expected an argument. He turned to the people. "I done called y'all together for us to judge the doin's of this here scout, and the backin' Carraway's been givin' 'im. I'm gonna say this: we elect a new wagon boss and send that almighty scout packin'. We don't need neither one o' them."

Buckner felt his scalp tighten, his stomach muscles pulled in against his ribs, and a red cloud began to form behind his eyes. Melanie had placed her hand on his forearm when they left the wagon; Buckner gently lifted it from where it rested and stepped toward the front of the mass of people.

"Wait, Kurt. Let's see what he has to say. We weren't with this train when we started and don't need to stay with them. Give the good people here a chance to be counted."

Buckner slanted a look at her, his eyes closed to a slit. "Ma'am, however this meeting comes out, I've had enough of Clanton. Either I'm killin' 'im, or he's leavin' the train. Either way, if I leave the train he won't be here either."

Clanton squared his shoulders. "First off, you gotta remember Buckner didn't give us no warnin' 'bout that fire 'til it was nigh too late. Some o' our wagons burned. Then he led us into the river in the face of a flash flood, we lost more wagons. To top that he let them red devils come into our camp and steal our horses. He caused one of our fine citizens, one o' the Bledsoles, to be run out of camp. That pore devil's carcass is probably a-layin' out yonder somewhere rottin'. In every case Mr. Almighty Wagon Boss has backed him up. I say we got enough."

Buckner's voice was soft. "An' who would you propose to replace Mr. Carraway, scum?"

Clanton's neck swiveled, his eyes probing the crowd. "Ah, Buckner, it ain't none o' your business, 'cause you won't be here, but I'm offerin' to take over leadin' this here train."

Buckner worked his way to the front of the circle of people. "Shut the hell up for a minute, Clanton. I'm gonna have my say." He scanned the crowd. "Folks, I'll step aside anytime you wish, but you have a contract with Mr. Carraway, and I want to tell you right here and now. You've got the best wagon master to be found anywhere. Don't let my presence make a difference how you vote, just look at the kind of leadership you've gotten from Carraway." He looked over his shoulder at Clanton. "Go ahead and call your vote."

Clanton stepped to the front. "Agin folks, I'm offerin' myself to lead you. Now we'll vote on it."

Bob Lee raised his voice against the swelling voices of the crowd. "Just a minute. We'll not vote until we all have a chance to nominate the one who we want to lead us. I propose that Mr. Carraway *and* Mr. Buckner have done a job for us that few could have done. This is a hard land, people, it's a land where only strong and often granite-hard men get the job done. I nominate Mr. Carraway, and if elected allow him to put whoever he wants in as our scout."

A rousing cheer exploded from the mass. Lee looked at Clanton. "Call your vote if there ain't no other nominations."

At the cheer, Clanton's face showed doubt, then he blustered. "Well, sounds like some o' you folks ain't very concerned he's bullied, beaten, and led you into danger." He slowly scanned the crowd. "All right. All in favor o' me takin' over this train, say yes." A very loud volume of yeses sounded.

Lee again stepped to the front. "No. You just don't get it, do you? We can't count voices. We'll have a show of hands. Now, those of you who want Clanton to take over, raise your hands and keep them raised. Mr. Swafford and Mr. Ford, step forward and help count."

Each of them counted. "How many you count, Swafford?"

"Eighteen."

Ford nodded. "That's what I got too."

Lee nodded. "Tallies with my count also." He again looked at the crowd. "Now, those of you who are satisfied with the leadership Mr. Carraway has provided, raise your hands."

The three of them again counted. Swafford reported forty-seven, as did Ford. "Again tallies with my count." Lee looked at Clanton. "You lose, Clanton. Now that Mr. Carraway is still our wagon master, I think he should take over the meetin'."

Carraway strode to the spot the others had used to speak from. He nodded. "Thanks, folks. Reckon the smart thing to do would be to run those of you who voted for Clanton outta camp—I can't do that. I'm still determined to get y'all to California in the best shape I can. Reckon it ain't the smartest thing I ever done, 'cause we'll sure as shootin' have more trouble from you, but you're welcome to stay with this train if you want." He chewed down on a fresh chaw of tobacco, again looked at the crowd. "We're gonna stay here a couple o' days. Rest up, wash up, an' be ready to roll the mornin' of the third day from now. An' in case you're wonderin', Mr. Buckner's still our scout." He nodded, headed for the fort, and turned back. "Those of you who want to leave, don't let the sun rise on your wagons sittin' alongside those in my train. Move 'em out. Got that?" Carraway's jaws knotted on each side, and Buckner knew it wasn't from chewing on his tobacco.

The wagon boss went into the fort before Buckner sidled to the side of Clanton. "Reckon you're gonna leave, so I'm tellin' you somethin' now. Don't cross my path anytime, anywhere. If you do, pull your gun, 'cause I'm gonna kill you. No questions, no words, no nothin'. Just come a-shootin'. And if you're here in the mornin', I'm gonna beat the hell outta you." He'd held his voice to a soft conversational level, and the angrier he got the softer he talked. He stood there a moment, his gaze locked on Clanton's, then he spun on his heel and headed for Melanie's wagon. She caught up with him before he cleared the edge of the crowd, which had now gathered into small groups talking among themselves.

Melanie again placed her hand on his forearm. He liked walking this way with her, it added a bit of elegance to the otherwise drab life they led. "What did you say to him, Kurt?" The devil lurked behind her eyes. "Somehow, I can't believe whatever you said was very nice."

Buckner stared straight ahead a moment, then looked at her. "Ma'am, I read to him from the book. Told 'im a few things Mr. Carraway neglected to say. Don't figure he's gonna be with the train when we waken in the mornin', that, or this train's gonna find out what real trouble's like."

Melanie shook her head. "You amaze me, Kurt Buckner. You can be the perfect gentleman, and then you're as savage as the Comanche. I do believe Mr. Carraway is right. You *are* one of the most dangerous men on the frontier."

Chapter 15

A FEW MINUTES later, Ned, Tilde, Melanie, and Buckner had finished cleaning their area and all sat by the fire enjoying a drink, even though Tilde grumbled Buckner was leading her into the jaws of perdition.

Melanie gazed into her drink a few moments, then looked up and locked gazes with Buckner. "You really think Clanton and his bunch will leave?"

"They'll leave. Clanton can't afford to stay here, it would be a show of weakness. But if they leave they're fools. They won't have enough rifles in that bunch to defend themselves, an' they're not out of Comanche territory yet." He set his cup on the ground, packed and lighted his pipe, then again looked at Melanie. "If I thought they'd listen to me, I'd try to talk them into stayin' with us. The Comanche look for undermanned wagon trains. We'll be all right. We have plenty of firepower left, but they won't." He made a slicing motion with the side of his hand. "Oh, hell, Melanie, I don't care anything about the grown folks in that bunch, it's the kids I'm worried about. They don't deserve to die because their folks're stupid."

"I thought you wanted Clanton to leave."

Buckner nodded. "I do. He's trouble wherever he is, and he doesn't have any children."

Melanie shivered and pulled the hem of her dress under her feet. "It's getting chilly." She took another sip of her coffee laced with bourbon. "Why don't you talk to them, show them they're asking for trouble?"

He shook his head. "They won't listen to me. Clanton has them convinced I'm the cause of their troubles."

"I'll talk to them then."

Buckner stared into the fire, nodded, and looked at her.

"Might work. It's worth a try anyway. Want me to walk over with you?"

"No, Kurt, remember they blame you. They won't listen to me with you there."

She stood, went to the wagon for a shawl, and walked toward the other vehicles.

In ten minutes she was back. "They wouldn't listen. Said if you left they'd stay. They're leaving in the morning."

"Figured as much."

The next morning with ten wagons gone, a hole gaped in the neat parking pattern Carraway insisted on. There were twenty-five wagons left, with an ample number of guns to defend the train. Though there were more men than women, Buckner figured every one who voted for Carraway, forty-seven of them, could all use a rifle.

Sitting in the shade of the wall, Buckner had to smile at the term they'd used to describe this two-day layover. Rest. Every man, woman, and child busily worked at various chores. The women washed clothes, the men worked on the wagons, greasing wheels, checking axles and wagon tongues, splicing harness, while the children stood by to get things their father or mother might need, or they searched the riverbank for driftwood.

Buckner yawned, stood, stretched, and headed for the river where Melanie scrubbed a large pile of clothes. "Want me to help, Melanie? I'm right handy at scrubbin'."

She glanced at him, then back to the laundry that had piled up since the last rest day. "Kurt," she glanced over her shoulder at him, "even if I counted this a man's job, I wouldn't let you help." She blushed, right prettily, Buckner thought. Then she continued, "I have articles of clothing in here I'd rather you didn't see."

He laughed, let it fade to a grin, and shrugged. "Thought I'd offer. Reckon I'll see if Ned needs help with anything."

The next day was a different story. The chores taken care of, the men played cards, the women gossiped, and the children enjoyed different games: tag, blindman's buff, foot races, and some of the boys even found things to fight about. To Kurt, they were now getting the much-needed rest they'd laid over for.

The next morning Buckner rode well ahead of the train. Melanie had fixed him a good breakfast, he'd had a cup of coffee with Bonney and Cantrell, and he'd noticed the people were all up at the time Melanie started his breakfast. They looked westward with rested faces and new hope.

About two hours ahead of the train, Buckner again came on grass. He grunted, glad to leave the scorched earth behind. Riding in the black ash all day made for dirty clothes and blackened skin.

He rode several miles from Timpas Creek, but parallel with it, heading southwest. The livestock were watered, every wagon had full water barrels. Water wasn't his worry, Indians were. He figured the Indians, if there were any, would stay close to water, so he stayed clear.

Time for his nooning he sat in the shade of his horse, munching on a sliced venison sandwich. Melanie had fixed it for him. He squinted into the bright sunlit day, searching the horizon and all that lay between. A guess put the Clanton bunch somewhere close. That morning he'd covered as much ground as Clanton's wagons would cover in two days. "Surprised I haven't seen them." His thought came out as a mutter.

Chewing the last bite of sandwich, he glanced to the west. Smoke, a black cloud of it, marred the pristine blue sky. Another prairie fire? His gut tightened. He studied the column billowing into the heavens. It continued to spiral upward from about the same spot. "Oh, damn, looks like Clanton's already gotten them in trouble." While mouthing those words he grabbed the saddle horn and, at a dead run, vaulted into the saddle.

He kept below the crests of the rolling hills, watching the smoke column, gauging how close he was to it. Finally, thinking it would be just over the next hill, he quit the saddle, crawled to the top, removed his hat, and peered over.

Close to the creek, a small group of wagons bunched together. A steady rattle of rifle fire from the settlers broke into the savage yells of a sparse war party circling them. Two wagons burned fiercely, now only skeletons of what they had been minutes before. Buckner reached for his Winchester. As fast as he could lever shells into the chamber, he aimed and fired. He fired his last shot and crammed fresh loads into the magazine. By his count there had been about fifteen warriors, now they were down to eight. He had gotten four of the seven now on the ground.

The leader of the war party gave a hand signal and they withdrew, upstream of the immigrants. They reined their ponies in and looked back at their failed attempt. Buckner figured they talked about the worth of continuing the raid.

He held his fire, a brassy taste of tear in his throat, hoping they hadn't had time to guess only one rifle fired at them from his position. After talking it over a few moments, the Indians kneed their ponies away and headed south. Buckner hadn't been aware he held his breath, but when he let it out, it came in a whoosh.

He let them get out of sight before he mounted and rode to the cluster of wagons.

"What the hell you doin' here, hero? Thought we got rid o' you."

Buckner stared at the filthy hunk a moment, then looked at the men and women standing in a group. "Folks, this is what I was afraid would happen. I'll take it on myself to invite you to stay where you are 'til the train catches up with you. Those of you who wish may join up with us again—that invite goes for all 'cept you, Clanton."

"Don't listen to him. For all we know he brung them Indians down on us."

One of the men stepped forward. "Don't be any more of a fool than you already are, Clanton. If it hadn't been for Buckner's rifle them Indians would still be here."

Clanton backed a step. Buckner backed right with him, he didn't want the likes of Clanton at his back.

Another man looked at the ground a moment, then swept the rest of them with a bitter glance. "Me an' my missus got no way o' goin'nowhere." He looked at the skeletal remains of one of the wagons. "That there was all I had in this world. Ain't got nothin' now."

Buckner felt no sorrow for the man. He'd asked for what he got, but he couldn't leave him out here, him, his wife, and the two dirty, ragged kids standing at his side. He shifted his gaze to the rest of the sorry-looking group. "Who had that other burned-out wagon?"

"Me." The man who answered looked of the same stripe as the other.

Buckner asked, "Any o' you got room for these people far as Trinidad? That's as far as they, or any o' you, go with our train."

Clanton spoke up, "We ain't takin' on no deadwood."

Another man said timidly, "One of the families can ride with us." And another volunteered to take on the other family.

"They damned shore ain't ridin' with us. Now I done told you," Clanton bellowed.

Buckner watched Clanton through slitted lids, knowing he would have to do something to keep control. Clanton reached for his handgun. Buckner, without thinking, drew his .44 and clubbed the brute alongside his head. He dropped like a poleaxed steer.

Buckner stooped, not taking his eyes off the group, pulled Clanton's pistol from its holster, stuck it in his belt, and picked up Clanton's Henry rifle. "That garbage there got any family, a wife, children?"

Several of the people shook their heads. "He's got no kids, just a wife," one of them said.

"All right, how many o' you want to rejoin Carraway's train?" Every hand in the bunch grabbed for the sky.

Buckner nodded. "Okay. But I'm tellin' you right now, any of you whine, growl, or in any way create dissension, you'll pull off to the side of the trail and we leave you right there. The best you can figure on, regardless how you act, is stayin' with Carraway no farther than Trinidad. There we leave you. Got it?"

Clanton stirred. Buckner kept his eyes on him until he sat up. "As for you," he continued as though Clanton had heard

every word, "take your wagon out of here, you're goin' it
alone from here on in."

"You cain't do that. Gimme my guns an' I'll show you."

Buckner smiled. "I'm gonna do you the only favor I'll
ever do you. I'm not givin' you your guns 'cause I'd have to
kill you right then. Now climb onto your rig and get outta
here."

The small party stood there, silently, and watched the
man in whose hands they had placed their lives ride off
mouthing curses against them, but mostly against Buckner.
They watched until Clanton disappeared over the brow of
the closest hill.

Buckner toed the stirrup and swung to his saddle. "I can't
stay with you people. I got a job to do. Every one of you get
a gun in your hands and keep it there until we catch up with
you. You see anything, shoot. Before we get in rifle range,
I'll fire three shots, evenly spaced so y'all won't shoot at us.
All right?" They nodded. "Something else," he continued.
"Bury those Indians lying out yonder. They gonna get pretty
ripe 'fore long." He kneed his horse around and rode off.

The sun sank below the mountains long before Buckner
made it back to report to Carraway. "Beginnin' to worry
'bout you, son. It's nigh on to ten o'clock."

Buckner smiled tiredly. "Yeah, I know, boss, but I been
kind o' busy." He went on to tell about the Indian fight, but
played down his part in it. Then he told Carraway about the
survivors of the fight and what he'd promised them.
"Carraway, I told 'em they couldn't travel with you any
farther than Trinidad. I hope you'll back me on that. You let
any o' those whiners back in the train, an' you gonna have
trouble from then on. Cut 'em loose in that town and they
won't be any worse off than they were when you headed
'em west."

Carraway stared at Buckner a moment, then shook his
head. "Buckner, they just ain't no give in you atall." He
chewed his cud a couple of times, turned his head to the side
and spit a stream of juice at the fire. "Let me think on it
while we travel. Fact is, I think you're right, but don't know

as I'm hard as you. Don't know whether I could stand to look at them faces when we ride off from 'em."

"You think on it, then, old-timer. Right now I'm gonna see if Melanie saved me any supper." Despite his words, he knew there would be a drink waiting for him at the wagon, and after the drink Melanie would dish up his supper.

On his way to the Studebaker, he smiled into the night. That woman is spoiling me rotten, he thought. And the hell of it is, I'm getting used to it, liking it more every day, getting so I don't want to ever do without the pampering. His thoughts continued along those lines until Melanie materialized out of the dark, and yes, she held a granite cup out for him. He smelled the bourbon before he put it to his mouth.

"You're spoiling me, girl."

Her face caught the glow of the fire. She looked at him, a slight frown worrying her forehead. "Kurt, I was getting terribly anxious for your safety." Her words caused him to repeat all he'd told Carraway. They walked to her fire and she sat next to him while he drank his evening drink. She sat as close as propriety would allow.

"You drove Clanton out of their camp without a weapon?"

He nodded.

She looked at his cup. "You want another drink?"

"No, but thanks. This is enough."

"Kurt, he might get killed out there without a weapon of any kind."

"Reckon you're right 'bout that. An' if your next question is gonna be, don't I feel a little sorry for him, the answer is no. It'll just save me havin' to do it later."

Melanie frowned and looked at him straight-on. "Kurt Buckner, I believe you're the hardest man I've ever known."

CHAPTER 16

SIX DAYS LATER, Carraway formed the train in four neat rows at the edge of Trinidad, at the north end of Uncle Dick Wootton's Raton Pass toll road.

Before cutting the settlers loose to enjoy the town, Carraway called a short meeting. "We're gonna be here 'bout a week. You folks, buy what provisions you need. If your clothes are gettin' a little thin, this is a better place to buy new ones. They get pretty expensive in the towns ahead of us.

"Most of all, check your wagons, especially the axles and the brakes. Raton Pass is directly ahead of us. Soon's we leave here we start climbin'. It's a hard climb, but I guarantee you, goin' down the other side is harder—and a lot more dangerous.

"When I say check your brakes and make sure they're like new, I ain't just whistling Dixie. Do it. Also, I want every one o' you to have a good block an' tackle, Make sure the manila line is not frayed. If you can afford it, I'd like it to be new. Yours or someone else's wagon will need help getting down slow-like instead of runnin' hell-to-breakfast down the side of that mountain. That happens, yore rigs gonna end up a pile o' toothpicks. Got it?" At their yell of understanding, Carraway nodded. "Good. Now, one more thing, save enough hard cash to pay Uncle Dick's toll. Now, all o' you have a good week and be ready to roll Monday mornin'."

Buckner walked around the end of the wagon, reached up to help Melanie down, then held his arms up and helped Tilde. He stood there, fidgeted a bit, then began to pack his pipe.

"Kurt, you got something to say to us, spit it out." Melanie stood, hands on hips waiting to hear what he had to say.

136

"Well, ma'am, it's like this, I don't want either o' you out and about town 'til I've had a chance to scout it out." He looked at Mama Tilde. "I'm gonna put y'all in your room and I want you to keep your handguns within close reach every moment until I come back and tell you everything is all right. Tilde, don't let Melanie out of your sight until I get back."

Round-eyed, Tilde reached in her reticule and pulled out her little gun. "Yes, *suh*, I ain't gonna let nothin' happen to our little missy, not never, Mistuh Kurt. I gonna . . ."

Melanie cut in, "What's all this about, Kurt? Clanton won't dare harm either of us."

Kurt gave her a straight-on look. "Melanie, it's not Clanton I'm concerned about. Now do as I say. I'm not just being bossy."

A slight smile crossed Melanie's face. "If you'd call me Melanie all the time, I think I would always do as you said."

Buckner felt his face turn red, and to cover his embarrassment, he took her elbow and steered her toward Wootton's Inn. "Come, we'll get you settled."

He checked them into the inn. Melanie scanned the room and was pleased with what she saw. It was spacious, airy, and looked out on the main street. She tested the bed. It felt like they'd put fresh corn shucks in the mattress, and it smelled clean. She looked at Mama Tilde. "Better'n I thought it'd be."

Tilde snorted. "Humph, anything would be better'n that hard floor of the wagon. We gonna have more fresh air in here too, what with not havin' to keep canvas down so's nobody gonna look at us while we sleep." She shook the wrinkles out of one of Melanie's dresses and hung it on the rod provided for the purpose. Without taking her eyes off the job she was doing, she said, "You shore do let that man know what yore feelin's are every chance you get. Why, girl, you 'most come right out an' tell 'im you're his'n anytime he'll reach out an' take you."

Melanie sat on the edge of the bed. "Mama Tilde, I know some of the things I say to him are not downright proper, but he's gonna know before he gets ready to leave us exactly how I feel." She frowned. "Wonder why he's always so standoffish, yet protects us like a mother hen."

Tilde stopped hanging clothes and faced Melanie. "Little missy, he protects us 'cause it's his job, an' yeah, I been noticin' how he looks at you. He cares, but if you want my say-so, I'm of a mind he's scared to death he's gonna lose some o' his freedom to jest git up an' roam whenever he wants."

Melanie's eyes filled with tears. Tilde put her arms around her and hugged. "Now, don't you cry, ain't no man worth even one o' yore tears."

"Mama Tilde, I'm about to cry to keep from pitching a fit. It makes me so d-d-damned mad a woman can't just go up to a man, like a man can, and say what she thinks—or feels. Before long, if I have to, I'm gonna do just that."

Tilde stepped back, put her hands on her hips, and glared at her. "Melanie, don't you never do nothin' like that. That'd be the worsest thing you could do. A man likes to think— has to think—he's the one who's doin' the chasin'." She shook her head. "No, ma'am, you ain't gonna do nothin' that stupid."

Melanie knew when Mama Tilde called her "Melanie" she was putting her foot down hard. She changed the subject. "Wonder why Kurt's so adamant we aren't to do anything until he looks the town over? I don't think Clanton is dumb enough to harm a woman."

Tilde hung another dress on the rod. "Missy, it ain't that Clanton he's worryin' his head over. You done forgot why you hired him to begin with?"

Melanie gasped. "You don't think he suspects the Odoms have tracked us this far, do you?"

Tilde nodded. "I believe just that, girl." She smiled. "At least he's gonna make bird dog sure they ain't no birds in the brush. Gotta give 'im credit for bein' smart 'nuff about them things even if he ain't woman smart."

Melanie sighed. "Well, I guess we better do like he said, and stay here." She dug in her reticule and put her gun on the table beside her. She'd noticed Tilde kept hers in her hand, even though it was awkward trying to hang clothes and hold it at the same time.

Buckner worried whether Melanie would do as he'd said. She was a strong-minded woman, but on the other hand had shown she trusted him. Yeah, he figured she'd stay put until he told them it was safe. He looked at Ned. "How 'bout you checkin' the wagon, while I look the town over. Don't want to keep Tilde an' Miss Melanie caged in that hotel room any longer'n I have to."

Ned nodded and grinned. "Reckon I can handle that, Mr. Kurt." His grin widened. "Reckon I could do 'thout even lookin' at it, jest feel it."

"Pay special attention to the brakes, that's a right steep grade we gotta get down."

"I got it, Mr. Kurt."

Buckner headed for the main street, wishing he could make Ned and Tilde talk to him without sticking the mister in front of his name. He shrugged. It was ingrained in them, and old habits were hard to break.

At the end of Trinidad's main street, Buckner stopped and studied the town. It had grown some since he last saw it. He looked especially at the saloons. He figured the Odoms would most likely be in one of them, but if not he'd check out the cafes, dry goods stores, even the blacksmith shop, but he'd look at the saloons first.

He came up dry on checking the saloons, then he went into every store, and from there he checked the cafes. He saw Clanton in the first cafe he checked, turned and left before hard talk could start, but he saw not a sign of the Odoms. Hope swelled his chest. Maybe they had gone on down the trail. He crushed the budding chance they were gone. Despite not seeing them, he figured the town was where they would make their bid to get rid of Melanie. They were city men, and were more comfortable where buildings were available to hide a man.

After two and a half hours, he headed for the hotel.

Outside Melanie's door, he rapped softly. "Who is it?" The voice was Melanie's.

"Buckner." The door opened a crack, an eye looked him over, and the door opened. Melanie stood there, her revolver hanging at her side. Buckner glanced at Tilde. She still had her gun trained on him. He grinned. "Y'all take instruction real well."

"Where have you been, Kurt Buckner? I went from worrying about us to worrying about you."

He slanted Melanie a look. "Lot o' stores an' waterin' holes in this town, little lady. I checked 'em all. The only one I saw was Clanton. I left before he could start trouble."

Melanie's eyes rounded. "For once? You mean to tell me you didn't walk into the middle of it flailing away? Oh, I'm so proud of you." He let her sarcasm slide off his shoulders like water off oilcloth.

He smiled. "Reckon I interfered with your shoppin'. Well, go on, do what a woman does best, but keep your handguns handy. I'm gonna have a drink and play a few hands of poker. I'll find you in time for supper. I'm buyin'."

At the door of the hotel he left them and headed for a saloon he'd been in earlier, quiet, cool, and clean. It hadn't smelled of stale whisky and tobacco smoke.

When he stepped through the batwing doors, he slid off to the side and let his eyes adjust to the changed light, not figuring someone would take a shot at him, but wanting to find a poker table with an open seat. The clink of poker chips came from the back of the room.

By the time he could see the tables clearly, he could also see the people in the room. His gaze flicked from person to person. A couple of the men from the wagon train stood at the bar, but he saw no one else he knew. He walked to a table with an empty chair, stood and waited to be asked to have a seat.

It was a small game, two-bit limit. Buckner sat there until he figured it was time to look for Melanie and Tilde. He'd won a few pots, lost a few, and ended up a little over three dollars richer. He'd come back after supper and find a bigger game.

Dark hadn't settled in when he headed for the hotel, but the alleys stood in deep shadow. Buckner walked close to the buildings on his side of the street, checked the darkened openings on the opposite side, looked around the corners on his side, and then hurried to the next storefront. The same feelings and sharpened senses came to him that he'd had only a few short months ago, when his only concern was his safety and the bounty he'd get on the man he was then hunting.

Melanie and Tilde were in the mercantile store when he spotted them. "I'll get Ned and we'll eat at the small cafe down in the next block."

"We'll wait here for you," Melanie said. She held up a sheepskin coat. "Do you like this? Will it keep a person warm in the mountains?"

He nodded. "It'll do the job." He walked away, saying over his shoulder, "Be back with Ned in a few minutes."

He'd taken only a few steps outside the door when a rifle shot tore the evening sounds. Glass in the storefront shattered. Buckner ducked low, ran for the door, realizing the shot wasn't meant for him. Melanie, had she been in clear sight through the window?

He hit the front door running. "Melanie, Melanie, are you all right?"

From behind a stack of jeans, Melanie answered, "Right here, Kurt. We're both okay."

"Stay there. Gonna see if I can find who fired the shot." On the way back out the door he tore several lengths of wrapping paper from the roll on the counter, wadded it up, sprinted for the door, went through it, and dodged to the side. He zigzagged across the street toward the alley the shot came from. He didn't expect to find the sniper, but thought he might find some clue as to who did it.

Before entering the alley, he stood a moment at the corner of the store adjacent to it, peeked around the corner into the dark shaft, saw nothing, and went in, gun in hand. He drew no shots. Searching his pocket he found a lucifer, dragged it across the seat of his pants, and held its fire to the wad of paper.

A gleam caught his eye. He picked up an empty .44-40 cartridge. A crowd had gathered outside the alley, and when they saw the alley was empty they started crowding into it. Buckner waved them back. A couple persisted. He pointed his handgun at them. They lost all curiosity and backed into the crowd.

Buckner, bent low over the ground, looked for footprints in the dust, and soon found what he looked for. The print of a narrow low-quarter shoe showed clearly, and a few steps away he found another, then he saw where whoever wore the shoe spun and ran. Clanton wore boots. The shot had clearly been meant for Melanie, and he knew of only two others who wanted her dead, but there was no hope he'd find them tonight. He dropped the still-burning wad of paper to the ground, snuffed out the flame with his boot sole, and walked back to the store.

His face feeling like old, brittle paper, he walked up to Melanie. "That shot was meant for you. Now you know why I wanted you to stay in your room." He looked down at the hole in the pile of jeans. "Doesn't look like I did much of a job taking care of you, does it?"

A man rushed through the door. He wore a badge. "What's going on here? Someone just told me a woman had been fired at."

"You're a little late, Marshal. This young lady was the target. I know who did it and I'll take care of it." His words dropped between them like granite boulders.

The marshal, iron-gray hair, leathery skin, and a little stooped, stared at Buckner from steel-blue eyes. "Know how you feel, son, but I'm the law here. Cain't let you go man-hunting in my town."

Buckner returned his look. "Marshal, you don't know what the man looks like who fired the shot. I do. You're only one man, and one man can't cover this whole town, maybe two of us can't, but if you'll accept my help we can try."

The old lawman never broke his gaze from Buckner's; he held it a long moment more, nodded and pointed toward the back of the store. "Let's go back there and talk." He looked at Melanie. "For your own safety, ma'am, I'd like to keep me and your friend here between you and the door, so join us back yonder, if you will." He looked at Tilde. "You a friend of the lady?"

Tilde straightened her thin little body. "Her best friend, Mr. Marshal."

"You come with us too, then."

In the back of the store, Buckner described the Odoms and told the marshal why they wanted Melanie dead. Then he painted a picture of what he'd found in the alley. "One of the men is constantly wiping his nose on his shirtsleeve, don't know as the other one has any peculiar traits, but I do know this, Marshal. They were both up at Bent's Fort a couple days ahead o' us. Quint Cantrell an' Billy Bonney told me that, an' I've never known either of 'em to lie."

The old man had been studying Buckner while he talked. Finally his eyes crinkled at the corners, he said, "Reckon I never heard either of 'em would lie either. Same goes for you. Took me a while, but I finally figured it out. You're Kurt Buckner, ain't you?"

"That's me, Marshal."

"Reckon what throwed me was I heered you was still man-huntin'. Didn't know you'd done gone back to scoutin' fer wagon trains."

"I haven't. I traded my services to Carraway for lettin' Miss Melanie an' her wagon join up with his train."

The marshal looked toward the door, then back at Buckner. "If even half what I hear about you is true, Carraway made one heck of a deal. Tell you what, we'll both look for them two men. Cain't say as I ever heered of no one who'd shoot a woman." He snapped his head in a quick nod. "Yep, we'll find 'em."

Buckner smiled. "Thanks, Marshal. But not tonight. It would be a waste of time to do anything now. We'll start in the morning. These ladies have not eaten yet, so I'm gonna take 'em to the cafe down the street, then I'm gonna tuck 'em in bed and stay right outside their door until mornin'."

The four of them headed for the door when the marshal asked, "You got a shotgun, Buckner?"

"Nope."

"After you eat, come by the office. I got a sawed-off twelve-gauge Greener I'll let you use."

Buckner smiled, knowing he showed little amusement. "Much obliged, Marshal. I'll take you up on that." He looked at Melanie and Tilde. "Come on, ladies, know you must be starved."

Two hours later, Buckner had them back at their room. They'd stopped to let Ned know what had happened, and he was to take care of things at the wagon.

After ensuring there was no way to enter their room through the window, Buckner went to the door. "I'll be just outside, ladies. If you need anything, call me."

Mischief lurking behind her eyes, Melanie smiled. "Well, Kurt Buckner, I can see you're not a man of your word."

"What'd I do now?"

"Why, you told the marshal you were going to tuck us in bed—I'm waiting."

Buckner felt his face catch fire. He twisted, grabbed for the doorknob, missed it, grabbed again, and went through the doorway, closing the door behind him. He heard a giggle mixed with a louder guffaw he knew to be Tilde's.

He slipped down the wall to take up his vigil for the night, muttering, "That woman's gonna drive me crazy 'fore I get her settled."

Time dragged. Two, three hours passed, he nodded, wished he had a cup of coffee, nodded again, then came fully awake. The stairs had squeaked. Buckner rolled over to the deeper shadows of the hallway, and trained the Greener toward the top of the stairs only twenty feet away.

Another squeak. His fingers tightened on the triggers. He didn't want to kill an innocent man, but he sure as hell figured to get a guilty one.

A hat brim showed first, then the whole man followed. It was Odom's brother. Buckner pulled both triggers, and cursed himself for not waiting a moment longer—he might have gotten them both.

The charge of double ought buckshot knocked Odom back onto the stairs. The sound of his body tumbling head over heels thumped each time he turned another flip.

Buckner, reloading the shotgun, ran through the cloud of powder smoke hanging in the still air and hit the top of the stairs running. Paul Odom was pushing through the front door. Buckner loosed another barrel at him. The glass shattered in an outward spray. Odom kept running.

Buckner got to the boardwalk in time to see his prey round the corner of the hotel. He ran to the corner, stopped, poked the Greener around the corner, and fired the other barrel down the space between the buildings, hoping the shot would spread enough, maybe, to hit the runner.

He followed the slugs into the space. Empty. A slight light at the other end would have silhouetted the man. Buckner ran to the other end, peered around the corner of the building, and looked in every direction. Odom had disappeared. He retraced his steps to the hotel foyer.

"You wrecked my door. No telling what you wrecked upstairs. You gotta pay for them."

Buckner dragged a look down the length of the bookish little man who'd signed him in to the hotel. "You're a helluva excuse for a human being. You don't give a damn whether there's someone hurt up there, do you?"

He went to what was left of Odom, stood there and looked at the damage a double charge of buckshot could do. They'd done the trick. This Odom wouldn't stalk any more women. He stepped toward the stairs. The acrid smell of gunpowder still filled the air. He sniffed and looked over his shoulder. "Get your door fixed. I'll pay for *it*—nothing more. Can't figure why Wootton would hire anybody like you."

At the top of the stairs he met Melanie and Tilde. "What happened, Kurt?"

"Half o' our trouble's lying at the bottom of the stairs, but it's not the one I really want. Anyway, that one won't be botherin' anyone ever again."

CHAPTER 17

MELANIE STARED FROM Buckner to the body at the bottom of the stairs. "One of the Odoms?"

"Yeah, but the one we really want got away. Goin' after 'im in the mornin'." He sighed. He was tired, sleepy, and the pungent smell of gun smoke still hanging in the stale hall air didn't help his tight, roiling stomach. He'd rather be smelling grass, cured on the stem, and fresh pine scent blowing off the mountains.

He smiled tiredly at Tilde. "You can put that six-shooter away for now. Figure Paul Odom won't be back, not tonight anyway." He broke the breech and checked the loads in the Greener. "Y'all go on in an' get to bed. I'll stay outside your door, so don't worry."

"You're tired, Kurt. Give me that shotgun and I'll watch. You get some sleep."

"No, ma'am. Do like I say now. Get to bed."

They closed the door behind them, and Buckner slipped down to sit outside it.

As he thought, Odom didn't come back during the long night. Darkness finally paled to a gray translucence. Objects changed from ghostly to solid.

He stirred, grunted, time for breakfast, but at the same time wondered which he'd like most, a good sleep, or food. He'd not leave Melanie and Tilde here alone. That turned out not to be a worry. He heard them moving around inside.

It wasn't long until the door opened. "Oh, you poor man. I know you must be dead. Now why don't you get to bed?"

"Ma'am, I been tireder, an' I got a full day ahead o' me. Let's go eat."

They ate. They all had the first eggs they'd had since Dodge City. Buckner had a half dozen of them along with steak and potatoes. Melanie and Tilde stared at his plate, then looked at theirs. Melanie giggled. "Here I've been starving you to death on the trail and didn't even know it."

He grinned sheepishly. "No, ma'am, you haven't. I'm just 'specially hungry for eggs." He frowned. "I sorta figured to go after Odom today, but after thinking on it during the night I don't reckon it'd be a good idea to leave you here in town. He might not have left."

"Is it not possible to take us with you?"

He shook his head. "Melanie, this country around here is more rugged than you can imagine. Besides, I'll be travelin' on foot. I know what his horse tracks look like an' I can track him better from ground level. Think we all ought to stay in town today, let me do some lookin' around here. The Odom horses might still be in the livery or some other stable. Gotta look."

After breakfast, Buckner took them to the general store where he bought copies of the weekly paper, and a book. Melanie had a puzzled look. "What's all the reading material for?"

"Gonna stash you an' Tilde in the marshal's office while I look." He pulled his pipe from his pocket, and before pushing tobacco into its bowl he gave them a look. "I know all this is spoilin' our stay here, but we can't take any chances. One o' you gettin' shot would be a lot worse."

Melanie placed her hand on his. "Do what you have to, Kurt."

He left them with the marshal and headed for the hotel. Children were not out playing yet, and there had been no reason he could think of for anyone to walk between the hotel and the store next door. That space was the first he checked— and there he found the same footprints as those he figured belonged to the person who had taken a shot at Melanie. Odom again, but that came as no surprise.

The fine dust, this early in the morning, preserved the footprints in mint condition. Buckner followed them down the back of three stores. There, he lost them in tracks left by horse and mule teams which used the backs of stores to unload provisions.

He circled the area most churned up by the teams and

again picked up the low-quarter shoe tracks. He lost them and found them again four times before he lost them for good when they crossed a street. Try as he might, they disappeared in the heavy traffic of the day.

Buckner leaned against a storefront, trying to put himself in Odom's place. He would have been in a hurry. Buckner didn't think he would tarry for the slim chance he'd get another opportunity today. If he had been Odom, he'd find a place to sleep where he'd likely not be found, or he'd leave town. Buckner nodded. He settled on the leave-town option and headed for the livery stable.

Inside the big double doors, a crippled old cowboy met him. "What can I do fer you, mister? You ain't ridin' no horse. You want to rent one?"

Buckner shook his head. "Lookin' for a man. Figured you might a seen 'im."

"What's he look like?"

Buckner grimaced. "Reckon the thing you'd notice most is, he's a dirty bastard, always wipin' his nose on his shirtsleeve."

Before Buckner could further describe his quarry, the liveryman nodded. "From your words, stranger, I don't figger he's a friend o' your'n."

"Well, cowboy, I don't usually call my friends 'dirty bastards.' You see 'im?"

"Yep. Him, an' I reckon the other man wuz his brother, they kept their horses with me four, maybe five days. This mornin' the one you spiked out for me, come in, in a big hurry. Took all three horses an' left. Headed toward the pass." He twirled a corn shuck cigarette, lit it, and grinned at Buckner. "That there other one is gonna be madder'n hell when he finds his horse gone."

"Won't be mad, he's dead. I blew 'im apart with buck-shot."

The old hostler slanted Buckner a sly grin. "Judgin' by what you jest said, neither one o' them wuz friends o' your'n."

"Reckon you could say that." Buckner tipped his hat and headed back to the marshal's office.

Before saying anything, even though they all looked questioningly at him, Buckner went to the old dented, blackened coffeepot and poured a cup. "You ladies can go on about your shoppin'. Odom won't be botherin' you today."

"Didn't hear no shots, son. You kill 'im?"

"No, but I found out enough to be pretty sure he left town."

Melanie came to him and looked into his eyes. "What're you going to do now, Kurt?"

"Go after 'im."

"Now? Kurt, you need some rest, and besides, he's probably long gone by now. He may be too afraid to try again."

Buckner looked at her a long moment. "Ma'am, you don't believe that any more'n I do." He rubbed his brow and dragged his hand down the side of his face. "I gotta hit the trail. Figure he's gonna find himself a spot he thinks he can get away from real fast, a place where he figures he can pick us both off. I'm gonna find him first."

Melanie's eyes flooded. "If anything happens to you, Kurt, I'll die."

"Yes'm, reckon I will too." As soon as he said it, he realized it was a bad joke. "Aw, ma'am, I was just jokin'."

He was too late. Melanie let the dam burst. Tears poured down her cheeks. She held out her arms as though to put them around him and quickly drew back. Buckner, without thinking, pulled her to him. She sobbed.

"Aw now, honey, don't cry. Sometimes I'm too dumb to know when to joke." He stood there helplessly, holding her, stroking her hair and back. Why couldn't he keep his damned mouth shut when he didn't really have anything to say?

"Oh, K-K-Kurt, I-I worry so much about you. It-it was me who got you into all of this mess to begin with. E-even if it meant I'd never meet you, I wish I hadn't dragged you into my troubles."

He ran his hands soothingly down her back again. "Now

don't you worry. I'm a lot better at this game than Odom
will ever be."

The old marshal, who'd been standing there shuffling
from one foot to the other, broke in, "Ma'am, you can
believe Buckner there. They ain't another man in the West
better'n him when he sets his mind to get you. Ain't no need
for you to worry."

Buckner stepped back and handed Melanie his handker-
chief. "Here now, ma'am, you dry your pretty eyes and
don't ever let me see tears in them again."

Melanie's lips crinkled at the corners, obviously trying to
force a smile. "You won't see them, Kurt, unless *you* cause
them."

"Well, I'm sure not gonna be the cause. Now, Tilde, you
take our young lady out and get your shoppin' done. I'll be
back in three, four days maybe, before the train pulls out
anyway. Tell Carraway where I've gone, an' if I'm not back
by the time the train pulls out, you folks take your place in
it. I'll find you down the trail a ways."

He went back to the hotel, made sure his moccasins were
in good shape, and rolled his bedroll. He then cleaned and
oiled his Winchester and Colt, took his riding boots off and
put on a pair of heavy-soled walking boots. He didn't even
consider taking the dun. A horse would be next to useless if
Odom left the trail, and that's exactly what Buckner thought
he'd do.

At the edge of town, using the Raton Pass trail as the
focal point, Buckner cast back and forth looking for horse
prints he recognized. After about a half hour, he decided to
get a little farther out of town; there had been too much
traffic in close.

He held to the outside edge of the trail, figuring there was
no way Odom would leave the road on the inside. He would
have to go straight up the mountain if he did, and neither
man nor horse could take that punishment.

Buckner walked less than a quarter of a mile when horse
tracks left the roadway and angled into a ravine. He felt
certain he'd lucked out, but to make sure he followed them,
and after about twenty feet or so squatted by the horse's

hoofprints. He ran his fingers around the inside of the indentations where the steel shoes cut into the soft earth. Here where the ground was soft, he could make sure he followed the right man. Still in the mountain's shadow, the hoofprints were moist—they'd been made since sundown the night before. He studied each print. In but a few minutes he identified the three horses Odom and his brothers had ridden. His chest swelled and tightened. His scalp tingled. The horses would be Odom's death knell.

On the trail, by changing horses frequently, the nasty carpetbagger could have left a posse far behind, but off the trail, in this rough country a man on foot could travel faster, and safer.

Buckner shifted his bedroll to a comfortable position on his shoulders and studied the landscape ahead. Off to his right, the Purgatoire River angled west, away from the trail. To his left the valley deepened sharply away from the road, and soon a rider would find it impossible to climb the talus slope back to the trail.

Buckner figured Odom didn't know this country and might take the route to his left, south, thinking to stay close to the roadway, find a place to climb the slope, leave his horses at the bottom, shoot his prey, get back to his horses, and make his escape.

He stood, studied the trees, ravines, and rocky slopes ahead for sign. Maybe Odom stayed close, letting the posse pass him by. He thought it would never enter the carpetbagger's mind that his pursuit would be a lone man.

After being as sure as possible his quarry wasn't sitting in some sniper's nest waiting for him, Buckner slipped from one scrub cedar to another. He'd gone less than a half mile when the tracks veered to the south.

Figured that, Buckner thought. That's a city boy ahead of me. He'll not get too far where he knows other humans are. He probably couldn't find an outhouse in bright daylight without a deep path running to it.

Buckner picked his way through the brush, searching ahead every few feet. It was slow going, but with three horses Odom wouldn't make any better time.

Throughout the long morning and afternoon, the horse tracks got no fresher, nor were they any older. Buckner nodded and grinned. Soon, Odom would begin to think he'd outwitted his pursuers, get careless, maybe even slow down. Fact was, he'd have to slow his pace or cripple his horses on the rough ground. That was when Buckner figured to start having fun with his man.

He followed the horse tracks until dusk settled into the bottom of the valley. The tops of the peaks around him were still bathed in sunlight when Buckner spotted a place he wanted to camp. He followed the tracks for another half hour to make sure Odom hadn't decided to camp not too far ahead of him, then backtracked to the spot he'd picked.

His camp lay in the middle of large boulders; a stream ran only fifty yards or so from where he unrolled his blankets. He had to fight himself to keep from going ahead and finding Odom, but he was tired, sleepy, and might make mistakes that would get him killed. He figured to rest and meet the carpetbagger on an even basis. He ate a sparse supper: coffee, hardtack, and jerky. He'd eaten less many times.

Finally, already between the blankets, it occurred to him Odom had had no more rest than he. The blankets felt good. He'd probably reached the six thousand foot level, and there was a chill to the air. They had been climbing steadily since leaving Trinidad.

His small fire, well hidden by the boulders, cast off an occasional flame from the embers, and its smoke, little though it was, drifted its scent close to him. Buckner smiled, inhaled deeply, savored the cedar smoke and moist earth smell close to his face.

His saddle rested under his head, and his provisions hung from a limb, high enough he thought foraging animals couldn't reach them. Even though tired, any sound, however slight, would waken him. Lying there, relaxed, the tension seeped from his body.

Sometime during the night, Buckner woke to a snarling, grunting racket. He'd put his rifle by his side when he went to bed. He moved his hand toward it now and gripped it in the small part of the stock, his finger curled around the trigger, his eyes never leaving the bulky, black shape standing on its hind feet swiping angrily at the package of provisions. When the bear apparently decided he couldn't reach them, he dropped back to all four feet, sniffed a couple of times, and waddled from the camp.

The next morning, Buckner woke refreshed, feeling as though he could fight that bear of the night before—and win. Every muscle felt loose, pliable. He stretched, went to the stream, washed his face, wet his hair, combed it back with his fingers, dipped coffee water into his pot, and went back to feed a small amount of wood to the coals from the night before. Before putting wood on the coals, he tested the air, making sure it came from the south and downslope. No trace of wood smoke would alert Odom. He placed the broken limbs on the fire and blew the coals to life.

After eating, he packed and shouldered his bedroll. He was far enough into the wild country to close on Odom, then he'd begin to toy with him. He'd do this the way Melanie wanted it.

Buckner picked up the trail from the night before, now making certain to make no noise. Odom probably thought pursuit had passed him by and would not be in a great hurry. He'd be more interested in finding a place to bushwhack Melanie.

Rocky, brush-studded mountains rose steeply on both sides of the narrow valley. Buckner's job got easier. Odom wouldn't try to climb either side, he'd stay where the horses had better, softer footing. Also, climbing the sides of either slope would put him in sight of anyone on the trail above.

The scrub cedar gave way to pines. In them a man could hide easier. Buckner slowed, searched every tree trunk for movement, looked at every roll in the earth's surface, checked every scarecrow of logs cast down haphazardly by a blowdown. He stopped behind a tree, shivered, and pulled farther into his sheepskin. He wondered if Odom had warm clothes, and doubted he did. The carpetbagger knew nothing about this country, and had probably judged it by the flat, arid, hot plains they traveled for several hundred miles.

Also, the eastern mountains Odom had crossed were nothing like the ones they were now into.

Buckner smiled. The thin, dirty man would soon find out what discomfort really was.

Mid-afternoon Buckner came on horse droppings. He broke a couple of them with a stick. They gave off tendrils of vapor to the cold air. For the present, Buckner was closer than he wanted to be.

The base of the pine looked to have a comfortable matting of needles. Buckner squatted, then sat. He wanted to get far enough away from Trinidad to cause Odom fear when he carried out his plan. One more night should do it. He pulled his pipe out, filled it, lighted it, and sat enjoying a smoke, the first since leaving Trinidad.

The next day he stayed only a quarter of a mile behind his quarry. Buckner had him in sight most of the afternoon. Every once in a while, Odom would pause, look back, and again knee his horse ahead. On those occasions he telegraphed his intent by twisting in his saddle. Buckner had only to slide behind a tree and hold still until he heard the horses move ahead.

While shadowing Odom, Buckner mentally recorded places to camp that night. The sun sank behind the peaks, leaving purple shadows in the valleys and ravines. Under the trees night would come early. Buckner stood within fifty yards of Odom and watched him make camp.

To wait for dark to erase the sharp outline of objects at first seemed a good idea, but on second thought, making camp well off the path they'd made coming in, in the black of night, cancelled the thought. He went back the way they'd come, climbed the slope to a shelf he'd noticed earlier, and spread his blankets. Then he went back to level ground, picked out a landmark he could find in the dark, an extra large boulder, studied his surroundings another moment, and gripping his Winchester headed toward Odom's camp.

Though he was wearing heavy-soled, mid-calf boots, his progress through the woods made no more noise than the shadows creeping in with the setting sun. Soon Buckner again stood looking into the thin renegade's camp.

The aroma of meat broiling, the smell of coffee boiling, both mixed with the pungent smell of juniper smoke caused Buckner's taste buds to water. He swallowed several times, wishing for a hunk of what was probably venison hanging over the fire.

His plan would deprive the carpetbagger of all means of survival, but he first wanted to put him afoot. Thin-soled, low-quarter shoes were all right for sidewalks and city streets, but out here—Buckner grinned at the thought of what walking would do to a man's feet. His first step was to run the horses off, then he'd move to the next step.

While watching Odom eat, then waiting for him to settle into his blankets, Buckner thought how satisfying a cup of that coffee sitting only a few feet from him would be, along with his pipe.

He shrugged off the desire for both, and waited, his gaze glued on every move the carpetbagger made. Finally, the thin man tossed more wood on the fire, moved the coffeepot to the side, looked at the large piece of meat left, wrapped it in oilskin, pulled his blankets closer to the fire, and crawled between them.

Buckner grinned, watching how tight Odom pulled the blanket around him. Probably the first time he'd been warm in a while. His smile widened. He'd give the man reason to work up a good sweat.

The blankets covering the carpetbagger's chest soon rose and fell evenly, then an occasional snore.

Buckner would have to go through the middle of the camp to reach the horses, a bad break, and then he wanted to drive them back the way they'd come, another problem. He waited until certain Odom slept deeply. He should be more than tired after the day's travel.

Finally, his gut muscles tight, his scalp tingling, Buckner moved into the camp. He didn't want to kill Odom—just yet. But if he woke and grabbed for a gun . . .

A glance at Odom, then again searching the ground for sticks or stones that might make a noise, he ghosted toward the fire. There he scooped up the oilskin-wrapped meat, picked up the coffeepot, drank a couple of swallows, and set it back where he got it. With the edge of his shoe sole he pushed a small stone from his path. Several times he worked his boot soles down through the pine straw to push aside small sticks. He'd heard twigs no larger than his little finger crack like a pistol shot. Fifteen or twenty minutes later he stood on the other side of the camp.

The tethered horses looked at him, their ears peaked. Buckner held his breath; a snort might waken the carpetbagger. Then one of them did what he feared, he gave off a fluttery blow. Buckner looked over his shoulder at the thin killer. Odom stopped snoring, pulled his blanket tighter, sucked in a deep breath—then snored again.

Buckner stroked each horse's neck, gave each a light pat, and thought to mount one and drive them through the camp. He changed his mind. The horse might stumble on rocky ground, break a leg, toss him, cause him to lose his gun. He shook his head. He'd take his chances afoot, with only a little help from the broncs. After a moment's hesitation, he raised his arms and yelled, "Teehaaa!" They broke into a run, missed Odom's blankets, and headed out the other side with Buckner hanging to the neck of one.

CHAPTER 18

FROM THE CORNER of his eye, Buckner saw Odom roll to the side, grabbing for his rifle.

A split second of flickering firelight, then darkness. Buckner dropped his hold on the horse, faded into the dark, found a boulder, and hid behind it.

A wild shot split the air, then another, then pounding footsteps passed him. Odom chased his only means of transportation, but, Buckner grinned, he'd never catch those horses here in the dark of the canyon. If the terrified horses didn't break a leg, they'd probably run until they reached Trinidad.

He stayed behind the large rock, then footsteps retraced their way to the camp. Odom built up his fire, a dumb thing to do. The thin renegade should know there was someone, or even several people, beyond the firelight wanting to do him harm. Buckner shrugged. It was what he'd expect of a man who knew nothing of survival. Now he'd see how the filthy outlaw fared with thin-soled shoes.

Odom hunkered by the fire, pulling his blankets around his shoulders. Buckner almost felt sorry for him, almost lost his resolve to make him suffer. The carpetbagger sat there forlorn, shivering.

A hard, cold knot formed in Buckner's chest. Any sympathy he might have had disappeared. A woman-killer, a renegade, a thief, deserved any punishment put on him. He watched until Odom lay by the fire and pulled his blankets tightly around him. After a while he again heard snoring.

Buckner wanted to go to his own blankets, but thought to cause Odom one more bit of misery. He waited a few minutes to make sure the renegade slept soundly, then again approached the camp.

Using as much care as he had the first time, he crouched

157

by the sleeping man, picked up Odom's rifle lying on the ground beside him, reached for the holster beside the now useless saddle, took the handgun from it, and tucked it behind his belt, then faded into the darkness.

The walk back to his own camp took a while, but he hardly noticed. He now had Odom without horses, without weapons, and without proper shoes for walking over rough ground. He wondered if the carpetbagger would go back to Trinidad, or try to find another town somewhere. Buckner thought he'd go ahead, knowing the law would be waiting for him in most of the places he'd been.

Back in camp, Buckner gnawed on the venison he'd taken from Odom, wrapped the leavings, turned in, and soon slept.

The next morning, he made a small, smokeless fire and fixed breakfast. The trail lay below, and Uncle Dick's toll road sliced across the mountain's shoulder three or four hundred feet above. He could see Odom if he tried to return to Trinidad, and if he went in the opposite direction Buckner knew he could catch him anytime he wished.

After waiting long enough to be fairly certain Odom headed away from Trinidad, he packed up, put out his fire, and left camp. His approach to the renegade's camp was as silent as the one of the night before.

The camp stood empty, but the carpetbagger had left his fire burning.

Buckner looked the camp over, poured water on the fire, cringing at the thought of allowing a man to roam the woods who apparently gave no thought to brush or forest fires.

He wasn't ready to put his prey out of his misery—yet. He wanted him to suffer awhile. Not, he thought, that the hardships would cause the thin, nasty man to rethink his life and correct his ways. Criminals don't reform, they just hide their crimes better. "Not gonna give 'im a chance to do that," Buckner muttered.

Odom's tracks were not hard to find, and as Buckner thought, they continued away from Trinidad. By mid-afternoon, the tracks weaved a bit, and by dusk it was obvious the renegade stumbled frequently and weaved farther to the sides. Buckner grinned.

That night, he stood in the dark and watched Odom set up camp, take his coffeepot and go to the stream, a hundred or so yards away, for water. Buckner waited until he bent over to dip water into the pot, then he walked to the renegade's bedroll and bundle of provisions, picked them up, and melted into the shadows beyond the firelight.

Odom walked unsteadily and gingerly on blistered raw feet back to the fire, stopped, stared at the spot he'd dropped his bedroll, dropped the coffeepot, threw back his head and yelled, "What you want with me? Why're you treatin' me like this? Shoot me. Do anythin'."

In the dark, Buckner shook his head and whispered into the night, knowing the renegade couldn't hear, "Not yet, trash, not yet."

Odom built his fire larger, sat by it close enough to roast raw meat, and shivered. He didn't even have anything to make coffee. Buckner wondered how he kept from burning himself.

That night, the bounty hunter camped within sight of the killer's fire. He figured the outlaw's thoughts and feelings were too numb by now to worry about his surroundings. He would be concerned with nothing but his own misery.

Buckner sat by his small fire, hidden behind a bend, and thought of Melanie, and the other woman Odom had killed along with her husband. Angry bile welled into his throat. He should go down there and rid the earth of the shivering, miserable vermin. He shook his head. He'd not make it that easy on the man. Let him suffer another day. He'd stuffed Odom's bedroll under a stumpy juniper. Pack rats would eventually tear it apart.

The next day was a repeat of the one just past, only by sundown Odom had gone to his knees and crawled. As close as Buckner was, he saw the renegade remove his shoes, groan, then sit on a rock and cry. Buckner wondered if his tears were from anger, frustration, no guts, or all three.

The slim outlaw finally straightened, looked both directions of the canyon, went to his knees, crawled another fifty feet, fell to his belly and beat the ground with his fists. Buckner walked to him and stood looking down.

"Roll over, scum."

The outlaw twisted his neck to look up at Buckner. "Who're you? Why you doin' this to me? I ain't never done nothin' to you." The whimper might have been pitiful coming from any other man, but the tall bounty hunter stared quietly while Odom rolled over and sat.

He pulled his .44, thumbed back the hammer, real slow-like, letting the ratcheting sound crash in on the sorry mess sitting before him. Odom's eyes widened, stared into the maw of the heavy handgun, then his lids drooped to slit over his eyes. "Don't care. Go on, kill me. I cain't walk ten more feet."

Buckner's finger tightened only a fraction, then he let the hammer down softly. "You just think you can't walk any farther—but you will. Not gonna kill you, Odom. Gonna let the law do that. We hang men out here for killin' women-folk, an' I know of one you killed, an' another you tried to kill."

"No! That was my brother who killed that woman back yonder in Virginia, an' I wasn't nowhere around the other night when he tried to kill that Corbin girl."

"Put your hands behind you. Gonna tie you for the night, then we head back to Trinidad—walkin'." Odom crossed his wrists in back of him. Buckner tied his hands, kicked him to his stomach, and tied his feet.

"Didn't you catch the horses?"

"Didn't try. Knew *I* could walk. Figured at the time to kill you, but after thinkin' on it awhile, believed a good hike down to Trinidad would be good for you. Then, I figured a bright new yellow rope stretchin' that filthy neck o' yours would be a right nice thing to look on. Give others like you somethin' to think about."

"Cain't walk, mister, cain't hardly crawl."

"You'll do one or the other, 'cause I sure as hell am not gonna carry you. Now you lie there nice an' quiet while I fix myself some supper. First food you get will be jail slop. Try to sleep, it'll rest you up for your walk tomorrow."

Odom lay there sniffling while Buckner watched to see if not being able to get his shirtsleeve to his nose would drive the man crazy. After a while, he fixed supper, enjoyed his pipe, and turned in.

Three days later, Trinidad's main street thronged with people who fell silent and pushed back toward the boardwalk on each side, opening a path for the tall, square-shouldered man dragging by the collar what must have been a human being in the near past.

Buckner walked slowly, so tired he could hardly put one foot in front of the other. He looked to neither side, his bedroll weighed heavy on his shoulders. His left hand clutched his Winchester, while his right clenched Odom's shirt close to his neck. The fingers of his right hand cramped so he wondered if he'd ever straighten them.

Smells of cooking food and brewing coffee came to him, but didn't penetrate his senses enough to cause hunger. A small dog walked to him and wagged his tail. Buckner barely noticed the pup. Crowd noise swelled along the street, but he didn't hear it. He sensed the sound by vibrations on his body. All these things were at the back of his mind.

In front of the marshal's office, he loosened the fingers of his hand enough to drop Odom to the dust, stumbled up the steps to the boardwalk and pushed through the doorway.

"My God, man, where you been? You look like you been through hell."

Buckner flopped into the chair facing the marshal's desk. "One of the men who tried to kill Miss Melanie is lying out yonder in the street. I want 'im hung."

"Gotta try 'im first, son, but we'll get it done. Sit still while I get 'im in here."

Buckner flexed the fingers of his right hand while waiting for the lawman to drag Odom to a cell and turn the key. When the marshal returned, he peered closely at Buckner. "I reckon you could use . . ."

Buckner cut him off. "Sir, I don't even know what handle to call you by."

The leathery-faced old man smiled. "Call me most anything, Buckner, but my name is Canfield, Ben Canfield."

His grin broadened. "What I wuz gonna say is, reckon you could use a bath, good supper, an' a hefty glass o' bourbon 'bout now. Not 'specially in that order."

Buckner smiled through his fatigue. "I smell that ripe, Canfield?" He nodded. "But yeah, you nailed those things dead center. Reckon first, a drink . . ."

The front door burst open. Melanie stood there. "Are you all right, Kurt? Please say you are."

"Melanie, you do break into a conversation at the worst times. I think Marshal Canfield, here, was about to offer me a drink."

Melanie popped hands to hips. "Kurt, you're the most exasperating . . ." She stopped. Her gaze raked him from head to foot. "Gracious. What in the world happened to you? You look like you've been dragged through a knot-hole."

Buckner looked at Canfield. "If you were about to offer me a drink, Marshal, pour that coffee cup a little more'n half full and hand it here, if you weren't," he turned his attention to Melanie, "maybe you'd be kind enough to go to my room and bring me that bottle I got stashed there."

Canfield reached in the bottom drawer of the desk that looked like it had not only crossed the plains in a covered wagon, it looked like it had started its journey on the Mayflower. He took a full quart of bourbon from the drawer, pulled the cork, poured his old granite cup full, and before he could hand it to Buckner, Melanie took it from his hands.

She took it to Buckner, held it to his lips, then looked primly at the marshal. "If you have another cup, Marshal, I'll have a sip," she glanced at Buckner, "only, of course, to cover the awful odor of a man who in the past I've known to be most fastidious about his personal cleanliness."

Tired though he was, Buckner guffawed. "Don't let her kid you, Canfield. If you don't give her a drink, I'm afraid she'll take mine." He hesitated. "She'd do that whether I was clean or not just to spite me."

Canfield poured Melanie and himself a small drink in some spare cups and reached for a pitcher of water. He looked questioningly at Melanie.

"Pour some of that coffee into it, please," she said, looking at the blackened old pot sitting on the heater.

He obliged, then splashed water into his own drink.

Looking worried, Melanie studied Buckner a moment. "Please, Kurt, what happened? We've all been so very worried."

"The important thing right now is, you don't have any more worries about Odom shootin' you. I brought 'im back with me—alive. I want 'im to stand trial an' hang." He looked into Canfield's eyes, daring him to object. "If the jury doesn't bring in a guilty verdict, I'll let 'im get outta town an' hang 'im myself." He took a swallow of his drink. "An', ma'am, you wanted 'im to suffer for what he did to your friend? Well, you can rest easy on that count."

She nodded. "I thought as much, but that doesn't explain why you look as you do."

He smiled, even though he felt like sliding down in the chair and going to sleep. "Sometimes, ma'am, we do stupid things. I did one a few days ago. I stole Odom's horses and ran 'em back to town, makin' him walk. When I took 'im into custody, he was near crazy with pain, but I swore I'd make 'im walk—or crawl—back to Trinidad, swore I'd not carry him one step. I lied to myself, and to him. I dragged 'im by his collar for two days. Reckon I'm 'bout as sorry-lookin' as he is."

"And about as dirty."

"Well, ma'am, I can take care of the dirt in 'bout an hour, I can take care of my hunger in another hour, an' I can take care of this drink and another one in another hour, but my tired is gonna take all night to get rid of."

Melanie looked accusingly at Canfield as though he were to blame for their thoughtlessness. "Oh, how cruel of us." She reached to set Buckner's cup on the desk, but he swished it beyond her hand. "Let me help you to the hotel."

"Not 'til I finish this drink and one more."

"I thought we might have one together after you clean up."

He grinned. "We'll do just that, but only after I sit here and relax a bit."

They talked and drank quietly while Buckner had his drinks. He brought them up-to-date on all that had happened while he was gone, and Canfield told them the circuit judge wouldn't be through Trinidad for another three weeks.

Buckner frowned, shook his head, and said, "Won't work, Marshal. I promised to scout for that wagon train as far as the Cimarron Canyon Cutoff, gave my word on it. Reckon I won't swear out any charges on Odom. I'll take 'im with me an' take care of 'im myself."

"Kurt! You can't mean you'd hang him yourself?"

"Reckon that's what I mean, ma'am."

"But you . . . you . . ."

"Buckner, think I might be able to save you doin' somethin' like that." Canfield frowned. "Ain't sure, but we done it before."

Buckner slanted Canfield a doubtful look. "Better be good, Marshal."

The old lawman gave back a look as good as he got from Buckner. "Think maybe, under the circumstances, the mayor could serve as judge." He frowned, obviously pondering the legality of his suggestion. "Course, we did things like that pretty often 'fore we got so civilized. Now, with a new mayor and all, I don't know."

Buckner took a swallow of his drink. "Tell you what, why don't you put it to 'im in the mornin', and if he agrees I'll make formal charges then." He shrugged. "If he doesn't agree to doin' it that way, then I'll take Odom with me. Do it that way an' I'll be judge, jury, and executioner."

Melanie, fire in her eyes, said, "The people in the train accused you of doing just that once before. Setting yourself up as God. You can't do it, Kurt."

He gave her a straight-on look, no give in it. "All due respect, ma'am, I'll do it my way. Won't stand for anyone interferin'."

She lowered her eyes, looked into her empty cup, and nodded. "I thought perhaps you would. You're a very hard man."

They finished their drinks, and feeling the bourbon sitting warmly in his stomach, Buckner stood. "Reckon I better get a bath 'fore Miss Melanie leaves here without me, Canfield. Try your idea on the mayor in the mornin'. See you then."

He and Melanie left together. She didn't walk close to him and take his arm this time. He thought it was because of his hardheaded attitude toward Odom. Of course it could have been because of his ripe condition.

When they went into the lobby, he noticed the door once again had glass in it. He stopped at the desk and told the clerk he'd pay for the glass when he came down for supper, but right now he wanted a tub of hot water taken to his room. He looked at Melanie. "Supper in 'bout an hour?" At her nod and smile, he said, "See you then."

While waiting for his bathwater to be brought up, Buckner checked his black suit, his only suit, to see if most of the wrinkles had hung out. For some reason, he wanted to look good for Melanie.

While waiting for his bathwater, he cleaned and oiled his guns, whetted his knife, washed his face, and, looking into the cracked and clouded mirror, shaved.

Although bone tired, for some reason he wanted the comfortable, relaxed feeling he had when around Melanie. He frowned. He'd better break that habit.

An hour later, clean, dressed with a great deal of care, he looked in the mirror approvingly, strapped on his six-shooter, and headed for the stairs.

CHAPTER 19

⚬ ──────────── ⚬

BUCKNER PAID THE bill for repairing the front door, and while waiting for Melanie sat on the sofa under the old Regulator wall clock. He faced the stairs.

When Melanie, Tilde, and Ned came to the top of the stairs, Buckner swallowed hard a couple of times. He didn't even look at her two companions. Melanie wore a white, fitted blouse, a black grosgrain ribbon threaded through some loops at the base of her collar and tied like a man's tie in the front. A wide, black patent-leather belt circled her waist he would've bet he could span, belt and all, with his two hands, and she wore a long, black, tailored skirt which barely brushed her instep. Lordy, her everyday beauty, dusty clothes, often smudged face, sometimes tired or worry lines in her face on the trail, all faded into cloudy memories. She once again looked the elegant lady he'd met in Newton. He stood.

She walked directly to him and took his arm. "My, what a suave, well-appointed gentleman." The devil lurked behind her eyes. "I'm supposed to meet the scout for that wagon train which rolled in a few days ago. You haven't seen him, have you? He's a ruggedly handsome man, sometimes needs a shave badly, and at least once since I've known him, he was way overdue for a bath."

Buckner gave her a sour look, then thought of a comeback. "That's strange, ma'am. I was sittin' there lookin' for a young woman, who most o' the time is dusty, dirty-faced, an' less often has a chance to bathe than the gentleman in question." He looked at Tilde and Ned. "The lady I have in mind was accompanied by two companions also, but they were not nearly as finely dressed as you two." They both laughed, but Ned, bent, slapped his knees with both hands, and roared.

"Mr. Kurt," Tilde said, "I 'spect that there woman you talkin' 'bout wuz throwed out with a tub o' awful dirty bathwater few days ago."

"All right, you got me back, Kurt. Where are we going to eat? I'm starved."

"I hear Uncle Dick Wootton sets a right nice table. Let's give 'im a chance, and it's right here in the inn. More convenient."

"Sounds good to me, Kurt."

In the dining room Buckner ordered coffee for them all, and when it was served spiked each drink with a liberal amount of bourbon from a silver flask he took from his coat pocket. Tilde grumbled, but she wasn't so set against it to refuse.

Melanie studied him a few moments. "You know, Kurt, you're an absolute contradiction."

He slanted her a puzzled look. "How so, fine lady?"

"You shed being and looking the barbarian like a snake does its skin, and in its place appears a fine, polished gentleman."

Before Buckner could answer, in almost one voice, Ned and Tilde grumbled, "Contradiction, barbarian, don't know what them words mean. You cussin' Mr. Kurt out, Miss Melanie?"

Buckner laughed. "No, good friends, I think Miss Melanie was, in her sharp-tongued way, paying me a sort of compliment." He gave Melanie his attention. "You judge me by my clothes, lady. Don't ever make that mistake. I'm the same man whichever of the two descriptions you want to hang on me."

While having supper, Melanie asked Buckner about Wootton, who was he, and what right did he have to put a toll on the road across the pass?

Buckner frowned. "I've known Uncle Dick quite a while, an' just because he runs this inn don't figure him for a tenderfoot. He's been an Army scout, trapper, rancher, and back in the fifties, '52 I believe, he drove nine thousand sheep to California. Got there with eighty-nine hundred of 'em."

"And that gives him the right to put a gate across the road to the pass?"

Buckner smiled. "Melanie, he built the road, hacked it out of solid rock with a pick and shovel. He charges whites to travel his road, lets Indians use it free."

Melanie studied on his words a few minutes, nodded, and smiled. "Sounds fair enough." About then, Wootton walked to their table.

"Howdy, folks." He looked at Buckner. "Didn't know you wuz in these parts, boy. How you doin'?"

"Doin' fine, Wootton. Scoutin' for Carraway right now. Gonna take a look at that country around Eagle's Nest, see how a horse ranch might go in that area."

Wootton frowned. "Don't know, son. Cimarron, Eagle's Nest, an' Red River's loaded down with them runnin' from somethin', an' the law leaves 'em alone. Most men would have problems," he grinned, "but the way you throw a gun, you just might make it."

Buckner wasn't amused at all, and his frozen-faced look showed it. "I *figure* to make it, Uncle Dick."

They talked until supper was served. Wootton left, then busy eating, they sat silent. Finally, Melanie, still looking at her plate, asked, "Kurt, are you really as dangerous as Mr. Wootton suggested? Would the outlaws leave you alone just because of . . . of your talents . . . gun talents?"

Grinning, he said, "Not hardly, but I have a plan to do horse business with 'em. They'll leave me alone if I treat 'em fair, an' I figure to do that."

"But Mr. Wootton said they were outlaws."

He nodded. "Far's the law in concerned, yeah, but most o' those men are not really hard cases. They've stolen a few cows here an' there, or horses. Some might've even tried holding up stages or banks, but most have never killed or hurt women. If my ma and pa hadn't whaled the daylights outta me as a kid when I did wrong, I might a ended up the same way."

She shook her head. "Like I said, you're a contradiction. Bounty hunter with sentiments like that, humph."

"Ma'am, I always picked the men I went after. *They* were more of the stripe of the Odoms."

A slight commotion at the door, and Tom Clanton along with four of his cohorts from the wagon train walked to a table. The four were men Buckner thought all along were cut from the same cloth as Clanton. He'd been surprised when they let the brute go on alone after the Indian fight. He shrugged mentally, thinking, they didn't have the guts to back the big bruiser when the chips were down, but they clustered around once the trail danger ended.

Clanton and his friends pulled chairs away from the table, and before sitting, Clanton looked toward Buckner's table and said in a loud voice, "Well, there's the big hero again with his woman. They gettin' right cozy."

Buckner clenched his fists. His jaw muscles knotted and worked. He would not fight with Melanie sitting there. He took a swallow of coffee and looked down at the table.

"Ignore him, Kurt, please. He's not worth soiling your hands on."

The smile he gave her, despite it being a smile, showed more anger than he could hold in. "Ma'am, I'll ignore him for right now—if he'll let me, but the time's gonna come soon, real soon, when I'm gonna take 'im apart."

"Kurt, if you could see your eyes. Oh! You scare me when you look like that."

"Melanie, what he said 'bout us is somethin' I can't—won't let go. Let's finish our meal and get outta here 'fore I forget to be a gentleman. He's already spoiled a night I wanted us all to enjoy."

"Don't worry about it, Kurt, we'll have more."

That thought pleased him.

They finished supper and went to the door. "Ned, escort Miss Melanie to her room if you will. I'm goin' to my room an' change clothes. Don't want to ruin my only suit."

"Kurt, please, let it go. He only suggested you and I were more to each other than we are."

"Ma'am, don't reckon I'm of a mind to let it go. Men out here don't even talk 'bout fallen angels that way, much less a proper lady like yourself." He nodded good night. "See y'all in the mornin'."

He went to his room and changed to his range garb, looked at his moccasins and decided to keep his boots on. They might come in handy. He ran his trouser belt through his knife scabbard, tested the blade of his knife, then strapped on his gun belt. He went back to the dining room.

"You filthy bastard," his voice was soft, "head for the door, go outside, I don't want to wreck this place. Wootton's a friend o' mine."

"What you figure to do, big hero? You gonna try to whip my butt? Or you gonna use that there big six-shooter? Figure I can take you anyway you want it. You give me a sucker punch last time. You ain't gonna git a chance at that agin."

Buckner stared at Clanton's friends. "Any o' you want a part of me, I'll still be there after I finish with your sorry friend, an' if you got any idea 'bout pullin' a gun I'd like that." He spun on his heel and headed for the front door.

Outside, he turned and faced the veranda he'd just stepped from. Clanton bounded down the steps, not slowing his pace. Buckner set himself and started his swing before the huge man got to him. He bent and aimed his fist low, under Clanton's flailing arms. His punch went to the middle of the brute's gut, stood him up, his mouth sucking air just as in the first fight.

"Gonna ask you again," Buckner said, "you want six-shooters, knives, or fists?" He pulled his handgun pointing at Clanton's chest. "You want fists, shuck your hardware an' we'll get it on, otherwise say so an' I'll holster my .44. I'll let you make a move for your weapon, then I'm gonna kill you."

A voice from the porch said, "You other four stand easy. Try to take a hand in this fight an' I'll even things up a bit."

Buckner, not taking his eyes off Clanton, recognized Wootton's voice.

Then a voice he'd ridden across the plains with cut in. "Yes, suh, an' what Mistuh Wootton don't take care of, I'll jest sop up his leavin's."

Despite forcing this fight against bad odds, Buckner wasn't so confident that he didn't welcome having Ned and Wootton at his back. He grinned. "Odds are even now, trash. What way you want it?"

He stared into Clanton's eyes and saw indecision. He'd whipped the big man once with his fists, and the brute had never seen him use knives or guns. Finally, after what seemed forever, Clanton's hands went to his belt buckle and slowly pulled the end loose to drop his gun belt. Buckner holstered his Colt.

Seeming to play it out in slow motion, the hulk held on to his buckle with his left hand and grabbed for his handgun with his right.

Clanton's six-shooter almost cleared its holster before Buckner made his play. Not until then did his hand flash to his side. He fired twice, dusting Clanton front and back with both shots, each shot hitting the brute's right shoulder. The heavy slugs knocked the troublemaker back a couple of steps, while his shot went into the dirt almost hitting his own foot.

Clanton stared at Buckner, then looked down at the red stain spreading across his shirt. Wide-eyed surprise, then the realization that those bullets could have been in his chest just as easy showed on his face. His mouth worked as though to say something. He took a step toward Buckner. He tried to raise his handgun for a´ shot, strained, but couldn't make his damaged muscles do the job. His pistol fell into the dust at his side.

"Don't get to feelin' too good 'bout this, Buckner. I'm gonna get you, front or back, I'm gonna get you." His voice weakened with the last words, and he fell on his face into the dirt.

Buckner looked at the bully's friends. "Reckon if you don't want this garbage to bleed to death one o' you'd better find a doctor." To Wootton, he said, "If Canfield wants me, I'll be in my room. And thanks to you both for sidin' me." He brushed past Clanton's cohorts and went into the inn.

Sitting on the edge of his bed, Buckner emptied the shells from his Colt and pushed an oily rag through the barrel, then had one chamber cleaned and oiled when a knock sounded at his door. He pulled his Winchester onto his lap, muzzle pointed at the door. "Yeah?" He thought it might be the marshal, but no point in taking a chance.

"It's me, Kurt. Please let me in."

"A man's room is no place for a lady. Go back to your room." His voice came out rougher than he wanted, but after a gunfight he didn't feel too friendly.

"Tilde's with me. It's all right."

"Go away."

"Oh, damn you, Kurt Buckner, make me beg. I only want to see if you're all right. Besides," he could hear a smile in her voice now, "I brought you a drink of Uncle Dick's finest bourbon."

He sighed and stood. That woman never took no for an answer. He let them in with Ned bringing up the rear.

Buckner looked at the bottle Melanie held at her side. "Reckon you don't feel any shame at all using bribery to get what you want."

Her smile dripped it was so sugary. "You'd be surprised to know the things I'd used to bribe you, Kurt." He didn't like the sound of that, and his embarrassment showed in his red face. He hated that he couldn't camouflage it.

"Oh, come on, Kurt. I want to know you're not hurt. I knew when you left me you would go back downstairs to see Clanton. What surprised me was, you didn't kill him."

"Didn't intend to. Reckon after what he said, though, I still have it to do, somewhere, someday." He again glanced at the bottle. "You gonna stand there holdin' that bottle the rest o' the night? Despite what most think, whisky doesn't age once it's taken outta the keg. Pour me a drink, woman, an' if Ned'll go back to your room and get your cups you can have one with me."

He assured Melanie he was all right, even though he felt dirty inside for what he'd done. Clanton was big, dumb, and vengeful, and that combination would get him killed some-day. He hoped he wasn't the one to do it.

While they were having their drink, Canfield showed up. "Have one with us, Marshal. I'm tryin' to feel better, an'

Miss Melanie's just tryin' to satisfy a deep thirst she seems to have acquired on the trail."

"Mr. Marshal, that man is draggin' my pore baby into the depths of hades with his bad habits. Far's I know she never let the foul stuff touch her lips 'fore she met up with *him*."

Canfield laughed. "Well, Tilde, reckon he's gonna pay for it someday." He looked at Buckner. "Wootton told me what happened. Said you had to draw on Clanton or be killed." He smiled. "Wasn't much of a match, wuz it?"

"Didn't have to be a match at all, Marshal, if he'd a kept his big mouth shut."

They talked awhile. Canfield finished his drink and eyed the bottle.

"Yeah, pour yourself one, Canfield, reckon we'll have another one with you."

"I ain't havin' one. Done put my pore soul farther into hell than I'll evuh be forgiven for."

Canfield poured his drink and looked at Buckner. "Spoke to the mayor, says he'll hold court in the mornin', an' he'll have a new, young lawyer in town talk for Odom, just to make it legal. Lawyer's done gone to see Odom, see what defense he can set up." He swallowed the rest of his drink. "Wootton volunteered his dinin' room here at the inn for the courtroom." He chuckled. "Reckon the cagey old devil wanted to be sure he got a good seat."

They talked about the upcoming trial, decided Canfield would present the prosecution's side of the story, and they'd rely on the fairness of the town's citizens to do the right thing.

The next morning, court convened at ten o'clock. It looked to Buckner like the whole town tried to crowd into Wootton's dining room despite the beautiful, blue sky day outside.

The mayor read the charges: two murders and one attempted murder.

Melanie was the first witness called to testify. She told what she had seen back in Virginia, and what prompted her to pack up and run. When Tilde and Ned were called, they corroborated Melanie's story.

Then Buckner was called to the stand, and he told what had happened right outside the courtroom at the top of the stairs.

The young lawyer stood to cross-examine. In the middle of the lawyer trying to cross Melanie up in her testimony, a gnarled old cowboy stood and yelled, "You young whipper-snapper, we don't only hang murderers an' hoss thieves out here, we hang lawyer fellows for callin' pretty ladies a liar, an' that there is 'zactly what we gonna do to you, you keep on the way you're goin'."

The mayor, using his six-shooter as a gavel, pounded on the table in front of him, and shouted, "Order! Order in the court." He turned his gaze on the cowboy. "Know how you feel, old-timer," his voice came out soft and sympathetic, "but the young feller's job is to try to make things fair. Now sit down."

In the defense's closing argument, the young man pointed out that in each case there was only one witness, and asked the jury to consider Odom's testimony equally with the one in each charge against him. It didn't work. The twelve men, without leaving their seats, looked at each other and made a motion across their necks with their hands.

The foreman stood. "Mr. Mayor—er Judge, we done agreed the varmint is guilty an' ought to have his neck stretched." He looked out at the crowd. "An' anybody else what figures to mistreat one o' our womenfolk needs to take a lesson from watchin' it."

"Sit down, Tom. I'll pronounce the sentence." The mayor looked at Odom. "Ain't got time or money to build a scaffold, so come daylight tomorrow, we gonna string you up to that big cottonwood down by the Purgatoire." He again pounded on the table. "Court's adjourned."

Melanie, Buckner, Ned, and Tilde kept their seats and watched Canfield take the prisoner out the door.

Buckner looked at them. "Want coffee?" They nodded.

With coffee in front of them, Melanie stared into the black, steaming fluid. "The poor devil didn't stand a chance, and I did it to him. I'm sorry now that I did."

"Don't be, Melanie. He asked for it."

CHAPTER 20

• ——————— •

THEY SAT THERE, no one talking, each deep in their own thoughts. Finally, Melanie said to Buckner. "Kurt, it just doesn't seem right to take a human life, no matter what he's done."

"Ma'am, reckon I've taken lives a few times, but each time it was to defend myself—that was the right thing to do. This is no different. Your friends back in Virginia could not defend themselves; we can't do it for them now that they're gone, but we can make sure that trash doesn't do the same thing to another. It's these others he hasn't gotten to yet, they're the ones we're defendin' now.

He sipped his coffee, never taking his eyes from hers. "Hell, Melanie, he was gonna kill *you*. You don't reckon he would a been sorry 'bout that if he could a carried it off, do you?"

She shook her head. "No, Kurt, I know he would have had no guilt if he'd managed it, but I suppose I'm just a little softer inside than you. I know he deserves what he's getting. I guess I'm just sorry I had a hand in it."

A cloud hung over them. The gaiety and friendly banter they usually had didn't surface. After another cup of coffee, Buckner suggested Tilde take Melanie shopping, maybe it would raise her spirits. "Come on, Ned, let's check the wagon one more time. We got an eight- or ten-mile hard pull to the pass, an' then the damnedest ten-mile downhill ride you'll ever take, only I don't want any of us in the wagon. We gonna walk the whole twenty miles—up, and down. Gonna be hard on the womenfolk, but that way they'll get there alive." He thought a long moment, then said, "We'll saddle a couple o' horses in case either of them want to ride."

"Miss Melanie might, but ain't no way you gonna git

Tilde on no horse. When we wuz jest chillun playin' together, she told me then she wasn't ever gonna git on one o' them big animals, an' to my knowin', she ain't never."

Buckner grinned. "Maybe she's never been as tired as she's gonna get goin' over that mountain."

Ned slapped his knees and laughed. "'Spect you're right, Mistuh Kurt."

They inspected the wagon again, and Buckner decided another block and tackle would be a good idea. They went to the general mercantile store and took care of that, then they bought what supplies they would need for the next couple of days. Buckner bought a haunch of venison, knowing there would be no chance to hunt until the other side of Raton. He looked at boxes of ammunition and decided against adding that weight to the Studebaker. Raton should have plenty of both guns and .44 shells.

He looked longingly at a ten-gauge Greener, figured he was through with bounty hunting, put the thought aside, then bought it anyway. It would be good for bird hunting.

After shopping, at a loss for anything to do, Buckner told Ned he figured to play a little poker. He asked Ned to go with him, but Ned thought Tilde would shorten his life somewhat if he got to drinking *and* gambling.

Two tables had men seated at them. At one table, a two-bit limit game was in full swing, the chairs full. The other table had two seats empty. Buckner watched a few moments. They played for table stakes with a two-hundred-dollar takeout. Buckner went to the outhouse, closed the door, and pulled his money belt from around his waist. He took out two hundred dollars and carefully tied his belt back in place. Win, lose, or draw, two hundred was it. He walked back to the saloon and took a seat.

They explained the game rules to him. Five-card stud, or five-card draw, were the only games allowed, dealer's choice, dollar ante, table stakes.

Buckner had watched long enough to know it wasn't a friendly game, but who ever heard of a friendly game of poker. If you weren't there to win, why play? He also watched long enough to know it was an honest game.

He played carefully, never opening on less than kings, unless he sat behind the dealer, then he'd open on jacks or better. He won a few small pots, twenty, twenty-five dollars, and after an hour was a couple hundred ahead.

There had been several good-sized pots, but he'd dropped out figuring his hand wasn't strong enough. He'd never had more than two pair in that time.

Then, sitting to the dealer's right, he caught triple aces on the deal. The guy on the other side of the dealer opened for fifty dollars and two men called before it got to him. He studied his three aces and raised fifty. The opener called and raised another fifty. One of the two remaining players called, and Buckner called.

"Cards," the dealer said.

The opener stood pat, the player next to him took one card. Buckner needed help. He figured the pat hand held a straight or flush, and the man next to him as having three of a kind with a kicker, or a possible four-card straight or flush. Buckner took two cards.

The opener shoved a hundred into the pot. The one-card draw called and raised fifty. Buckner squeezed out his five cards. He'd caught a pair of nines. He called and raised a hundred, declaring he was all in for the pot.

The opener raised an eyebrow, smiled, and called the raise. The next player called the hundred Buckner raised, and put another hundred to the side. The opener called his raise.

They looked at Buckner. "We called your raise, Buckner, whatcha got?"

"Aces full of nines." He spread his hand in front of him.

The opener spread a king-high flush. "Beats me," he said and looked at the man who'd drawn one card.

The one-card draw said, "Queen-high straight." He grimaced. "Hell, I wasn't even second best." He grinned. "You win the big one, Buckner," and to the pat hand player, he said, "an' you, you sonuvagun win my other hundred."

Buckner played another hour, but won no more big pots. He won several small ones, enough to make his winnings about twelve or fourteen hundred dollars. He stacked his money, folded it, and put it in his pocket. He grinned. "Don't know when I've enjoyed myself more, men. I'm goin' to bed."

The man with the pat hand returned his grin with a grimace. "You ever come this way again, Buckner, let me know. I'll make it a point to leave town."

The other man nodded solemnly. "And I'll be right in his tracks."

They both nodded and said in unison, "Night, friend. See you again."

Although night and the hour was still early, Buckner headed for his room. He was tired, mentally and physically. He wanted a good night's sleep, then to lie around the next day, and get on the trail the next. He intended to see that Melanie didn't go to the hanging.

In his room, he stashed his poker winnings in his money belt, but kept out about two hundred dollars. If he could find a couple of books to read the next day he'd buy them, and he figured to buy a couple pair of jeans and work shirts. The two doeskin shirts he had were getting a little greasy-looking. He'd make himself another when he settled in one place long enough. He crawled between the blankets and soon slept.

The next morning, he woke at his regular time, about four-thirty, tried to go back to sleep, tossed and turned a good half hour, groaned and sat up. Might as well get up. He dressed and went downstairs to the dining room. Canfield and Wootton sat at a corner table drinking coffee.

"Don't you old-timers ever sleep? Most people in their right mind are still in bed, unless they got something special to do."

"Reckon you're one who has something special to do or you wouldn't be up either," Wootton growled. "Danged whippersnapper, always giving your elders a bunch o' mouth."

Buckner looked at Canfield. "You find anybody to do the hangin'?"

Canfield nodded. "A down-at-the-heels buffalo hunter said he'd take on any job long's it paid in gold, coin, or dust made him no never mind. Told 'im I figured we could arrange that, so he took the job." He cocked his head and squinted at Buckner. "You comin' to the hangin'?"

"Don't b'lieve so, Marshal. Gonna stay with Miss Melanie. The fact she helped send 'im to the gallows is eatin' her guts out. She's carryin' more guilt than a Baptist preacher in a cathouse."

Uncle Dick grinned. "Now I'd say she's gotta be 'bout the most guilty feelin' woman in the country, or that preacher man ain't near as godly as he'd have folks believe."

"Havin' been around Miss Melanie the last couple of days, I'd say a little o' both them statements are true, Wootton." Canfield's face got serious. "Buckner, think you're right, you better stay with 'er. Know she's havin' a hard time right now. Just keep 'er mind off'n it, an' don't let 'er go near the river today. We gonna let 'im hang there an' ripen 'til sundown so's all the no-goods can see 'im. We'll cut 'im down after dark."

They sat there, drank coffee, and talked of the old days. Wootton and Canfield knew Kit Carson, Jim Bridger, in fact most of the mountain men. When they started telling tales that happened before the War Between the States, Buckner only listened.

The objects in the corners of the room began to take on shape, and Buckner realized daylight pushed its way into the room. Carraway came in, followed by Melanie and her companions.

"Wanna push a couple tables together an' we can sit together?" Buckner asked, but hoped the three old-timers wouldn't take him up on it. He wanted to gauge how Melanie felt.

Wootton answered for them, "Nope, you go ahead an' see can you make 'er feel better."

Buckner nodded, selected a table, and seated Melanie. After ordering and waiting for their breakfast, Buckner asked, "Ma'am, why don't you an' I take those three thoroughbreds out for a run today. Figure they can stand the exercise." She studied him, looking right in his eyes until he felt uncomfortable.

Finally, she nodded. "That is a wonderful idea, Kurt. What time?"

"Oh, 'bout nine-thirty. I'll saddle 'em an' bring 'em here to the inn."

Four hours later, well out of Trinidad on the road to Walsenburg, they pulled the horses down to a trot after about a fifteen-minute gallop. They had the third horse on a lead rope.

Melanie's face glowed. Buckner thought if all the women in the world gathered in one place, Melanie would be head and shoulders above the rest in beauty. "Ma'am, if you don't mind me sayin' so, I reckon there's not another woman in the world as pretty as you."

Her face turned a rosy pink showing through the healthy glow. "Kurt, every woman likes a compliment." She cocked her head and smiled at him. "I had begun to think you hadn't noticed or cared that I am a fairly nice-looking woman."

"Reckon there's not a man livin' who wouldn't notice *you*. I just never told you before." He felt his face turn red, and he didn't like the way the conversation was going. Abruptly he twisted in his saddle and pointed toward two distant trees. "Race you to those trees," he shouted and kneed his horse into a run.

Melanie stared at his back and slumped against the leg rest on her sidesaddle. Her heart was a leaden lump in her chest. "Kurt Buckner," she said, wanting to shout, "you're the most exasperating man who ever lived. Why didn't you stay here and face me like a man? But no, you turn and run the minute you feel your freedom threatened. Why, I truly believe you're more afraid of me than a man with a gun." She leaned over her horse's neck and urged him into a run.

They exercised the horses until it was time to get back to town for their noon meal. If Buckner had thought, he would have brought something along to cook, not knowing how rowdy the celebration might be after the hanging. They rode slowly, stirrup to stirrup, both deep in their own thoughts.

The fact Melanie hadn't mentioned the hanging didn't mean anything. She probably hid her feelings from him. He frowned. One thing was certain, she didn't hide her feelings *for* him. What the heck was the matter with him? Most men would give their horse and saddle just for a smile from her, and here he was, running like a scared rabbit.

He glanced sidewise at her. She was the kind of woman a man needed to side him out here. Her inner strength showed in the way she faced every problem they'd run up against. He'd never heard her utter one word of complaint, she never whined, and she had always been there for him, quietly doing the things that had to be done.

Also, they each had the same goals: a horse ranch, a good solid home, children. Yeah, they had the same goals, but hers were for the immediate future and his were still out there in the hazy distance. He grimaced, not being able to figure out why he had to put those things off so long, they were the most serious things a man would ever try for. He smiled to himself. That was the reason he ran, a man just didn't rush into serious things like that. He had to give it more thought.

He came out of his thoughtful fog to see Trinidad directly ahead.

CHAPTER 21

◆ ━━━━━━━━━ ◆

THE NEXT MORNING, low clouds hanging to sides of the mountains, wood smoke perfuming the air, and the rolling crunch of wagon wheels painted a different picture for every member of the wagon train. They'd seen nothing like this since leaving home months before, and despite the hardships ahead of them they were in high spirits.

Buckner made sure Melanie's Studebaker brought up the rear. After reaching the summit, he didn't want a runaway team and wagon coming down on them like an avalanche. He walked at the head of Melanie's team on the outside. Ned walked on the shoulder side of the mountain. Buckner dropped back to talk with Melanie.

"Ma'am, if you an' Tilde want, you can ride until we get to the summit. I don't believe there's much danger until then. If you do ride, though, if anything happens, wagon breaks loose, anything, jump to the ground quick as you can. Don't wait." He pushed his hat to the back of his head. "You know we saddled horses for you, but I'd rather you didn't ride 'em. When we reach the top I want you walkin' — behind the wagon. No horse, no ride, just walk."

Melanie looked from him to the steep trail. "Yes, Kurt." A worried frown creased her forehead. "Do you think the rest of the people will do as you've said?"

"Well, ma'am, I've told 'em an' Carraway's told 'em. Those with any brains'll see the sense in what we've said. There'll be some who won't. They'll do as they please an' may pay a mighty high price for it." He walked back toward the lead steer.

The steep grade taxed every team, but the tough animals bent into their yokes and pulled. The families who'd chosen to use mules got along easier, for now. But Buckner knew when they got to the desert the other side of Albuquerque

the oxen would be better even though they couldn't stand
the heat as well. These old longhorn steers foraged better.

Sundown found them still climbing. Carraway rode the
length of the train cautioning each member to pick out as
level a site as possible, stop, and on each wheel, chock it
front and back with a large rock to prevent accidental
movement in any direction, then go about making camp.
"We'll night-herd the animals between the wagons and the
face of the cliffs, cain't afford to have none o' them fall over
the side."

Buckner made sure Melanie's wagon was properly se-
cured. He checked the wheel nuts, made sure the riveted
ends hadn't worked loose. He checked the iron tires to see
if they were still properly set. Tires tended to work loose in
this dry weather due to wood shrinkage. When through
checking everything, he walked to the small fire Ned started
for Melanie. "Ma'am, everything is in good shape. Figure if
you'd just fix coffee we could make do with jerky an'
hardtack tonight, maybe tomorrow night too. Then, if I got
it figured right, we'll be in better country for cookin' a full
meal. Same goes for breakfast." He stepped toward the front
of the train.

"Aren't you going to wait for a cup of coffee?"

"I'll find Carraway first. Figure there won't be Indian
trouble for a while. Want him to know I'm gonna stay with
your wagon 'til we get on flat an' level ground again."

Melanie watched his broad back melt into the velvety
darkness. Every time she looked at him, her heart swelled,
and a warm knot grew in the pit of her stomach. He was the
only man she'd ever met who needed no nurturing or special
care, but something inside her *demanded* she do things for
him, anything to make his life easier.

She clenched her fists tight at her side, telling herself he
didn't need anybody or anything. He could be in the middle
of the most barren wilderness and still survive. She sighed.
That very quality was one that drew her to him, but he had
to need more. He had to need *her*.

"It sho does get hard on you, don't it, honey? But you jest
watch what I tell you, little one, when he thinks he's done

got you an' all these here other people where y'all gonna be safe, then he gonna come to you. I b'lieve he's done made up his haid thataway." Tilde put her thin arms around Melanie's shoulders.

"Mama Tilde, I want to believe that so much b-but he never really looks at me." She stopped, peered at the fire a moment, then smiled. "Well, he did tell me he thought I was pretty."

Tilde laughed. "Aw now, didn't I tell you? He's beginning to see you." She glanced at the coffeepot sitting next to the coals. "Now when that there coffee gits to boilin' right good, you pour him some o' that whisky, 'bout half a cup o' it in with his coffee an' have it ready for 'im when he gets back."

"Mama Tilde! Gracious, I believe you're beginning to like him."

Tilde chuckled. "Child, reckon that man's done cut a path for me straight to satan's nest, an' to put a cap on it, he's done captured a part o' *my* heart too."

Melanie put her arms around Tilde and hugged her. "Mama Tilde, I love you so much."

"I know, child, I know. Now you remember Mistuh Kurt told you that high as we are, that coffee's gonna boil long 'fore it gets hot, so taste it an' make sure it's hot 'fore you serve him some."

A half hour or so passed before Buckner returned to their fire. When he walked into the firelight, Melanie handed him a cup of coffee. He took a small sip of it, slanted her an amused glance and sat, leaning against his saddle. "You remembered."

Melanie only smiled.

The next morning about ten o'clock they reached the summit. As each wagon topped out, Buckner and Carraway had them stop, check their brakes, and hook a block and tackle to the back axle, the other end of which they hooked to another team, or tree at the side of the trail, and eased the wagons slowly down to the next relatively flat place where they again chocked the wheels and moved the anchored end of the block and tackle to another tree or team of horses. Each wagon had to be treated in this manner until they got them all stopped in one line farther down the grade. Then they'd go back to the lead wagon and repeat the whole thing again, one wagon at a time. Everyone walked now.

Buckner and Carraway both rode their horses, riding from front to back of the train, and back again, helping wherever they were needed.

By nightfall, all but ten wagons were at the bottom of the grade. Those ten again camped in the middle of the trail.

In the murky light of dawn Buckner again checked Melanie's rig and started back down when the man in the lead team yelled. It was a frightened, heart-rending thing to hear. Buckner put spurs to his gelding. He came on a man staring in horror at his wagon and team careening down the slope. Buckner, in only a short moment, gauged his chance of reaching the rig before it crashed into the wagons at the bottom of the grade—or went over the embankment. It would be tight. He urged his dun faster.

The wagon, outrunning the oxen hitched to it, was close to running up on the aft pair. It pushed all eight steers ahead of it.

The chance of getting to the lead oxen and crowding them to the side of the cliff was slight. Buckner, guts tight, throat swelled, pulled his .44 and rode alongside the team. He thumbed off two shots so fast the sound blended as one. He knew exactly where each slug had gone—one behind the right ear of each steer.

The two steers immediately in front of the wagon dropped to their knees. The oxen ahead of them broke free and continued down the trail at a dead run. The wagon rode up on the carcasses of the two dead steers, slowed, teetered, and fell to its side—but it stayed on the trail.

The man whose wagon it was that lay on its side ran up panting, white-faced. His face showed anger, not fear or relief.

"What the hell you kill my oxen for? You done yore job there'd never a been no danger." He looked at his wagon lying on its side. "Probably done ruined ever'thing inside my rig. Things we wuz gonna use in Californy."

Buckner tasted the bitter bile of anger and fear well into

his tight throat, anger at the stupid yokel facing him, fear for the people below who had been two .44 slugs away from death and ruin.

By now people from the wagons behind were running to see if they could help. Buckner speared the owner of the wrecked wagon with a look that seemed to burn even his own eyes. "Mister, I'm gonna inspect your block an' tackle. Your line broke putting every man, woman, and child down below us in danger of losing everything they own, not to mention their lives."

He sucked in a gulp of air, trying to get a handle on his temper. "We may be able to salvage your wagon, an' you got six oxen still alive. You wouldn't have any of that if I hadn't shot your two steers." He breathed deeply again. "Now I'm gonna tell you somethin'. I explained why I did what I did. I don't often do that so don't push your luck with me. I don't take pushin'."

Carraway rode up the steep incline at a gallop and dropped off his horse in front of Buckner. "Fast work, Buckner. Didn't think you had a chance of keepin' the whole shebang from goin' over the cliff, yourself along with it."

Buckner, still trying to get a rein on his anger, said, "Tell this stupid bastard that. Don't tell me. I did what I had to do."

Carraway squinted at him. "Whoa up, boy. Who turpentined your rear end?"

"Reckon I did, Mr. Carraway. I was terrified me an' my wife an' kids'd done lost every'thing we owned." The young man who went by the name of Benning, and was not much over twenty years old, looked Buckner in the eye. "Sir, I apologize. I know whatever we got left, we owe it to you. Not many men I know would've taken the chance you did. You could a been killed."

To admit he felt like a long-eared jackass would have been an understatement. Buckner returned the man's look and grinned sheepishly. "Mr. Benning, it takes a man to admit he was wrong. I accept your apology, an' add mine to yours. I should've known you were talkin' from fear. Let's forget it." He looked at the crowd gathered around. "C'mon, let's get that wagon back on its wheels."

After they righted the vehicle, Buckner looked at the broken line. It was old and frayed. He looked up into Benning's eyes. Benning lowered his. "Sir, I didn't have enough money to buy a new one an' was ashamed to tell anybody."

Buckner studied the boy awhile longer. "Son, don't ever let pride stand between you an' your family's welfare an' safety. I would a lent you one o' ours."

Benning nodded. "Yes, sir. I'll never do nothin' like that again."

It took the rest of the day to get all the wagons to the bottom. But they all got there in one piece, and after checking the provisions, and things he and his wife planned to start their California life with, Benning told Buckner nothing important had been broken.

They spent that night on the New Mexico Territory side of the pass and, watching each member of the train's company, Buckner realized how much stress the crossing had put on each of them. They laughed more than usual, talked louder, and all showed extreme fatigue.

At Raton, Carraway asked if anyone had a reason to lay over a day or two, but urged them to keep going. The Sangre de Cristo and Jemez mountains of New Mexico and the San Francisco Mountains of Arizona would be no problem, too early for snow, but by the time they reached the California ranges it might be a different story.

Benning was the only one who needed repairs, and he said he'd work on his rig each night after they stopped rather than hold the train up for another day.

They camped that night on the fringe of the small settlement of Raton. Melanie fixed a good supper, and while having coffee afterward, she sat closer to Buckner than usual, close enough for her shoulder to brush his when either of them lifted their cups to take a swallow. Buckner didn't move from her.

The next morning, he told Carraway he'd make one more sweep of the country ahead, but didn't figure the Jicarilla

Apache would be roaming that far east. "When I get back, I'm cuttin' out. Gonna take Miss Melanie on to Cimarron, then through Cimarron Canyon, an' on to Eagle's Nest. Figure we'll set up to ranch over yonder somewhere."

Carraway grimaced. "Shore hate to see you go, boy. Don't need to tell you they's been many a time since you joined up we'd a been in a heap o' trouble without you."

Buckner smiled even though he didn't feel like it. He never liked to leave an old friend. "Figure it's time I set my roots somewhere. A man can't roam all his life."

A grin split the full width of Carraway's face. "Figured that young filly wuz gonna capture you sooner or later." He pushed his hat back and scratched his head. "Cain't b'lieve it took so long, as pretty as she is."

"Aw, hell, Carraway, I never even mentioned anything like that to her. Even if I was of a mind to wed 'er, I got no notion she'd have me."

"Been watchin' 'er, Buckner. She takes care o' you like a mother hen. Yeah, figure she'd have you."

"Seemed kinda like that to me too, but a man never knows." Buckner toed his stirrup and swung aboard. "See you in time for our noonin'."

His ride took him across grasslands, parallel with the Sangre de Cristos, with the Turkey Range sticking into the sky ahead, making a purple, cloud-like pattern on the horizon.

Buckner studied ridge lines, shoulders of hills, edges of arroyos, anywhere an Apache might hide, but mostly he looked at the ground around him. It had been a good while since rain fell on the hard-baked soil. Through the long morning not a single pony track showed in the soil. He turned toward the train, letting the gelding into a gull gallop.

Melanie had sandwiches and coffee ready when he rode up. They ate while he told her they'd gone a little past where he intended to turn off toward Cimarron, but he figured they'd only lost an hour or two, and anyway they looked at it, Cimarron sat about forty miles away.

Finished with his sandwiches, which consisted of slices

of warm venison between two halves of biscuit, he said he was going to talk with the settlers.

Carraway called them to muster around. Buckner and the wagon boss stood by Carraway's fire waiting for them to gather. Finally, Buckner swept the gathering with a glance. "Folks, just want to say Miss Melanie an' her companions, along with me, will leave you now. I know I've been hard on some o' you, but want you to know I always figured it was for your own good. You're new here in this country, while I'm an old hand. I know what it takes to live to see the sun come up in the mornin'. Your wagon boss is the same kind o' man as me. Do what he says—always, an' he'll get you there." He pinned each of them with a straight-on stare. "Hope none o' you have hard feelin's toward me." He walked off.

Before he led Melanie's wagon off to the southwest, every man and woman in the company came by to shake his hand and thank him.

In only a few minutes their wagon dropped over the crest of a hill. Buckner looked back. Carraway's train was no longer in sight. "Well, ma'am, we're 'bout where we started, all alone out in the middle o' nowhere. 'Cept right now, we're only about a week an' a half, maybe two weeks from where I'll show you the prettiest horse country you'll ever see."

"What'll you do then, Kurt?"

A lump came in his throat. Was she in such a hurry to see him ride off? He swallowed. "Don't know, ma'am. Figured to help you get settled 'fore I go anywhere, then, well, I just don't know. Haven't given it much thought." She seemed to draw away from him with his last words, sort of like, well sort of like she would be glad to see him go.

The four days it took to reach Cimarron, Melanie took just as good care of him as always. Supper was ready when he rode in from scouting, she had a drink with him, she told him to take care before he left in the mornings, but she, somehow, had put a barrier between them.

Buckner wondered what he'd done to cause her to change, and he hurt inside. His heart swelled when he looked at her, his throat tightened. Why hadn't he said something to her when she plainly showed she had some feelings for him: Why the hell hadn't he let go the dream of seeing the other side of every hill? Waking beside her every morning would be more exciting than seeing every hill in the universe. Cimarron lay only a quarter of a mile ahead.

CHAPTER 22

$\bullet$ ———————— $\bullet$

THERE WERE MANY in this town who rode outside the law. Buckner didn't intend to leave Melanie alone any longer than he had to, but there were things he had to do if they were to ranch in that country the other end of the canyon. He got Tilde and her settled in the hotel, and said he'd be back in time for supper.

Getting the oxen corralled and fed, with Ned helping, didn't take long. Next he wanted to see Black Jack Slade, if he was in town. Slade could be here, or Eagle's Nest, or Red River. Buckner hoped for Cimarron.

Rumors said Slade headed up all the outlaws in the region. If that was true he had to sell the outlaw leader on his proposal, or he and Melanie could kiss ranching in the Eagle's Nest country good-bye.

The town was small enough he figured if Slade was here he'd find him. He headed for the best of the two saloons, went through the batwing doors, and stood a moment to let his eyes adjust to the room's darkness. He felt no sense of danger, but friends of those he'd taken to the law might have a different idea. He slipped the thong from the hammer of his .44.

While his eyes adjusted, his sense of smell also tried to get used to the odor of stale alcohol and sweaty bodies. A few moments later the large room came into focus.

He swept the large room with a glance. A few here were men he'd met in other towns, but none had reason to bring a fight to him—and he lucked out, Slade sat at one of the poker tables in the back of the room. Buckner walked back and stood watching. Slade, a handsome but dangerous man, looked up.

"Well, look what the cat dragged in. Howdy, Buckner, you here on a friendly visit, or you lookin' for someone?"

Buckner grinned. "Friendly, Slade. I'm outta that business." His grin widened. "You can put that six-shooter you're holdin' under the table back in its holster."

Slade raised an eyebrow. "Must be slippin'. Most wouldn't a noticed me slip it outta its holster."

"Noticin' things like that keeps me alive, amigo." Buckner motioned to the empty chair. "Mind if I sit in?"

Slade grinned. "I can spend your money good as anybody else's. Sit down."

Buckner played carefully, staying about even. Slade played about the same kind of game. After several hands in which they both threw their cards in, Buckner looked questioningly at the outlaw leader. "Any chance we could find a place to talk?"

"Say what you gotta say. Here's good enough."

Buckner shook his head. "This's somethin' you might want to keep under your hat. I know damned well I do."

"Okay. I have a room upstairs. We'll talk there."

Only moments later they had cashed in their chips and sat across from each other at a table in the second floor room.

Slade pinned Buckner with icy eyes. "This better be good, I don't like leavin' a good poker game."

"Ah bull, Slade. You weren't enjoyin' that game any more'n me. Neither of us were catchin' decent cards." Buckner crossed his arms and leaned on the table. "Slade, I never heard you'd lie to a man. I'm bankin' on that."

The handsome outlaw nodded. "Go ahead. Reckon lyin' ain't one o' the things people accuse me of."

"Okay, here it is. I'll promise you somethin', an' in return I want a promise from you. Here's the . . ."

Slade interrupted, "Hold it 'til I get us a bottle up here. Looks like we gonna be friendly for a while." He went to the door and yelled over the bannister to the bartender. "Send a bottle of your good stuff up here, none of that swill you serve across the bar."

A very firm "Yes, sir," sounded from below.

They waited for the whisky and glasses. When they each sat with a drink in front of them, Slade nodded. "Go ahead."

"The deal is, I and a friend of mine want to start a couple

o' horse ranches somewhere around Eagle's Nest. Want you to leave us alone and let us run our ranches."

Slade opened his mouth to say something. Buckner held up his hand to silence him. "Wait and hear me out, Slade. The horses we'll raise will be mixed bloods, thoroughbred and mustang—fast an' tough, the kind o' horses you and your men need occasionally." Tongue in cheek, he added, "Can't imagine what you need such fast horses for, but it's none of my business."

He took a sip of his drink, and again looked at Slade straight-on. "Like I said, I want your men to leave us an' our horses alone. We'll sell 'em to you at a fair price. You, or your men, don't have the time to raise good horseflesh. 'Nother thing: we won't sell to any o' your men wanted for murder, or botherin' a woman. I know most who ride for you, an' they're mostly pretty decent boys, so keep the others away from us. I want your word you'll work it that way."

He sat back, packed his pipe, and lighted it, took another swallow of his drink—and waited.

The tall, dark-haired outlaw stared at the table, obviously thinking hard on what Buckner proposed. When he looked up, his face was solemn. "Buckner, this'll put you ridin' the fence 'tween us an' the law."

Buckner shook his head. "Don't figure it that way. I got a right to sell my stock to whoever I chose."

Slade lapsed into thought again. When he looked up, Buckner could see he'd made a decision. "Like you said, when I give my word, I keep it. Give me a week to contact a few of my men, if they say it's a deal, that's it, we're in business. Stay here in Cimarron 'til I can get an answer from them. It'll take 'bout a week."

Only minutes later, Buckner saw one of Slade's men ride out of town. He figured he'd have his answer as promised.

From seeing Slade, Buckner hunted up a tall thin man, dressed in a black broadcloth suit and a black hat. Most would take him for a gambler, or a gunfighter. Buckner talked with the man for several minutes. "One thing about this," Buckner said, "I may not need you at all, but I want you to ride with us just in case. Whatever happens, though, I'll pay what I promised." He stared at the man a moment. "Another thing, don't want you to mention what business you're in. It might upset the ladies."

The black-suited man shrugged and held out his hand. "Sounds good to me, partner. I'll do it your way. Gimme enough time before you leave so I can fix my bedroll."

Four days into the week, Buckner, sitting in a chair on the hotel veranda, studied a wagon on its way into town. He recognized the man driving it. "Damn," he mumbled under his breath. This was one thing he'd hoped to avoid, another confrontation with Clanton.

The mouthy settler pulled his rig to the side of the general store, parked it, and headed for the saloon. Looking at him, Buckner couldn't see that the shoulder wounds bothered him any.

He sat there awhile longer. He might be able to dodge Clanton for a couple more days, but most likely would run into him somewhere in town. He had no desire to hole up until he left in order to keep from killing the trash, but the fact remained, he didn't want to kill him. If he chose where they met, it would lessen the chance some bystander would get hurt.

Buckner breathed another soft, "Damn," uncrossed his legs, stood, and walked toward the saloon.

Before pushing through the batwings, he pulled the thong from the hammer of his side gun, wishing there was some other way to keep from losing it short of having a holster flap. He eased the big .44 in its holster, making sure it would jump to his hand if needed, then went through the doorway.

Finally, seeing clearly, and with his back to the wall he studied the crowd. Clanton stood at the bar, his voice sounding above all others.

What Buckner was about to try put a sour taste in the back of his throat, but he had to try. He wanted to show Clanton up for a blowhard, shame him into leaving the country. The bully's words came to him. ". . . gonna beat that Buckner to death with my bare hands. He shot me over yonder in Trinidad, didn't give me no chance, jest pulled iron an' let me have it."

"Mister, I've knowed Kurt Buckner a number o' years; never knowed 'im to draw first, an' I never seen the day he couldn't beat the likes o' you with his *left* hand, let alone his right, an' still let you get yore gun almost clear of the holster before startin' his draw."

Buckner's gaze flicked to the cowboy doing the talking, and recognized him as a young hellion he'd known down Juárez way, Bob Stevens was his name.

Buckner's voice, soft and silky, penetrated the crowd noise. "Thanks for those words, Stevens. I'll take it from here."

Every face along the bar snapped in his direction, and those men closest to Clanton pulled away from him, leaving a good five or six feet on both sides. Buckner, in slow, measured steps, closed the distance between him and the mouthy one.

Standing only a foot from him, Buckner stared into eyes now showing a spark of fear. "What's the matter, Clanton? You could a drawn on me while I walked toward you. No guts?" In a backhanded swing he slapped Clanton's cheek, opening a cut along his cheekbone. He slapped again, the print of his fingers showing white, then turning an angry red on the other cheek.

"You got your chance, big man. Swing at me, or do you remember the beating I gave you along the trail?" He slapped again. Clanton, his back pressed against the bar, bent backwards. His hands went to his face to ward off the stinging punishment Buckner dealt out. Buckner slapped him twice more, then reached to the big man's holster and took his six-shooter. He emptied the shells onto the floor, tossed the gun to the counter, and leaned into Clanton.

"Gonna tell you somethin'. The men in here who saw this will spread the word throughout the West. There's not a town you can go to but what you'll be known for a coward. If you're smart, an' you've not shown much of a tendency in that direction, you'll get in that wagon o' yours an' you won't stop this side the Pacific Ocean. Even there, people will know you for what you are. Now, get outta here."

Clanton reached for his empty revolver on the counter.

"Leave it."

Clanton drew back his hand like he'd touched a hot stove, pushed away from the bar, and in a stumbling run left the saloon.

Stevens looked hard into Buckner's eyes. "Man, you ever get a mad on at me, just shoot me. That man ain't gonna do no good wherever he goes after this."

Buckner stared at him a moment. "Figured it that way, Stevens." He glanced down the bar and left.

A week later, Black Jack Slade approved Buckner's proposal, and Buckner led Melanie and her companions deep into one of the most beautiful canyons he'd ever seen. The thin, black-clad man rode well ahead of them.

The third evening into the canyon, they sat by the fire, having coffee. The thin man declined Buckner's invitation to share the bourbon, he did however have a cup of coffee.

The barrier Melanie had erected still stood between them. Wondering if he'd ever penetrate it, Buckner finished his drink and said to her, "Ma'am, reckon if you're of a mind to, we could take a walk down the river 'fore it gets too dark. It's a mighty pretty stream."

Her face showing surprise, she finished her coffee, put her cup to the side, and stood. "I'd like that, Kurt. It might work the stiffness out of my bones from sitting on that hard wagon seat all day."

Wanting any touch she might give him, he said, "Ma'am, you'd best take hold o' my arm, it gets pretty rocky along the bank."

Darkness slipped into the canyon, and under the trees night laid its hold on the land, while the trail still held on to the last faint light of the setting sun. Buckner and Melanie walked where trees often crowded them to the stream's edge. Here, night surrounded them.

The ripple and splash of water over stones sang a soft song into the velvet blackness of their surroundings. Buckner stopped and faced Melanie. "Ma'am, gonna say somethin'. Know you've taken a dislike to me in the past couple o' weeks, seems like you've sorta put a distance 'tween us. Don't know why, but there's somethin' I got to say."

"Well, say it, Mr. Buckner."

He shuffled his feet a moment, then looked at the shadowy loveliness of her face. "Ma'am, ever since I first saw you back in Newton, reckon I been in love with you. I fought it mighty hard 'cause I figured you wouldn't like the way I live my life, an' would wanna change me. Don't know that I could promise to change, ma'am.

"I studied on it a good long while an' finally figured I better give you a chance to tell me yourself I wasn't the kind o' man you could live with the rest o' your life. Then somethin' happened—that's when you drew away from me. I know now I've waited too long." He stood back from her. "Know now, ma'am, you won't have me but I'm gonna ask anyway. Ma'am, I love you, an' want to marry you."

Melanie stood, hands on hips. "Mr. Buckner, I have a question."

"Yes, ma'am?"

"When we're lying close to one another at night, I don't think I could marry a man who called me ma'am. Do you think, under those circumstances, you could call me Melanie?"

"Ma—uh, Melanie, that man back there in camp, I brought 'im along in case you said yes, just in case, knowin' there wasn't much chance. He's a preacher."

"Yes, Kurt, a thousand times yes. I thought for a long time you were going to make me ask *you*." With those words she threw herself into his arms. For a long moment, her lips and body pressed close to him gave him her answer better than any words.

When they finally stood back from each other, breathless, Buckner drawled, "*Ma'am*, let's go see that preacher man."